Praise for Denise Patrick's
The Importance of Almack's

A Perfect 10! "...one of the best Regencies I have ever read ...filled with information and splendid descriptions. Denise Patrick sets Society on its ear and leaves the reader furiously turning pages to see what happens next... THE IMPORTANCE OF ALMACK'S is a Perfect 10 that I very strongly recommend."
~ *Vi Janaway, Romance Reviews Today*

4½ Hearts! "Ms. Denise Patrick has written a great novel which is not only a poignant look at extended family but also the importance of true love. I highly recommend this book. . .you will definitely not be disappointed!"
~ *Brenda, The Romance Studio*

4 Angels! "...I loved The Importance of Almack's ...and that is hard to come by when there are few historical romances that fall into my keeper pile but Denise Patrick managed it ...it ended beautifully ...Great job!"
~ *Lena C., Fallen Angel Reviews*

4½ Stars! "...a highly enjoyable tale ...Each page tantalizes you, revealing just a little bit more of the puzzle and at the same time creating new twists and sub-plots ...a real page turner."
~*JR Hyatt, Historical Romance Club*

3½ Klovers! "This Regency set historical was truly lovely both in the sweetly toned romance, the vibrant personalities of the players, intelligent and witty dialogs and the exciting twists and turns ...the author masterfully weaves an unfolding story of deceit and a web of lies from a twenty year old scandal. I was immensely entertained by the story and the very likeable leads and their friends..."

~Marilyn Rondeau, (RIO) ck2s Kwips and Kritiques

The Importance
of Almack's

Denise Patrick

A Samhain Publishing, Ltd. publication.

Samhain Publishing, Ltd.
577 Mulberry Street, Suite 1520
Macon, GA 31201
www.samhainpublishing.com

The Importance of Almack's
Copyright © 2008 by Denise Patrick
Print ISBN: 978-1-59998-795-8
Digital ISBN: 1-59998-518-7

Editing by Jennifer Miller
Cover by Dawn Seewar

First Samhain Publishing, Ltd. electronic publication: July 2007
First Samhain Publishing, Ltd. print publication: May 2008

Dedication

To Sarah-Jane and Emma-Jean. Those who know who you are, also know how much you are missed. Without you, this book would have never been written. I still miss you both more than anyone will ever know.

All on that magic List depends;
Fame, fortune, fashion, lovers, friends;
'Tis that which gratifies or vexes
All ranks, all ages, and both sexes.
If once to Almack's you belong,
Like monarchs you can do no wrong;
But banished thence on Wednesday night,
By Jove, you can do nothing right.
—Henry Luttrell

Chapter One

Yorkshire, March 1816

The stranger lay completely still as Pamela approached the stream. Positioned on his side, he faced away from her. She hesitated before continuing down the embankment. The sound of Midas's hooves, only slightly muffled by the foliage, should have disturbed him but apparently did not. Urging the horse forward, she studied the area, ready to bolt at the first sign of danger. When Midas balked at moving closer, she concentrated on the stranger, willing him to move. He didn't.

Thankfully, there were really no places for accomplices to hide if he wasn't alone, and she looked around her carefully before dismounting.

For a clear day, the mid-morning sun provided almost no heat, and although it was not unheard of for Yorkshire to still have snow on the ground in the middle of March, she was glad there was none today. When the man still didn't move at the sound of her approaching footsteps, she feared the worst.

What was he doing out here? Where had he come from? How had he gotten here?

"Dear God, don't let him be dead."

The first thing she noticed as she dropped down beside him was that he was the handsomest man she'd ever seen. Midnight waves covered his head, a lock of the dark hair falling forward over his forehead. His sharp, slightly angular features were softened by his repose, but she had the feeling he could freeze with a look, and she found herself wondering what color his eyes were. He was dressed in the height of fashion, a dark brown riding jacket over a white shirt and cravat; his black boots were scuffed but expensively made, as were the leather gloves he still wore.

"Please, God, don't let him be dead," she repeated as she grasped his shoulder.

With little difficulty, she pushed him on to his back then put her ear to his chest. His heartbeat was faint, but there. Relief flooded her limbs. Looking him over carefully, she finally noticed a dark stain on the shoulder of his jacket. Shock immobilized her for a moment as she realized he'd been shot.

"Now what?" She checked the area again. "Lord Crandall isn't going to like this."

Thankful the man was only unconscious, she quickly tore off a strip of her petticoat and hurried down to the stream. Soaking it in the icy water, she folded it into a pad as she moved back toward him. She knelt beside him and unbuttoned his jacket, only to realize she couldn't get it off. She cursed roundly, and in a very unladylike manner, the fashion that dictated clothing fit like a second skin. Rocking back on her heels, she stared down at him in frustration. At least he didn't have a fever, but she wondered how long he'd been unconscious.

Unbuttoning his shirt, she was momentarily distracted by the first naked male chest she'd ever seen. Ridges of muscle and bone covered by tanned skin and dusted by dark curly hair caused her mouth to go dry. Cleaning the wound would be nearly impossible, but she noted the bullet had apparently gone completely through the soft tissue of his shoulder and the bleeding had slowed to a trickle. Sliding her hand beneath the shirt as best she could, she pressed her wet pad against the wound and wished she knew whether she was helping or hurting.

Squinting up at the sun, trying to judge its movement, she hoped Barlow had not disregarded her parting comment.

"I won't be out long," she'd told the stable master. "You can send Seth out after me if I'm not back in an hour. I'm only headed down by the stream." She'd wanted some time alone. A chance to be outside in the cool, crisp air and enjoy the gradual coming of spring.

He was too large to lift, but she managed to move him out of the pool of dried blood she found beneath him. She shivered as the cold air began to seep through the thin riding habit she wore. Retrieving her heavy woolen cloak from Midas's back, she returned to her stranger to wait. Time crawled and she wondered again if Barlow remembered.

She didn't dare leave him. He was chilled already and she chafed first one hand, then his other to warm them. The bullet hadn't killed him, but he could freeze to death if he remained out here much longer.

She grunted as she shifted his broad shoulders, trying not to jostle his injured shoulder too much, and turned him onto his side, supporting his head in her lap and attempting to share her cloak. Leaving his good shoulder resting on the ground, she hoped she wouldn't get any blood on her skirts. Once back at home, she didn't want to have to make explanations.

"Please don't die," she whispered and looked around, hoping she'd been gone long enough that Seth had been sent to find her.

Movement, and a groan, drew her gaze back to her patient.

Blue, was her first thought as she looked down into indigo eyes. She felt the shudder that racked him. "Don't move. You have a hole in your shoulder and I don't want it to start bleeding."

Kitt came to slowly. His head lay on something soft and warm, but the rest of him was decidedly chilled. Opening his eyes gingerly, he remained still, breathing in a light, flowery fragrance he didn't recognize. Taking a few moments to become accustomed to the light, he was stunned to find an angel leaning over him, her bright hair haloed by the sun. His shoulder throbbed, causing him to groan before he could catch himself.

She spoke, her voice gentle, but his brain registered only a few words as a shudder went through him.

"I'm glad you're awake."

"Where am I?" He was amazed at how strong his voice sounded compared to how he felt.

"Near Clark Hall. Where'd you come from?"

"London."

"That's a long way. What happened?"

"I was set upon and treated to Yorkshire hospitality," he answered tersely.

"Oh," was her only comment, but her eyes narrowed slightly.

The silence stretched and he regretted his shortness. She was obviously trying to help him. And he had no reason to believe she was in league with the footpads who'd relieved him of his horse and purse. Gritting his teeth against the pain in his shoulder, he tried to sit up.

"Be careful," she cried, reaching out to help him. "Remember, you've been shot."

Once in a sitting position, Kitt felt a little more in control of himself, but he was still cold. *I should be thankful,* he mused. *At least I'm still alive.*

The sun was high in the sky, reflecting weakly off the water of the small stream before him. It must be fairly late in the morning and he wondered how long he'd lain unconscious before she came along. He couldn't remember what time he approached the stream to water his horse. Right now, he thought grimly, he was lucky to even remember his name.

"How long?"

"I don't know how long you were here before I came, but I've been here for nearly an hour, I think. Are you hungry?"

The girl sat beside him. She wore a riding dress which had once been of very high quality, but the fine brown velvet was worn thin in many places. Her hair, a fiery gold and red mix, was pulled back into a loose knot at her nape.

Pamela felt the blood rushing into her face under his scrutiny. Wyatt never affected her like this, and she once thought herself in love with him. *Stop gawking!* she chided herself.

"I...I have some food," she stammered. "It's not much, but..." Rising as she spoke, she was surprised when he reached out and grabbed her wrist. The contact jolted her and, losing her train of thought, she dropped back to the ground as fear flashed through her.

"I'm sorry. Did I hurt you?"

"N-no," she stuttered, flustered by the tingling in her wrist where his hand held it.

"I'm Kitt. And you are...?"

"Pamela. Pamela Clarkdale."

"Pamela." The name rolled off his tongue. "I like that."

His deep voice sent a small frisson of awareness through her. She found herself blushing and chastised herself inwardly. *Stop acting like a lovesick fool! He's injured.*

"I...I have a little something to eat, if you're hungry," she said hesitantly. "It's not much...I didn't expect to have to share." She smiled as she chattered on. "But you can have some, that is...if you...I mean...if you're hungry, that is."

She knew he smiled at her nervousness.

"Relax," he told her gently. "I won't hurt you. Perhaps just a little water and I can walk to the nearest village to get some help."

Aghast, Pamela declared, "You can't walk all the way to the village with a hole in your shoulder. Besides, someone ought to alert Lord Crandall. He's the local magistrate."

He grimaced. "It's only a scratch." He moved his arm experimentally and his lips whitened in pain. "Well, maybe not. But I sincerely doubt the ruffians are still in the area—they took my horse and purse."

"I'm sorry." She rose to her feet and went back to where Midas stood. Unhooking the small sack from the pommel of the saddle, she returned to Kitt. Opening the sack, she produced an apple, some biscuits and a small flask which she filled with water from the stream.

She watched him eat the apple, all the while wondering what to do with him. Her father distrusted strangers and, to her mother's chagrin, refused to provide hospitality to travelers. Even one as injured as this gentleman would garner no sympathy from her father.

"I could take you to Lord Crandall's home," she offered. "He could send for a doctor."

If he thought it odd she did not offer to take him to Clark Hall, he kept it to himself.

"I don't want to cause any trouble. If you can just help me to the nearest inn, I should be fine." He started to stand as he spoke, but sudden dizziness assailed him and he collapsed in a heap.

"Be careful," she cried, moving to help him. "You're not strong enough to go anywhere alone. Seth should be here soon."

Nearly two hours later, safely ensconced in a small room at the rear of the stables, his wound cleaned and bandaged, Kitt discovered more about his savior. Miss Pamela was the oldest and apparently the favorite of the three children of Sir Maurice Clarkdale. The favorite among the servants, that was. Her younger sister Sheila was apparently the master's favorite, while her brother Stephen, needless to say, was the son and heir. Master Stephen, however, was off at a school, so only the two girls were at home.

Miss Pamela was twenty-three and still unmarried, while Miss Sheila was a beauty at eighteen and expected to make a grand match. The rumor among the servants was that the master was promoting a match between Miss Sheila and Lord Crandall, but that Lord Crandall had courted Miss Pamela. The fact that he hadn't proposed marriage worried those among the servants who saw Lord Crandall as Miss Pamela's chance to get out from under her father's thumb. With Lady Clarkdale gravely ill, the servants felt Pamela was being shamelessly taken advantage of by her father and sister. The two of them had essentially relegated her to the role of housekeeper and treated her more like one of the servants than the mistress of the house—which would be her proper role during her mother's illness.

Pamela hurried through breakfast and was headed for the stables when she heard her sister coming down the stairs. "Pamela? Pammy? Are you down here?"

Now what? Pamela thought as she turned back to meet Sheila at the bottom. "I'm here. Do you want something?"

"I can't find my new blue shawl," Sheila whined. "Have you seen it?"

"Why should I have seen it? Did you leave it in the sitting room? Or the salon?"

Sheila pouted, her blue eyes darkening in irritation. "How should I know where I left it? I didn't leave the house with it, so it must be here somewhere. That silly Bess can't keep track of anything."

Pamela looked up at the unadorned plaster ceiling in exasperation. Sheila was completely careless with things. When something went missing, she always blamed it on someone else, usually their overworked maid, Bess.

"Sheila, you have to help when it comes to these things. You can't just leave them lying around here and there and expect something to appear when you want it. Who do you think retrieves them?"

"Obviously not you. You're too busy playing 'lady of the manor' and ordering people around."

Pamela sighed. "We've been through this before, Sheila. Someone has to keep the household running with Mother so sick. You don't seem to care one way or another, unless you can't find something." Forestalling another outburst, she continued, "I'll check with the laundress. If she doesn't have it, I'll check with the housekeeper and downstairs maids to see if anyone has seen it. Until then, why don't you just wear your white one over that dress. It will look lovely." She eyed Sheila's blue and white striped morning gown. The blue shawl would have highlighted the pure gold of her hair, matched her eyes and, of course, accented Sheila's flawless skin.

Turning toward the back of the house, she heard Sheila flounce back up the stairs. With a sigh, she put those thoughts from her mind and went in search of the laundress and housekeeper.

An hour later she slipped into the room where Kitt sat on a cot with his back propped up against the wall. He no longer looked pale and his eyes were clearer. Smiling, she perched on the chair beside him.

"How are you feeling today?"

"Much better. The shoulder is still painful, but the seepage has stopped. Barlow says it is healing nicely."

"Good."

Kitt watched her as she settled onto the chair. Today she was wearing a gown many years out of date, which must have been altered to fit some time ago. Even so, the ill-fitting, odd-colored gown could not disguise the feminine curves beneath. Her skin was clear but, against the dress, looked sallow. Her red-gold tresses were restrained firmly into a no-nonsense bun at the back of her head. Her most interesting features, by far, were her eyes. He still could not put a color to the mixture of green and brown, but they intrigued him immensely.

"Would you like to send someone a letter? I could get you some writing paper and post a letter for you if you would like someone to know where you are."

The suggestion brought Kitt up short. In the three days he'd been here, it did not occur to him to write to let anyone know what happened. With his father's death four years ago, his only relative was a distant cousin. While on good terms, they were not regular correspondents. But his friends might wonder what happened to him if he suddenly ceased all contact. And he needed funds to get back to London. Having learned more about this unusual household from the stable hands, he realized there was little help to be had from that quarter.

"I would like that very much," he answered. "Thank you for thinking of it. I must confess I have been enjoying my convalescence somewhat and forgot others might be worried about my whereabouts."

"Do you have any family who might worry?"

"No, no family, but I do have friends and acquaintances who might wonder at my uncharacteristic silence."

"I'll go and get you some paper right now." She rose and shook out her dress.

"Thank you," he replied as she hurried out of the stable.

Kitt put his head back and closed his eyes. Pamela's face swam before him. He was drawn to her, he knew that. That she didn't seem to notice was almost comical. He was well aware the reason it never occurred to him to write to anyone was that someone might come to his aid if he did—and right now aid was the last thing he wanted. Picturing her smiling face, the concern in her eyes, the worry over his shoulder, gave him a pleasant feeling he'd never experienced before. Her natural warmth and generosity soothed his cynical, world-weary soul.

He nearly laughed out loud at his predicament. He was the Earl of Kittridge, the most sought-after peer in London, a rake, and confirmed bachelor...attracted to a slip of a woman who had no idea of his identity, imaginings, or feelings. At thirty, he'd had more than his share of women, but never had any of them looked at him like she did. Her thoughtfulness touched him.

Pamela returned with writing utensils and a small lap desk. As she put it down on the chair, he reached for it and their hands touched. Automatically, he gripped her hand gently as she raised startled eyes to his. His thumb caressed the back of her hand as he watched her. Awareness flared deep in her eyes and he realized she was not indifferent.

"I haven't thanked you for everything you've done," he said slowly, testing her reaction.

"I...you...you're welcome," she stammered. "I...it was not much...really." She swallowed and his eyes were drawn to the smooth skin of her throat.

Raising her hand to his lips, he savored the softness of the back of her hand before turning it over and placing a kiss on the pulse point on her wrist.

Pamela was so surprised she didn't react. For a moment she stared at the dark head bent over her hand, nearly giving in to the impulse to run her fingers through the inky locks. Sensation sizzled up her arm as he pressed his lips first to the back of her hand, then her wrist. She trembled, unsure whether her legs would continue to hold her up. When Kitt raised his head to look up at her, she was suddenly embarrassed at her response. Mumbling something about chores to do, she straightened and pulled her hand from his, then fled the small room. Once outside the stables, she paused to recover.

Her hand felt warm, and she looked at it as if it was a foreign object attached to her arm. Lifting it, she pressed the back of her hand against her cheek and felt again the tingling sensation of Kitt's lips settling there. She was lost in a daydream until the voices of the stable hands intruded.

She shook herself. *It's time to get to work,* she admonished herself as she headed toward the house. There was still Sheila's shawl to find.

"How's the patient today?" her mother asked when Pamela slipped into her room for a visit much later.

Sunlight streamed through large windows, casting bright patterns over the carpet and furniture. Lady Clarkdale sat in a large overstuffed chair, her small frame swathed in shawls, a colorful knitted throw covering her legs. The sun haloed her hair, the same pure gold as Sheila's. Not for the first time, Pamela wondered where the red in her own unruly mane came from.

"Mending." She sank on to a stool beside her mother's chair. "I sent a letter off for him to a friend in Devon. I told him to have his friend address his reply to Mrs. Creal. I just hope that I intercept it first when it arrives." She sighed. "I didn't know how else to do it."

A frail, blue-veined hand reached out and patted her on the shoulder. "That was for the best. But have you learned anything more about him?"

Only that he can make my heart stop, she nearly replied. Instead she said, "No. I haven't asked. I suppose I should inform Lord Crandall, but he said it wasn't important enough to bother the local magistrate." She looked up into her mother's faded blue eyes. "Do you think that means he's hiding something?"

"Possibly. But since we don't want your father to find out about him, for now it's best to leave things as they are."

Pamela pondered this for a moment. "I asked Barlow about him. He said Kitt had a fever the first night and talked about two people named Denny and Geoff, but little else. Since the fever broke, he's been a model patient. But he's obviously a gentleman, possibly a lord."

Lady Clarkdale's pale brows drew into a frown. "I wish I could meet him."

Pamela smiled. "I could smuggle him in."

Her mother smiled in return. "That would be nice, but it's too risky. We do not want your father to discover his presence."

"I suppose not."

Pamela and her mother shared a conspiratorial silence. Neither liked deceit, but when it came to hospitality, her mother felt the ends justified the means. Pamela did not understand her father's antipathy toward strangers, and her mother simply refused to turn anyone needing aid away. Fortunately, not many strangers ventured near Clark Hall since it was not close to a main road. The locals all knew better than to come here for aid, despite her mother's instructions to Barlow to come to her or Pamela if he knew of someone who needed help.

Their nearest neighbors were the residents of the small village of Timpvale, Lord Crandall and Squire Halston. The city of York was a two-hour ride away to the east, and the nearest posting inn was three miles to the south.

The door to the room opened, startling her from her thoughts. Sheila entered, coming to a stop as she noticed Pamela.

"Here you are! I thought you would be in the stables."

Pamela frowned. "Why would you think that?"

Maddie, her mother's abigail, followed Sheila into the room.

"You practically live there, except when you're playing 'lady of the manor'."

"Sheila!" Lady Clarkdale exclaimed.

"Well, it's true," she said defensively. "And I still can't find my blue shawl."

Pamela restrained herself from rolling her eyes. Sheila always expected her needs to be addressed first. If it didn't revolve around her or something she wanted, it didn't exist. Her self-absorption was further exacerbated by their father, who indulged her every whim.

"Your blue shawl, miss?" Maddie spoke for the first time. "Why, you left it in here just yesterday." The abigail crossed the room to the overstuffed chair in front of the fireplace and picked up something hanging over the back.

"Oh, Maddie. You're wonderful!" Sheila grabbed the shawl and draped it over her shoulders. Twirling for the admiration of the rest of the occupants of the room, she smiled brightly. "It's perfect."

Pamela struggled unsuccessfully to keep her irritation at bay, all the while reluctantly admitting that her sister *was* exceedingly beautiful.

"Sheila, a number of the maids and I spent a good portion of the day looking for that shawl. A good portion of the day, I might add, we could have spent doing other things."

Sheila looked over at her. "Oh, pooh. That's what servants are for."

"Sheila!" Lady Clarkdale's tone indicated her disappointment.

"How could you be so thoughtless?" Pamela said, angry now. "I swear I wonder how we could be so different. How can you be so unconcerned about what others have to do to satisfy your whims?"

"They get paid to do that."

"I don't," Pamela shot back.

"Girls..." Lady Clarkdale tried for calm.

"Maybe you ought to," came a voice from the doorway.

Their mother gasped as all eyes turned to the open door. "Maurice! You cannot possibly mean that."

Pamela noticed Maddie left the room as her father entered, closing the door behind her. She rose from her stool.

Sheila, unaware of the suddenly charged atmosphere in the room, turned to her father. "Look, Papa, I left my shawl in here when I was visiting Mama yesterday."

It took all of Pamela's willpower not to grab Sheila and shake her. How could one person be so selfish? It didn't take much looking to find the answer. Sheila had been outrageously indulged from the day she was born. All attempts to curb her selfishness by their mother, governess, or anyone else were ignored by their father.

Recognizing that her time with her mother was over for today, Pamela leaned over and kissed her cheek.

"I will come see you again tomorrow, Mama." Crossing the carpet to the door, she greeted her father. "Good afternoon, Papa."

His dark eyes narrowed at her, but he responded in a neutral tone. "Good afternoon, Pamela." Then he dismissed her by turning toward Sheila. "You run along, too, Poppet. I wish to speak to your mother."

"About me?"

Pamela didn't wait to hear any more. She opened the door and slipped out, closing it behind her. Heart heavy in her chest, she headed down the back stairs toward the kitchen.

She wished she didn't feel as if her father didn't like her, let alone love her as a father should. Why? It was a question she asked herself often. She wasn't the beauty that Sheila was, her hair was more red than blond, but she had his brown eyes, although hers had green flecks in them. She was sure being able to look him directly in the eye unnerved him, but there was nothing she could do about her height. Her brother Stephen was tall. Her mother said he took after their grandfather. So why did it seem so wrong for her to be tall as well?

Chapter Two

The night was quiet. Pamela pulled her thin shawl tightly around her shoulders against the chill, but hesitated at the door to the stables. Memories from the morning before came flooding back, causing heat to infuse her whole body. Without warning, her hand began to tingle. She shivered.

Slipping into the welcoming warmth, she found Kitt and Seth playing a game of cards in the back room. "Good evening. I'm not interrupting, am I?"

"You're just in time to see me lose yet again," Kitt replied good-naturedly. "I should be thankful we are only playing for fun or I'd be in debt to Seth as well as you."

She smiled as she dropped down onto the end of the cot. Kitt sat on the other end, while Seth occupied the chair. An upturned crate served as a table between them. In addition to the cards, she noticed two mugs of ale on the crate and wondered if she should have offered Kitt something of her father's. Comfortable in the room with the two men, she allowed herself to study Kitt as he played with Seth.

He was exceptionally attractive, with midnight blue eyes under dark, slashed brows. His cheekbones were high, sharp and well defined, and his tanned skin stretched taut over a strong, squared jaw. Full lips hid even, white teeth, and the lines radiating from the corner of his eyes told her he smiled quite a bit, and not just with his mouth.

She wanted to know more about him, but was reluctant to come right out and ask.

When the game was over, Seth left them alone. She noticed Kitt wince as he moved his left arm.

"How is the shoulder? Has Barlow looked at it again?" She was thankful the stable master was skilled with injuries. Her father didn't like doctors any more than other strangers, and if it wasn't for her mother's illness, wouldn't allow Dr. Leeds on the property at all.

"It is extremely sore, but has not developed any infection."

"Good."

Silence fell and a blush rose in her cheeks as she realized he was studying her. Fleetingly she wondered if he liked what he saw.

"Tell me about London," she blurted to cover her embarrassment at her thoughts.

A dark eyebrow rose. "What do you want to know?"

"Is it truly as big as everyone says?"

"That depends on what everyone says. But it is quite large. Much larger than York."

"Mama says there are so many things to do that you never get bored."

"That's true, up to a point. But a person can only go to so many parties and run into the same people so often before everything begins to pall."

"Oh, but I wasn't speaking of balls and parties. I suppose going to a few might be fun. But I would like to see the museums, shop in the bookshops, ride in the park and go to the theatre."

"You have no interest in a Season?" His surprise was evident.

"Well, I did hope for one when I was eighteen, but we were in mourning, then the next year Papa said I didn't need one."

Kitt heard the forlorn tone in her voice. Her disappointment was obvious.

"Why is that? Are you already betrothed?"

She shook her head. The red-gold strands gleamed in the lamplight, but her face was in shadow.

"No." A deep sigh emerged, causing her shoulders to slump. "Mama needs me here. She's too sick to do much, and the doctor says she's unlikely to get better."

He wanted to ask what was wrong with her mother but was reluctant to pry. "Perhaps your father ought to consult with a doctor in York or London."

"Papa doesn't like doctors. He only tolerates Dr. Leeds because Mama insists on seeing him. Once Grandpapa wanted to send a doctor from London, but Papa refused. Have you seen many plays?"

Surprised at the sudden switch in topic, Kitt paused before answering.

"A few."

"Is Kean really as good and as handsome as the papers say?"

"I am not a connoisseur, but I would say he is a very good actor. As for his looks, I'm afraid I have not paid them much attention."

She laughed, and he was surprised at the pleasing effect on his senses. Her eyes sparkled in the dim light and her cheeks took on a rosy hue. She was quite pretty when animated. His body reacted instantly and he had to shift his legs to make himself more comfortable.

"No, I suppose you would not."

He was conscious of her scent, which reached him from where she sat at the far end of the cot. Wildflowers. A mixture of which he could only pick out honeysuckle. It suited her. A few curls had escaped her knot and bounced against her shoulders, framing her face.

He ruthlessly squelched the urge to reach out and touch her and shifted again. She rose and looked down at him.

"I must get back to the house before someone wonders where I have gone to. I will wish you a good night and see you tomorrow."

He stood and approached her. Unable to stop himself, he tucked a stray strand behind her ears, brushing his fingers lightly over her cheek as he did so.

"Thank you again."

Her eyes widened. She stepped back. "Y...you're welcome." Then she turned and fled.

Kitt's shoulder was healing nicely by the next week, but he chafed at the inactivity as he waited for a response to his letter. Barlow, Seth, and the other stable hands were congenial, but after the first few days they left him to his own devices while they went about their duties. Pamela was a frequent visitor and he looked forward to the times she dropped in.

The stables were a hive of activity. Sir Maurice was either a connoisseur of good horseflesh, or incredibly lucky in his purchases. Barlow indicated that it was somewhere in between, that in actuality many of the horses were bought by Master Stephen. Pamela's mount, Midas, was such.

The spirited gelding was a dark glossy brown with two white stockings. Whenever Pamela came near his stall, he stuck his head out eagerly, awaiting the apples she frequently kept in her pocket for him. Midas, however, wasn't the only occupant of the stables Pamela bestowed her warmth and care on. Up in the hayloft there was a tabby with a litter of kittens she checked on regularly. And of course, there was Kitt.

He anticipated her visits as much as Midas did. Perhaps more.

In the past, female companionship never meant friendship. Women were for warming a man's bed, bearing a man's children, and running a man's household. Except for his godmother, no woman in his life had ever seen him as anything other than a deep pocket. As long as he satisfied them in and out of bed, and their arrangements were mutually beneficial, he paid them little heed. But Pamela broke the mold.

She was friendly, caring, intelligent and generous. Her smile lit up the stables, warming the frigid air with her enthusiasm. She gave freely of her time, often sitting up late with him playing chess or cards when he knew she needed to be up early. She had apologized for keeping him in the stables, blushing furiously as she tried to explain her father's distrust of strangers.

"I have slept in worse places. You needn't worry that my delicate sensibilities have been overset."

She changed the subject then, asking him again about London and the sights, which he obligingly described to her in as much detail as he could.

23

Her eyes lit up at his descriptions and he became warm watching her. He hadn't touched her since the day he kissed her wrist, but he hadn't forgotten the texture of her skin or the throb of her pulse against his mouth. He itched to take her in his arms and taste her lips, but restrained himself. After all, she was a gently bred lady—and she had saved his life. Only a thoroughly disreputable character would take advantage of her in such a manner, and he wasn't that jaded.

Was he?

"Papa has taken Sheila to York." Pamela passed her mother a cup of tea. "Shall I smuggle Kitt in to see you today?"

"No. I'm sorry, dear, but I have a terrible headache. I need to rest a little. But perhaps you could take him out for a bit. I'm sure he wouldn't mind some time outside."

Pamela giggled. "You make him sound like a pet that needs to be let out on occasion."

Her mother's smile was wan. "I didn't mean it that way, but..."

"Yes, I know what you meant, Mama. I was only teasing."

Pamela sipped her tea, watching her mother intently as she did so. She was surprised to find her mother still in bed this morning. Although she rarely left her room, Lady Clarkdale usually rose and dressed each day. A headache explained the departure from her routine, but something else was not right. Pamela could feel it. Her mother obviously had something to say, but was hesitating. Putting the delicate cup back on its saucer, Pamela returned both to the tray.

"What's wrong, Mama?" When her mother merely looked up at her, she felt her heart slow. "There is something wrong, is there not?"

Lady Clarkdale put down her cup and saucer, too. Pamela noted that her hands shook before she rested them on the pale blue coverlet of her bed.

"I don't know. I have been wondering why there has been no word from Lord Crandall lately. I thought he was courting you."

Pamela went still at the mention of Lord Crandall. He was their nearest neighbor, and the local magistrate. Two years ago, as a frequent visitor to Clark Hall, he had singled Pamela out for marked attention. But in the last year he hadn't put in an appearance, except once. A week ago she'd encountered him in the front hall, but her mother knew nothing about it and Pamela would not worry her by repeating it.

At twenty-six, he was the best catch in the local area. With his dark hair, dark eyes, and athletic figure, she wondered why he bothered with anyone here when he could go to London and take his pick of the beauties there. Two years ago, when she thought he was courting her, she allowed herself to fall under his spell and think she was in love. Now she knew better, and since finding Kitt she had given him no thought whatsoever—except to wonder whether she should send him a message concerning Kitt. When Kitt insisted it wasn't necessary, she'd put it from her mind.

"I don't know." She chose her words carefully. "But I have not given him much thought lately. I have been too busy."

"Midas will be unhappy with me for leaving him behind, but Barlow didn't think you ought to be riding just yet with your shoulder."

Pamela and Kitt were walking through the meadow behind the stables, headed for a small wood that lay just beyond. The day was comfortably warm, and she'd left her cloak behind, opting for a shawl over her day dress of dark brown twill. Kitt wore his newly laundered and mended riding jacket with his left arm in a makeshift sling.

Checking with cook to see that all was under control in the kitchen, and leaving instructions with Mrs. Creal, she took her mother's advice and invited Kitt for a walk. She knew if any of the household staff saw her leaving carrying a small basket they would assume she was taking apples to the horses in the stables. In actuality, she'd brought food for a picnic.

They entered the shelter of the trees. "Are you tired of convalescing yet?"

He stopped and looked up at the cloudless sky through the canopy of branches.

"I would be prevaricating were I to say 'no', but I'm not sure I'm so thoroughly bored that I would welcome the crowds and noise of London again."

"Ahh, a true politician." She smiled. "I suspect you would handle yourself well in Parliament."

Kitt chuckled with pleasure as they began walking again.

"Do you truly have no family at all, or just none who will worry?"

"My parents are dead, as are my grandparents. And I was an only child, as were both my parents."

Pamela digested this information. There were times when she wished she was an only child. Perhaps then her father might pay her some attention. As it was, he had to be reminded occasionally that she was part of the family. It was possible Sheila was right. Maybe taking on not only her mother's responsibilities, but also some of Mrs. Creal's caused her to be so busy with the household that her father was beginning to see her as one of the staff rather than his daughter. Except for mealtimes, their paths rarely crossed.

Too often he had to be convinced she needed new clothes, and she knew that while he brought small trinkets back from York occasionally for Sheila, only in the past when her mother accompanied him had he thought to buy her anything. She often wondered if he would even miss her if she simply disappeared.

She sighed, wishing she knew what it would take to please him. Sheila seemed to do it effortlessly, yet nothing Pamela did evoked even the smallest bit of approval from him.

Lost in her thoughts, she scarcely noticed Kitt turn and look down at her as they walked. Spring had been slow in coming this year. Many of the trees were only just now beginning to grow new foliage. Birdsong wafted through the wood and small animals scurried across their path up ahead.

They entered a clearing, startling a doe and two fawns feeding on the new shoots of tender grass. The deer froze for a moment and then swiftly disappeared into the brush on the other side.

Kitt stood in the middle of the clearing and watched Pamela approach a tree, beneath which sat three old crates. As she bent over, his practiced eye admired the outline of her bottom beneath the brown material. Moving one of the crates as he joined her, she reached into a hollow at the base of the trunk and came up with a package. When she handed it to him, he realized that it was a blanket wrapped in oilcloth.

She spread the blanket in a patch of sunlight, then brought one of the crates over and placed her basket on top. A second crate joined the first and she spread her shawl over it. Opening the basket, she set out a light luncheon of meat pies, fruit tarts, dried apples, and almond biscuits.

"It's not much because I couldn't bring a bigger basket. But I don't think we'll starve."

"You've obviously done this before." Kitt lowered himself to the blanket.

She grinned and her eyes sparkled in the sunlight.

"This was probably Stephen's and my favorite place to play as children. Barlow helped us to bring the crates here the summer I was seven. Stephen was five. We thought we were going to take them apart and build a playhouse, but Barlow convinced us that we could use them just as they were. Now that I'm older, I'm glad we didn't dismantle them. They come in handy as tables or chairs occasionally."

"And the blanket?"

"Oh, that was my idea two years ago. It was easier to leave it here than to carry it out all the time. I leave it in the stables over the winter, but I brought it back out here not long ago." She had finished emptying her basket and now set it aside. "I must have known you were coming."

The small clearing was dotted with patches of grass and he suspected wildflowers carpeted it in the summer. The air smelled faintly of cool, damp earth and he breathed deeply. In the distance, he could hear water tumbling over rocks.

As if she read his mind, she said, "The stream that I found you beside runs through here over that way," and pointed in the direction the deer had gone. Producing two small cups from the bottom of the basket, she rose to her feet and shook out her skirts. "Help yourself while I get us some water."

He scrambled to join her, but she waved him back.

"No. I can do it faster. Besides, if we leave the food, it may not be here when we get back."

He grimaced as he watched her disappear around a tree. It went against his nature to allow her to go off alone, but knew she was right. This was her home. She probably knew every inch of this forest, whereas he wasn't sure he knew his way back to the stables.

"What does your father do in York?" he asked when she returned.

Setting the brimming cups down on the upturned crate, she sank on to the blanket and reached for a meat pie.

"He owns two factories there." She handed him the meat pie before helping herself to one. "He goes to meet with his foremen and bankers, I think." She bit into the pie, chewing and swallowing before she continued. "Although this time I think he went because Sheila wanted to go."

He wondered if she knew her voice changed whenever she spoke of her sister. It was not exactly bitter, but there was a sardonic bent to her comments which alerted one that all was not well in that corner.

"Does he ever go to London?"

She shook her head. "Not that I can remember. He says he doesn't like all the noise and people in London."

"And your mother?"

"Mama prefers not to go either, although now that she is so ill, she could not go anyway. I think my grandparents have been asked to sponsor Sheila for a Season."

If he hadn't been watching her, he would not have noticed the hurt reflected in her eyes as she spoke of her grandparents and sister. The workings of her family were a mystery to him, but one he felt was not his concern. At any rate, he was unlikely to encounter her sister in London. It was doubtful the daughter of a knight would move in the same circles he inhabited. Once home, he would relegate these weeks to a fond memory.

As they made their way back to the stables later that afternoon, Kitt contemplated the atmosphere of contentment surrounding them. Never had he spent so long with a woman without touching her. Yet the afternoon flew by as he and Pamela talked, discussed, and even argued across a spectrum of topics. It was unfamiliar territory—the notion that he could merely talk to a woman without the sexual undercurrent and innuendo which regularly peppered *ton* conversations.

Although their conversation wasn't littered with subtle insinuations and invitations, his mind and body were not completely oblivious to Pamela's appeal. She had a low, husky voice, which made promises he knew she had no idea how to keep. Her face, while not beautiful in the accepted sense, drew his gaze often, and her tall, long-legged form was perfectly proportioned for his taller-than-average build. There were many in the *ton* who might not give her a second glance, but many others who would be only too happy to squire her about.

As they ducked into the stables via a back door near his room, their shoulders brushed and he felt a jolt clear to his boots. Hearing her sharp intake of breath mollified him somewhat, but he had to restrain himself from hauling her into his arms and tasting those soft, full lips.

When she slipped away, he returned to his solitary cot. He'd felt fine for most of the afternoon, but now tiredness pulled at him and his shoulder ached a bit.

"I'm getting soft," he muttered to himself. "It's time to make my way home." Settling on top of the rough blanket, he stared at the rough-hewn beams criss-crossing the ceiling until his eyelids drooped.

Pamela stood just inside the door to the stables, her back against the rough wood. The familiar smells of hay, horses, and men surrounded her, the darkness a welcome blanket. Tonight, however, they failed to provide the comfort she was accustomed to.

Tears ran in rivulets down her cheeks, seeping out from beneath closed lids as she fought the urge to burst into noisy sobs. Sheila's squeal of delight rang in her ears as she heard, again, her father grant Sheila a wish he'd long denied her.

A Season. Their grandparents were to sponsor Sheila for a Season in London.

Five years ago, when she should have come out, they were in mourning for an aunt she'd never met. Even though he'd had no contact with his sister, her father insisted on a full six months of mourning when word came of her death in Scotland.

The next year her mother had fallen ill—the first of many illnesses which gradually reduced her to a frail shadow of her former self. Pamela was needed then to keep the household running smoothly. And she had been doing so ever since.

Her mother wanted her to have a Season, but her father stood firm. Pamela was needed at home. For the last few years, the excuse was Sheila was still in the schoolroom. But when Sheila turned eighteen shortly before Christmas and the last governess was dismissed, she erroneously assumed both of them would come out this year.

Now she faced the unmistakable fact—Sheila would be allowed to go to London while she, Pamela, was expected to remain at home and continue to run the household.

"It's not fair!" She sniffed and dragged the back of her hand across her eyes. "Why does she get everything?"

She did not begrudge her sister anything. The clothes, the trinkets, the gifts, even the Season. She only wanted to share it. But Sheila *never* had to share. What Sheila wanted, Sheila got. And it was hers alone. As children, Pamela and Stephen often shared their toys and games, but not Sheila.

Pushing herself away from the door, Pamela took a shaky breath, wiped her cheeks with the back of her hand, and made her way down the row of stalls. Moonlight streamed in through high windows, but she needed no light. The stables were as familiar to her as her own room. She could traverse them blindfolded. As she reached Midas's stall, the horse snorted and she stopped.

"Did you know I was coming?" She stroked his glossy coat and he nudged her with his nose. "No apples tonight, I'm afraid."

Burying her face in the horse's neck, she regained a bit of her equilibrium. At least she'd not had to share Midas. Sheila was afraid of horses and never learned to ride. Closing her eyes, she remembered the day Stephen brought him home three years ago.

"What do you mean, he's for Pamela?" their father had argued. "What does *she* need with a horse like that?"

"She doesn't *need* it, but I want her to have him."

Her father blustered and complained, but in the end Stephen won, and Midas remained when he left. That her father resented Stephen's high-handedness was obvious, but he said nothing. A year ago, he'd tried to sell the gelding, but Barlow squelched it by letting the prospective buyer's groom know that the horse wasn't her father's to sell. She was thankful he'd never found out it was Barlow who'd been so disloyal as to reveal that bit of information.

The horse nickered and she was suddenly aware of no longer being alone. Raising her head, she found Kitt standing beside her. His face was in shadow, but it didn't matter. In fact, it was probably for the best as it meant he couldn't see her tears.

"I heard Midas and came to investigate. His voice rolled through her, easing the pain. His presence was comforting in an odd way and she moved toward him without thought. When his arms closed around her and she rested her head against his uninjured shoulder, the sigh that slipped from her lips released all her pent up anger, disappointment, and disillusionment.

Kitt remained still as Pamela relaxed in his arms. Only three days ago, he would have given half his fortune to have her where she was now. Why she was there, he didn't know, but he was sure her father or sister had something to do with it.

His mind told him she needed comfort. Unfortunately if the blood hammering in his veins and the increase in his heartbeat indicated anything, it was that his body had other ideas. Sliding his hand up her spine, he pressed her soft curves more fully against him. Her breasts were pillowed against the hardness of his chest, and he swallowed as his body reacted to her nearness.

She took a deep breath as his hand reached her neck and began toying with her habitual chignon. When the knot came

31

loose, spilling the silken curls down over his hand, she raised her head. He could not see her face, but his mouth unerringly found hers.

Two things hit him at once. One, she'd been crying. The salty taste of tears on her lips was unmistakable. And two, she was not resisting. The second fact sent a wave of heat through him to rival the most potent of brandies. His imagination was a poor second to the actuality of her soft lips beneath his.

He tightened his arm around her waist, ignoring the small stab of pain in his shoulder as he did so. Cradling her neck in his other hand, he angled his head and deepened the kiss, sliding his tongue across the seam of her lips and, when she parted her lips in response, surging into the warm cavern beyond. She shuddered in his arms as he gently explored, rubbing her tongue with his and drinking in the tiny moan that bubbled up from her throat.

She was an innocent. It was evident in the way she clung to him, following his more experienced lead. Her hands crept up to his shoulders, her fingers sinking in momentarily before snaking around his neck and burying themselves in his hair.

His hold on reality slipped a notch and he moved from her lips to trace a path along her jaw. Her head fell back, steadied by his hand, allowing unobstructed access to the soft skin of her throat. The scent of wildflowers surrounded him. He took a deep breath and was unable to stop the rush of blood to his loins. When he tasted the skin at the hollow of her throat, she whimpered and her hands spasmed against the back of his skull.

Moving back up, he caught her lips again, sinking into the moist opening and taking complete possession. How long they were locked together he wouldn't guess, yet he was thankful for the small part of his brain that remained alert.

The slight sound only barely registered, but Midas's muzzle against Pamela's back brought him down to earth with a jolt. He raised his head, his eyes searching the gloom beyond as Pamela rested her head against his shoulder again.

He could hear her dragging in large breaths. His blood pounded in tempo with his heart, and another part of his body demanded he continue what he started. He ignored it. Moving his hand in circles, he rubbed her back. The repetitive motion allowed him to bring his wayward impulses under control and regain his stability.

As calm and quiet returned to his body and mind, he searched for something to say that wouldn't cheapen the moment. Pamela solved his dilemma by stepping back. His arms tightened for a fraction of a second, then relaxed and let her go. She looked up at him for a very long moment before she said in a soft, slightly shaky voice, "I'm sorry to have disturbed you. Good night, Kitt."

Then she turned and disappeared into the gloom before he could react. The closing of the stable door echoed loudly in the silence. Even Midas retreated into his stall, leaving Kitt standing in the darkened aisle, alone with his thoughts.

I'm sorry to have disturbed you. If he wasn't convinced of her innocence, he would have thought she'd said it deliberately.

Pamela took large gulps of icy air into her lungs. Her body shook, but not from the cold. After tonight, she might never be cold again.

Why? Why did she go to the stables? After her father's announcement over dinner, she retreated to her room, but Sheila followed. Excited by her good fortune and oblivious to Pamela's disappointment, she wanted to talk about London and everything she expected to see and do. The stables were the only place she knew to go where Sheila would not follow her. Mumbling an excuse about checking on Midas, she'd fled.

Such was her distraction that she hadn't stopped in the kitchen to collect a dried apple or two for him as usual. When Kitt appeared, it seemed inevitable she would end up in his arms. After fighting a growing attraction to him for the last two weeks, tonight her resistance was nonexistent.

She glanced up at the house. Moonlight limned the gray brick, the windows dark hollows in a multi-faceted face. If her father was still up, he was in the library, which faced the front.

Trudging toward the house, she could still feel the heat in her cheeks.

I'm sorry to have disturbed you. What was she thinking? He was probably even now laughing at the inane comment.

33

More so, she was sorry for the impact that disturbance had on her. Slipping through the rear door near the kitchen, she climbed the back stairs on silent feet. Sheila would be asleep by now, hopefully having chattered away at Bess or their mother for the evening.

She reached her room and entered. The embers in the fireplace flared to life as she stirred them, then she undressed before the fire. Her brush lay on the mantle above the fireplace and she picked it up before sinking to the rug before it. Sitting in the pool of warmth, she brushed her hair and relived the encounter in the stables.

So that's what it felt like to be kissed. If anyone had tried to explain it to her, she would never have believed it. Not without the use of words like "exhilarating", "hot", or "mindless". Nothing she'd ever experienced prepared her for the wonder of being in Kitt's arms, for the sensation of being held captive by nothing more than his lips. It was magical. It was glorious. It was heaven.

A log fell in the grate and she blinked, emerging from her thoughts to realize that she'd finished brushing and plaiting her hair and now sat staring into the dying flames.

"Stop acting like a lovesick fool!" Rising from the rug, she replaced her brush on the mantle, then crossed to her bed and climbed in. She thought the kiss might have left her too excited to sleep, but she fell quickly into a dreamless slumber.

Pamela hated being late. It threw her entire day off schedule. Hurrying through her toilette, she ate in the kitchen rather than the dining room. She was thankful she hadn't run into Sheila yet this morning as she hurried through the instructions to Mrs. Creal and the maids for the day, then headed upstairs to check with Maddie on how her mother fared.

Her hopes her mother might already be awake this early were dashed when Maddie told her Sheila had visited the night before and stayed late. Sighing, she returned downstairs to the kitchen to speak to the cook, which was where Bess found her a short time later to relay the message her father wished to see her in the library.

Frowning, she left the kitchen. Her father rarely sent for her or Sheila. If he had news, he usually waited until a meal time to pass it along, as he had last night. As she crossed the front hall, the butler was receiving the post from the local postboy.

"Sorry I didn't get it here yesterday," the boy said. "The coach didn't get in 'til late."

She waited until the door was closed, then approached the butler. "I'll take that, Dobbs. I'm headed for the library and I'll give it to Papa."

The butler handed over the small bundle and she turned toward the library. Flipping through the small stack, she noticed a letter addressed to Mrs. Creal from someplace in Devon. It must be for Kitt, she thought. Slipping it into a pocket, she continued on to the library and knocked at the door.

Entering at her father's call, she found him sitting at the large oak desk answering correspondence. The day outside was overcast, the light coming in through the windows not enough to work by. A lamp on the desk was lit, casting a pool of yellow light over the letter he was writing.

Pamela's eyes wandered the room fondly. The floor-to-ceiling bookshelves were crammed full, but she knew her father read very little. The combined smells of leather and polish wafted around her and she breathed deeply. She loved the library. Unfortunately, she rarely spent time in here, so busy was she with her mother and the rest of the household.

Her father finished his letter and sanded it.

"You sent for me, Papa?"

He looked up and brown eyes met hers but he did not answer.

"The post just arrived." She put the letters on the desk. "I thought to save Dobbs the trip."

Her father gave her a hard look. He didn't invite her to sit, so she remained standing before the desk, feeling like she was eight again and had been summoned for being naughty.

"I understand you've been dallying with a young man in the stables."

The statement out of the blue, in an accusatory tone, stunned her.

"I have not." Her retort was automatically defensive.

"Are you saying Sheila made it up?"

"Sheila? What does she have to do with this?"

"She said she saw you allow a young man take indecent liberties with your person in the stables. Was she lying?"

Pamela felt as if the rug had been pulled out from under her. "What was Sheila doing in the stables? And when?"

"Does it matter?"

"But she *never* goes out to the stables."

"Is that why you felt free to conduct yourself indecently there?"

"It depends upon what you consider indecent." She knew she was stalling.

Her father reddened and blustered a bit. "Are you saying Sheila lied about seeing you kissing a young man in the stables?"

Pamela stared at the surface of the desk, unable to meet her father's eyes. It would be so easy to say yes. Sheila only told the truth when it suited her, and was not adverse to twisting it or outright lying. But Pamela refused to stoop to her level. "No."

There was a long silence during which Pamela could feel his eyes boring into her. "I see," was all he said before rising to his feet. She looked up warily. "I suppose I should have a talk with this young man. Which one of the stable hands is he?"

"Why?"

"To see that he does the proper thing by you, of course."

"What?" Baffled, she stared at her father.

"Pay attention, girl! If you've been dallying with one of the stable hands, then he'd best be prepared to marry you."

"I haven't."

Crossing his arms over his chest, he narrowed his eyes at her. Fear rose in her throat at the look before she quashed it. She'd never been afraid of her father before. Why should she start now?

He came around his desk. She stepped back from him, but he walked past her toward the door. "We'll just see about that. Which one of the stable hands is he?"

She panicked. "He isn't one of the stable hands. "He's not from here. I-I found him down by the stream." The truth was the only thing that came to mind at the moment.

He turned. "What?" His roar caused her to jump.

"He...he was injured. S-someone had shot him and left him to die. I-I couldn't just...just leave him."

Pamela shrank back against the desk as he returned to her. "You brought a stranger into my house?" His voice seemed to vibrate around the room.

"I-I didn't bring him into the house." A blacksmith set up shop in her head, the pounding muddling her thoughts.

His hand shot out and fastened around her upper arm, pulling her toward him. "We shall just go out and see this young man. Is he still in the stables?"

Pamela nodded dumbly. Trying desperately to make sense of what was happening, she allowed her father to nearly drag her out of the house.

As they went out the rear door, the cold air jolted her and she realized where they were headed. She began to struggle.

"Let me go. Please, Papa, let me go. I haven't done anything wrong." They reached the stables and he dragged her inside. Struggling futilely, Pamela tried to pull away, but his hand on her arm only gripped tighter. "Papa, you're hurting me."

He didn't answer as Seth hurried toward them.

"Where is he?"

"Where is who?" Seth asked.

"Don't play the fool with me, boy. Where's the young man you've got hidden in here?"

Kitt came down the aisle between the stalls. "Are you looking for me?"

Pamela looked to Kitt. Embarrassment heated her cheeks as she continued to struggle to free herself.

"And just who are you?"

"Kitt—"

"From?"

"London."

"Well, then," he snapped dismissively. "You can return there."

"Papa, he's only waiting—" Pamela was cut off in mid-sentence as he flung her at Kitt.

"And take her with you!"

Pamela would have stumbled and fallen against one of the upright beams had Kitt not caught her. The momentary fear she'd felt in the library returned as Kitt steadied her.

"And why would I want to do that?" Kitt's voice was mild, but she heard the steel in it.

"As you are the reason her reputation is now in ruins, it would seem obvious that I expect you to repair it."

Flabbergasted, Pamela stared at her father.

"What do you mean, my reputation is in ruins? I haven't done anything wrong."

"I suppose your admission in the library means nothing?"

"It was only a kiss!" Pamela stepped toward her father to emphasize her point.

For someone his size, he moved quicker than she expected. Pain exploded in her head, sending her stumbling back into Kitt. Only Kitt's grip on her shoulders as he caught her kept her from blacking out.

"Wanton baggage! How dare you try—" Her father was cut short by Kitt who, after confirming that she was still conscious and able to stand, grabbed him by his shirtfront and cravat, nearly lifting him off the floor—not an easy feat, considering his girth.

Pamela watched in awe as her father's face turned first red, then bright purple, as he struggled to breathe and free himself from Kitt's grip.

A deadly silence ensued that was broken by Kitt's voice, each word falling ominously. "Touch her again and you'll regret it." Then he let go and her father fell to the hay-strewn dirt floor as Kitt turned back to her. "Are you all right?" His gentle voice calmed the furious hammering in her head.

Pamela nodded and he put his uninjured arm around her, pressing her against his chest.

Behind them, she heard her father scramble to his feet. Kitt turned to watch him. "Get out! Get out of this house and never come back!" His voice rose and Pamela didn't bother to turn back to face him. Even with her face buried against Kitt's warm chest, she could hear him quite clearly. "I should have known you'd be no better than your mother. Well, I won't have it. You will leave this house today!"

In a daze, she turned in the circle of Kitt's arms as her father continued.

"I have tolerated you long enough. No longer. I wash my hands of you once and for all!" Having finished his tirade, he turned on his heel to leave, throwing over his shoulder as he left, "The servants will be instructed that you are no longer a member of this household. Anyone who admits you to the house will be dismissed on the spot!"

Then he was gone, leaving her bewildered, slumped against Kitt's hard frame with only one thought in her head. *Why?*

The heightened activity caused some of the horses to fidget and fuss and Seth had tactfully disappeared during the confrontation. The banging of the door caused her to jump, but she still did not, could not, move.

What just happened? Lifting her hands, she pressed fingers against her temples. Another blacksmith had moved into her head and she closed her eyes against the pain. Taking a deep breath, she tried to sort out her thoughts. She savored the warmth and strength of Kitt's arms for a moment, then stepped away and turned to look up at him.

Pulling an envelope out of her pocket, she handed it to him. "I'm sure this is for you. I know no one in Devon."

He took it, barely glancing at it as he turned his full attention to her. The look in his eyes warned her of his intention before he began to speak. "I have caused you a considerable amount of trouble..."

"No you haven't. Papa always says things he doesn't mean when he's in a temper." She tried to smile, but at least her voice was firm. "You have no idea how many times he's disowned me, then wondered where I was when I didn't show for supper."

She noticed he relaxed slightly at her confident words, and continued.

"I shall go and tell Mama all about it. You'll see," she said with an attempt at cheerfulness. "Unfortunately, now that Papa knows you're here, you'll need to leave. I can have Seth take you to the Three Swans. It's the nearest posting inn. I'm sure you could get a coach to London from there."

Kitt's eyes narrowed at her and she saw the skepticism in his gaze.

He folded his arms across his chest. "I will not leave you unless I'm sure all is well."

"And why wouldn't it be?"

"Your father, as I recall, just disowned you."

She tried to laugh and hoped it sounded convincing. "Well, that's what he said. But he never means it. You can ask Seth or Barlow. He's threatened before to put me out, but he never means it."

She could see Kitt was still unconvinced. The hammering in her head intensified and she stopped herself from grinding her teeth in frustration.

"Very well. I shall go and tell Mama all about it. If I don't come back right away, you'll know it was all bluff."

He studied her for a long moment, considering his options. Finally, after a tense minute, he reached out and tipped her face up to his.

"I will wait for an hour. If you haven't returned by then, I will be on my way."

Pleasure rippled through her at his concern, but she knew it was only guilt. Moving closer, she lifted up on her toes and brushed her lips against his cheek. He stilled.

"Thank you."

"I am the one who should be thanking you. You saved my life. Never underestimate yourself on that score."

Unable to speak in the face of his sincerity, she nodded. Then she turned and hurried out of the stables.

Chapter Three

London, May

"Of all the cockle-brained, madcap schemes I've ever heard, this is one of the worst!" Pamela exclaimed.

"How many have you heard?"

Pamela stared up into Kitt's deep blue eyes above her, distracted by the extraordinarily long dark lashes framing them. She could feel the blood flooding her cheeks as she tore her eyes away to glance over the small overgrown garden.

"Well, not many," she confessed. "But I made up my share as a child, and what you're proposing is preposterous."

"Why?"

"Because...well, because it is!"

"How do you know?"

Turning away in exasperation, Pamela strolled to the small fountain and sat on the smooth marble edge. Dipping her hand into the cool water, she disturbed her reflection and felt her composure return. Why did things like this happen to her?

Her life had not been the same since the day she found Kitt lying injured by the small stream on her father's land. Standing up to her father hadn't seemed so bad, but being banished still hurt.

After that horrible scene in the stables, she'd slipped back into the house and upstairs to speak to her mother. That last conversation was never far from her thoughts these days. She could still hear her mother's whisper-soft voice.

"I didn't have a choice, but I trusted him to keep his word."

"Trusted who?"

Sitting gingerly on the bed beside her, Pamela had straightened the blue counterpane covering her mother's lap. When Maddie arrived a few minutes later with a tea tray, she poured, then put the delicate white and gold cup into her mother's frail blue-veined hands.

"Maurice. He promised he would treat you as his own."

Pamela knew she looked confused. "As his...?"

Tears welled in her mother's faded blue eyes. "He's not your father."

As the tears spilled down her mother's cheeks, Pamela learned her real father had been a nobleman and childhood friend of her mother's. Someone she loved dearly, but who had no prospects and so could not aspire to the hand of the only daughter of an earl who needed a rich son-in-law to refill the family coffers. Even though his own father was also an earl, he wasn't wealthy enough. As a younger son, his only choice had been the military.

"My father had a fondness for the cards back then and needed the money Maurice was willing to give in exchange for my hand. It was a feather in his cap to marry the daughter of an earl and my father was able to reestablish the family fortune."

Pamela had sat in stunned silence as the tale unfolded. Although she'd refused, her mother was not given a choice. Maurice had been persuasive, assuring her she could keep the child and he would raise it as his own.

Maurice hadn't been a very attentive parent, so his attitude toward Pamela didn't seem odd until she was well into childhood. Her brother, Stephen, had been born three years later, and Sheila two years after him.

"It was Sheila's birth, I'm sure, that changed everything." Her mother sighed. "But I just didn't notice."

Pamela was not interested in recounting the numerous snubs and hurts she'd suffered while growing up in her younger sister's shadow. Nor did she want to revisit the feeling she'd often had of being an outsider, of not belonging. She had but one question.

"Who was he?"

Closing her eyes, Lady Clarkdale sagged against the mound of pillows at her back. A small dreamy smile flitted across her bloodless lips, but when she had opened her eyes again there was only pain to be seen in the watery blue depths.

"It no longer matters. He's dead."

Pamela looked up as Kitt approached, his boots crunching over the narrow graveled path. The sun shone brightly overhead, cloaking him in its brilliance and casting his shadow before him. A light, cooling breeze feathered across her cheeks. As he reached her side, the shadow enveloped her and she felt as if he touched her.

"Do you want me to apologize again? Is that it? I've already..."

"No!" She gripped her wet fingers together in her lap. She'd end up in tears if he told her again that he should have waited longer. It wouldn't have mattered; she would not have returned. That was all water under the bridge, wasn't it?

"Then what is it?"

"I just can't see that it will work." She nearly groaned as his lips tilted upwards. She didn't want him to think she was weakening. "It won't work."

"Oh, yes it will."

"But why me? I'm a nobody. Your godmother's companion. Don't you know anyone else who you'd..."

He grinned as she stumbled over the question, revealing even white teeth between firm lips.

"Be willing to marry? No. No one in particular."

"But, but I couldn't. You shouldn't." She was stammering, blathering like an idiot. And she didn't like it one bit.

She rose to her feet as he reached for her and stepped away from him. She needed to get back inside and away from his potent presence. Time. She needed time.

"I...I'll think about it. Now I...I have to get back. Lady Parkington will be looking for me." Then she turned and fled.

Christopher Orion Covington, twelfth Earl of Kittridge, Kitt to his family and friends, watched her go in frustration. He'd already aroused her doubts as to his sincerity. And now she was suspicious of his motives.

He supposed it was his own fault it came out so badly. Whatever happened to his vaunted reputation as a ladies' man?

Pose as my betrothed for the next few months. If there's no way to break it gracefully by the end of the Season, we can marry.

Some proposal. What kind of sapskull would ask a young woman to marry him in such a ham-fisted fashion? Him, apparently! He might as well have told her he'd flipped a coin to decide whom to marry and she'd won the toss.

Kitt turned toward the house, following Pamela's hurried steps at a more leisurely pace. He'd have to come up with a way to convince her eventually. For now, he wouldn't push things any further.

The interior of the house was cool and as he passed the small parlor, he could hear his godmother's voice and Pamela's in response. Retrieving his hat and cane from the butler, he strode out the front door and down the steps.

Arden Street was quiet at this time of day. Not far from the fashionable district, it was the perfect location for his godmother, who did not always want to be part of the social whirl. Close, but not in the middle of things.

Claire, Lady Parkington, had been his mother's closest and dearest friend. That should have been enough for him to ignore her altogether, but he adored the elderly woman. When his mother died in Scotland, she had been the one to break the news to him. She had also been the one to arrange to bring the body home to Kitt Ridge. And she had been the only one to attend the funeral. His father couldn't be bothered to leave his current mistress's side.

In all fairness, Kitt hadn't blamed his father. His mother had run off with a Frenchman when he was twelve, leaving her husband and son to fend for themselves. He had been away at school so the day-to-day routine hadn't changed, but once he returned home, he and his father quickly turned Kitt Ridge into an all-male domain. They rubbed along famously without her. Who needed a wife when one could have a different woman every month, or week? Such had been his father's philosophy, dutifully absorbed by his son.

When Kitt needed the softer touch of a female—not one in his bed, but one to talk to—he turned to his godmother. His father made sure they never lost touch, but only because she'd hinted Kitt might be her heir and his father was afraid she'd change her mind if she never saw him. Kitt didn't care much one way or another. The family fortune was large enough and he wasn't a gambler or a spendthrift. Over the years, however, he grew attached to her and now made an effort to see she was comfortable and suitably entertained when he was in Town.

He reached his house on Grosvenor Square and was ascending the steps to the front door when he heard his name. Turning, he noticed a curricle had drawn up to the curb. He grimaced. He was more distracted than he realized if he hadn't heard it approach. Aware the door to his house stood open, his butler standing sentinel, he waited for his friend, Lord Denton Avery, Denny to most, to join him and the two entered together.

"How are you, old chap? Haven't seen you in a while," Denny greeted him.

"Been a bit busy. But I've been in Town for a whole month and this is the first I've seen of you."

Entering the library, he crossed to the decanters set on a sideboard near one of the tall windows. Burgundy velvet drapes were pulled back to allow the late afternoon sunshine to spill into the room and pick out the colorful royal blue, red and burgundy patterns in the Axminster carpet.

"Your usual?"

"Whiskey. Denny settled his large but trim frame into a comfortable chair not far from the spotlessly clean rosewood desk.

Kitt glanced back at his friend in surprise. "What happened to port?"

Denny grinned. "Just thought I'd become less predictable."

Kitt poured two whiskeys, turned to hand one to his friend, then seated himself in the matching chair across from Denny.

"So, what brings you up to Town?"

"Not much. Been buried down in Devon with Mama since Christmas."

"And how is the duchess these days?"

"On her way to Town and still as eccentric as ever. She swears she'll need me around to take care of her in her dotage because she doesn't think my nephews will be bothered." Denny took a sip of his drink. "Don't know how she can tell that already—they're only five and seven, but wild as can be. I told Muriel she ought to ship 'em off to the Colonies and set 'em loose among the savages."

"I didn't think your father was near to sticking his spoon in the wall the last time I visited."

Denny laughed. "Papa is as hale and hearty as ever and busy trying to keep Geoff from breaking his neck on those fool horses he insists on riding."

Kitt did not reply. He was used to Denny complaining about his family and had heard it all before. There was nothing alarming about it. Denny's was a close-knit family. He allowed his thoughts to wander while he sipped his drink and Denny continued rambling.

Had he frightened Pamela with his proposal? She hadn't struck him as the missish type, but he supposed he couldn't blame her for being wary of him. It was his fault that she was now on her own, forced to earn her own living, and his conscience pricked him again as he imagined what must have happened after he left Clark Hall.

If he closed his eyes, he could still see the inside of the stables.

"...so I came to find out for myself what you were doing up in the wilds of Yorkshire, in March, no less."

Denny's voice brought him out of his reverie and back to the present.

"Just passing through. I stopped in to see Wyatt on my way back from Edinburgh, but he was away and his butler didn't know when he was due to return so I didn't bother to wait and decided to continue on home."

Denny raised a golden eyebrow as if he knew there was more to the story.

Kitt grimaced. He didn't mind telling his best friend about his adventure, but he wasn't sure he was up to the ribbing he'd have to endure once he revealed how careless he'd been.

"Must have lost your purse along the way. Not like you to be so remiss." Kitt remained silent. "On the other hand, there was that time..."

"Damn it, Den! Leave it be."

Unruffled by Kitt's outburst, Denny merely shook his head, a speculative gleam in his eyes. He took another sip of his drink. "Must involve a woman—maybe two?"

Kitt groaned and leaned his head back against the chair. "I should put you out."

Denny's laughter was infectious and soon Kitt was laughing with him—much the same way they had as schoolboys at Eton.

"Very well. But I want to hear nothing from you about how negligent I was in getting myself robbed in the first place."

"Robbed?" Denny perked up at this admission.

"It is very lowering to be caught napping and relieved of all one's possessions like the veriest babe. It was fortunate I was riding a rented hack at the time, so did not lose any of my own cattle. But to then be accidentally shot by one of the thieves who looked too young to be let out on his own was quite aggravating."

Denny's green eyes nearly goggled at the blasé narration.

"Accident? You were shot by accident? How do you know it was an accident?"

Kitt chuckled. He could laugh at the farce now, but at the time it had not been amusing.

"The would-be ruffian was so nervous he dropped the pistol and it went off. Caught me in the shoulder. The next thing I remember was opening my eyes to find an angel bending over me. Thought I'd died and gone to heaven."

"Ah-ha! I knew it. There *had* to be a female in the story somewhere. Then what happened?"

"She bandaged me up and took me home. Hid me in the stables."

"The stables? You jest!"

Kitt shook his head. "No. The stables. Didn't want her father to know I was there. She tried to make excuses, but I later learned from the stable hands that 'dear old Papa' was a skinflint and would have put me out rather than extend hospitality to a stranger."

"Even injured?"

Kitt nodded.

Denny sat back in his chair.

"So, instead of availing yourself of Wyatt's hospitality, you chose to remain hidden in the stables? Why?"

Kitt paused for a moment, remembering the conversations with Seth and Barlow that convinced him to remain. If they hadn't hinted at Lord Crandall's interest in Pamela, he might have taken her up on the offer to notify the local authorities of the robbery and injury.

"Curiosity." Kitt took another sip of his drink. "I sent Wyatt a letter after I returned to London. If he wanted to pursue the incident, he could, but my guess is that the villains are no longer in the area." He finished his drink and waited for the inevitable question. He was not disappointed.

"And the girl?"

"What about her?"

"Did you at least enjoy yourself while you were there?"

"Not in the way you mean."

Denny looked genuinely disappointed and Kitt frowned. Did Denny really think he would take advantage of a woman who saved his life? He was certain had Pamela not come along when she did, he might have bled or frozen to death.

"Despite her ramshackle father, the 'girl' was a lady and not available for a dalliance."

"Hmmm."

Kitt's butler, Tibbs, entered at that moment carrying a salver upon which rested a note. Taking the paper, Kitt broke the seal, scanned the contents, and smiled.

"Is there someone waiting for a reply?"

"Yes, my lord. The lad said he was not to return without one."

"Very well. Tell him I accept, and I will be bringing along a friend."

"Very good, my lord."

After the door closed behind the butler, he turned to Denny.

"We are dining with my godmother tonight."

"We?"

"Yes, we."

"But your godmother has a lash for a tongue. I'm not of a mind to be harangued about my prospects—or lack thereof."

The smile hovering over Kitt's lips should have warned Denny there was more.

"Do you want to meet my angel or not?"

Pamela sat at her dressing table and peered at her reflection in the mirror as Tilly styled her hair. She wasn't vain about her looks, considering them fairly ordinary if not downright plain, but Kitt's attention over the past two days caused her to wonder what it was about her that seemed to draw him. Whatever it was, she wished he'd stop watching her whenever he visited. She was beginning to feel self-conscious.

Tilly finished anchoring the last curl in her hair and stepped back. "There you go, miss. Not as fancy as some would do, but—"

Pamela interrupted the maid's apologetic tone. "Oh, you know I don't need fancy."

The truth was she didn't feel the need for a maid either, but Lady Parkington insisted she have one. That lady was also responsible for the dress Pamela was wearing—a creation in leaf green with gold accents. Pamela didn't want to feel ungrateful, but she was sure most ladies' companions did not dress so fashionably.

On the other hand, she was thankful for the good fortune that landed her in Lady Parkington's employ.

When her mother confided in her the reason her father seemed to dislike her was because she wasn't his daughter, she'd been crushed. Years of trying to please someone who would never be pleased suddenly made sense. She also realized he meant what he'd said in the stables.

Horrified to learn of the altercation in the stables, her mother had hidden Pamela in her dressing room—refusing to see anyone while the two of them decided what to do. Pamela worried her father or Sheila might discover her, but with her mother and Maddie working together, she'd remained undetected.

Nearly a week later while perusing *The Times*, Pamela found an ad for a companion and answered it. Two weeks later, she left her home for Newcastle, wondering if she'd ever see it or her mother again.

Pamela turned away from the mirror and her depressing thoughts. She had long since apologized to Lady Parkington for the counterfeit reference letters she and her mother created in order to get the position. Her relief and gratitude at the elderly lady's easy acceptance had been tempered recently by the feeling that Lady Parkington was up to something. She just hoped it had nothing to do with Kitt Covington.

Chapter Four

Pamela paused in the doorway of the parlor, taking in the cozy scene before her. Lady Parkington sat in her favorite overstuffed chair, her small brown and black terrier, Pearl, in her lap. Dressed in a dark purple silk gown, diamonds around her neck and in her ears, she looked every inch the regal lady she was. Her hair was more silver than the blond of her youth, but her hazel eyes were still lively; often mischievously so. Kitt stood near the fireplace, his back to the door. From what Pamela could see and hear, another young man lounged in the chair opposite Lady Parkington.

Pearl noticed Pamela first, giving out a sharp bark before settling back into her mistress's lap. Kitt turned toward the door. He caught her eye and she felt a warmth unfurl deep inside. The black evening jacket fitted his broad shoulders without a wrinkle, and the white of his shirt and cravat were bright against the tanned column of his throat. Her mouth went dry at the sight of dark trousers molded to thickly muscled thighs. Had she noticed in Yorkshire how very tall and commanding he was?

"Don't stand there," Lady Parkington said sharply. "Come in, gel. We have guests."

Startled, Pamela shifted her gaze to Lady Parkington. She nearly rolled her eyes at the over-bright gleam in the lady's eyes. She'd seen that look before, and after only two months, she knew it usually meant mischief was afoot. What was she up to now? Moving across the room to her chair, Pamela glanced at the last occupant of the room, who seemed to be staring at her in wide-eyed awe.

Kitt performed the introductions as the man rose from his chair. "Lord Denton Avery, Miss Pamela Clarkdale."

"A pleasure to meet you Miss Clarkdale," Lord Denton practically purred as he bowed over her hand. "A very lovely pleasure indeed." Pamela looked up into warm green eyes as he straightened, still holding her hand. He was even taller than Kitt.

"Pleased to meet you, my lord." She favored him with a curtsy.

"That's enough, Den." Kitt's voice held a warning, and something else she couldn't identify. Possessiveness?

Lord Denton grinned and released Pamela's hand, but not before he winked at her. "Kitt's description did not do you justice. Please, call me Denny."

"Don't go flustering the gel, Denny," Lady Parkington snapped.

Pamela murmured something complimentary, then turned to greet Kitt, only to forget what she was about to say when her eyes met his.

"Me? Fluster a lady?" Denny's mock innocence was pure theatrics.

He was a flirt, Pamela decided. And probably the bane of every mama with a chick. With his golden curls and laughing green eyes, he would be nearly irresistible to a young, giddy debutante. Thankfully she was past that stage, if she'd ever been there at all.

"We have been discussing the Season," Lady Parkington said. "Kitt has agreed to escort us to the Halloran's ball next week."

"A ball?" She turned abruptly toward Lady Parkington. "Are you sure you want to go?"

Lady Parkington raised a haughty eyebrow. "And why shouldn't I?"

"But you said you liked living quietly," Pamela protested. "That you weren't up to parties and the lot."

"I've changed my mind."

Pamela knew from the tone of her voice the subject was closed—for now.

Carter appeared at the door. "Dinner is served, my lady."

Kitt helped his godmother out of her chair, but when he would have escorted her in, she waved him away. "I haven't talked to this scamp in an age." She looked to Denny. "Come along now and tell me what your mother and that scapegrace brother of yours have been doing recently. Is she still trying to keep you on a string?" Taking his arm, she allowed him to lead her out of the room, leaving Pamela with Kitt.

"Don't you dare say a word!" Pamela hissed at the grinning male beside her.

Kitt complied, bowing and offering her his arm, but his eyes were brimming with laughter, and she felt her lips twitch at his godmother's transparent ploy. How had she fallen into such a farce? His arrival two days ago as she and Lady Parkington were settling in had thrown her completely. Then the conversation outside in the garden this afternoon, and now this. Had he told his godmother about his proposal? Was that why she was suddenly amenable to Kitt escorting them to balls and parties?

Pamela wasn't sure she could endure too much time spent in Kitt's company. As it was, just walking beside him with her hand on his strong arm reminded her of what it felt like when he held her securely against his rock hard chest. On the heels of that memory came the remembered feel of his lips on hers and the heat that washed through her, turning her legs to jelly and her mind to mush.

She mustn't dwell on it. That was part of her previous life— the life of Miss Pamela Clarkdale, respectable daughter of Sir Maurice and Lady Clarkdale, not Pamela Clarkdale, bastard and outcast.

They entered the dining room and took their seats. The room was as cozy as the parlor, small and informal. Sitting down to a dinner of turtle soup followed by roast hare, then pork cutlets in a flavorful sauce, Pamela was quiet as the conversation flowed around her.

Upon leaving home, she'd traveled to Newcastle. At Kinsea Manor, Lady Parkington's home outside the city, she'd fallen in love with the sea. When it was time to leave for London, she'd been excited and worried. Three days ago they'd arrived in Town. And when Lady Parkington mentioned contacting her godson, Pamela thought little of it. It wasn't until Kitt arrived—and she discovered he was an earl—that she wondered if he'd had a hand in her new position.

"I heard Clyde is in Town."

Kitt's comment drew a sharp glance from his godmother. "Where did you hear that?"

"Someone mentioned him to me just the other day. I suspect he did so because he knew you and I were close."

"Don't suppose he's changed much," Denny commented.

"Possible, but not likely," Lady Parkington said. "He's very much his father's son."

Pamela listened to the discussion in silence. Clyde was Lady Parkington's son and the current Baron Parkington. He was apparently a gambler and Lady Parkington alternated between worrying he'd get in too deep and washing her hands of him.

"I also heard he had your nephew Gerald in tow," Kitt said.

"Don't suppose my brother approves. Provided he knows."

"How old is Gerald now?" Kitt asked.

"He must be twenty or twenty-one. Haven't seen him since last year. I missed spending this past Christmas with them."

"Lord Fallmerton didn't accompany Lady Fallmerton and Louisa to Town, so he's not likely to know that Gerald and Clyde are hanging about together."

Lady Parkington's head snapped up at that. "Charlotte's in Town, too?" And at Kitt's nod of affirmation, added, "Well, well, a veritable family reunion. I wonder how I forgot Lisa would be presented this year."

Kitt chuckled and turned to Pamela. "Charlotte is Lady Fallmerton, my godmother's sister-in-law. I would venture to say there is little love lost between them, which is why you may never see her. And Lisa is her niece, Louisa. I think the story is that when she was born her brother couldn't pronounce Louisa, but managed Lisa instead and the name stuck."

Lady Parkington snorted. "It's not that we don't like each other...we just see the world differently."

"Don't know why Clyde would be interested in ushering a cub about," Denny remarked. "The kinds of places he likes to frequent are not for a boy still wet behind the ears."

"Well, if he puts in an appearance, I'll give him a piece of my mind. Maybe I'll write to my brother and find out if he knows."

Kitt chuckled again and Pamela slanted a glance in his direction.

"Careful," he warned his godmother, "or you might find yourself playing nursemaid to the boy."

"Humph. Maybe *you* should take him under your wing. At least you won't drag him from gaming hell to gaming hell."

"I daresay his mother would be horrified," Kitt drawled.

It was Lady Parkington's turn to chuckle. "Just the reason for you to do it, but you'd only drag the poor boy from boudoir to boudoir." She laughed out loud as what looked suspiciously like a blush reddened his ears. "I don't know what would be worse."

"Clyde, definitely," Denny said.

As the last course was served, and a dish of strawberries and cream left for dessert, Kitt turned to Pamela. "I don't suppose you've ever seen an opera?"

"No."

"Then we shall make a party of it." He turned to Denny. "Are you free on Thursday?"

"For the opera? Now you know I don't understand all that caterwauling in foreign languages, but for the opportunity to escort two lovely ladies, I'll sacrifice."

There was much laughter at his expense, but he took it good-naturedly.

After the men left, the two women adjourned to the parlor to plan the next few days. At the top of the list was a shopping expedition.

"But...but you shouldn't be buying me clothes." Pamela stood beside the window overlooking the darkened garden. A slightly warped version of herself looked back. "And especially not ball gowns."

"You must have ball gowns to attend balls."

"But I'm only a companion. Surely you do not expect me to take part?"

"And why not? You're young and beautiful, you don't have a head filled with feathers, and you're a lady. Why shouldn't you?"

"You know why." There was no keeping the bitterness out of her voice. "I'm not a lady. You know that as well as I. No one will want me—not once they learn of my background."

"Pshaw! The right young man won't care."

Pamela wrapped her arms around her waist and turned around. "That's easy for you to say."

"And I'm right, too. Why, Denny would snap you up in a minute if you encouraged him."

Pamela laughed, as she was meant to, lightening the mood momentarily. "Denny's an accomplished flirt."

Pearl came trotting into the room and jumped into Lady Parkington's lap.

"True, but he's a gentle giant with a heart of gold."

Heart of gold or not, Pamela had no interest in encouraging Denny. He seemed nice enough and would probably be an amiable companion, but she was more interested in a pair of deep blue eyes and an even deeper voice. Too bad he only was interested in her as a shield.

Are you sure? a small voice within her asked. He had qualified his scheme this afternoon. If there was no graceful way out, they could marry anyway. Perhaps that was the best she could do. Marry someone who felt sorry for her.

She knew he felt guilty for leaving Yorkshire, though none of what happened to her was his fault. Even had she known at the time her father meant what he said, she wouldn't have returned to the stables. She was not, however, willing to explain to Kitt why his guilt was misplaced.

"I don't know that I want to go to balls." Her measured words drew a sharp glance from Lady Parkington.

"Nonsense! How do you expect to find a husband if you don't go to balls and parties?"

She struggled to keep her mouth from dropping open. "Who said I was looking for a husband?"

"But of course you should be looking for a husband. No girl wants to be at the beck and call of some disagreeable old lady forever. She wants a home of her own and babies. That's the way the world is."

Pamela pressed her lips together. That might be the way of the world, but only for those with unblemished backgrounds.

"Besides, your mother wants you to have a Season."

"My mother? What does my mother have to do with this?"

"We've been corresponding."

At that admission, Pamela crossed the room to sit on the stool beside Lady Parkington's chair.

"Why?"

"Because I wanted to know more than what you told me. And I thought if your mother helped you in the first place, she might still be willing to do so."

Pamela watched the older woman's soft, white hands stroke Pearl's brown-black fur. If the animal had been a cat, it would have been purring. "And what will happen should I meet my sister and grandparents?"

Lady Parkington waved her hand. "We'll worry about that when it happens. In the meantime, you've been terribly wronged my girl—and not just by your own family. Your mother wants to rectify it."

"How? She can't change the circumstances of my birth."

Lady Parkington snorted. "There's more to you than that. The *ton* isn't completely populated with fools."

Madame Marie's establishment on Bond Street was small compared to some, but she was a favorite of Lady Parkington's. Despite the "Corsican Upstart" raging across the continent, everything French had become the newest rage. Previously English dressmakers suddenly developed French accents, began calling themselves modistes, and establishments like Mme. Cheroit's and Mme. Marchand's sprouted along the famous shopping thoroughfare. Unlike her competitors, however, Marie was the real thing.

Greeted effusively in flowing French, Lady Parkington got right to the point.

"Miss Clarkdale needs a complete wardrobe."

Pamela's protestations fell on deaf ears and soon she was standing in a small room clad in only her chemise and being measured and draped in various fabrics and colors. Lady Parkington made herself comfortable with a pot of tea and the latest fashion plates.

Three hours later a very tired Pamela and an extremely satisfied Lady Parkington made their way back to Arden Street. Marie's promises of finished gowns by the end of the week filled their ears. They left with fabric scraps to match for bonnets, gloves, slippers, reticules, and a host of other paraphernalia which Lady Parkington insisted Pamela needed.

"Who is paying for all of this?" Pamela demanded as they entered the house.

"You needn't worry about that."

"But I do. I'm your companion, not a debutante."

Lady Parkington continued into the parlor, Pamela on her heels. "Never tell me you are paying for all this. I insist on knowing."

When she hesitated, Pamela added an ultimatum. "If you don't tell me, I shall refuse to wear any of it."

Lady Parkington sighed. "Very well. While I didn't promise not to tell, I did say I would keep it from you if possible. But since you are being pig-headed," she raised her chin and looked Pamela directly in the eye, "your mother is."

Pamela's mouth dropped open. "My mother! But..."

"No more questions."

And that was the end of the discussion. Lady Parkington refused to say any more on the subject and Pamela was well aware of how stubborn she could be.

Kitt's arrival for luncheon brought a more perplexing problem.

Pamela had taken Pearl for a short walk in the gardens. Pleased to find his godmother alone, he got right to the point.

"While I applaud your willingness to sponsor Miss Clarkdale, madam, I wonder what the rest of the *ton* will think.

Do you want to promote a rift in the family? I'm worried you may make enemies of Pamela's grandparents and your protégée will be the one to suffer. Marscombe will not enjoy looking foolish."

Never one to mince words, his godmother nevertheless surprised him by saying, "There wouldn't be a problem if you just married the gel."

Kitt sat back in his chair, studying the woman before him and wondering how much she knew or he should tell her. Finally throwing caution to the wind, he said, "I would, but she won't have me."

Surprise lit Lady Parkington's features. "Why not?"

"It's a long story." He was deliberately vague. "But you must have thought of this problem and how to get around it before you decided to leg-shackle her to me. I won't believe you haven't."

Recognizing that no explanation would be forthcoming, she capitulated.

"She's my companion for now, so there's no harm in her attending *ton* events with me. If anyone is bold enough to ask, I will say her mother and I are friends."

"And if Marscombe contradicts?"

"Not likely," she replied with a mischievous twinkle in her eyes. "It is possible Lady Clarkdale and I might have known one another as children. Although I was older, Merton Park and Castleton, Marscombe's country seat, march. I did think Nicky or one of my other brothers might have known her, but I haven't asked. It would have been long ago—even before Pamela was born."

"I see."

Kitt ruminated on the possibilities. Pamela's maternal grandparents, he'd discovered, were the Earl and Countess of Marscombe. They were sponsoring her younger sister, Sheila, this Season. The *ton* would wonder why they hadn't done the same for Pamela and the gossip and speculation as to why she was Lady Parkington's companion would be caustic. Bringing Pamela out might force the Marscombes into doing something, but he was concerned Pamela would be the one to suffer. That was the last thing he wanted.

He went back to the day before when he asked her to pose as his betrothed. It was a ploy to pull her into the Season, but also a way to thwart her sister's growing interest in him. He could have kicked himself for not checking on Sir Maurice Clarkdale's background. If he had, he would not have been surprised to meet Sheila at the Merridales' a fortnight ago. With the Season now only a month old, Sheila had made her interest known and was pursuing him doggedly with the help of her grandmother. Knowing what he did about her family, he concluded there was more to what happened after he left Yorkshire than he had guessed. When Pamela hadn't returned to the stables, he left, assuming she had been correct about her father. It obviously wasn't the case and he wondered how she met his godmother.

He wished he'd told her who he was and left her with his direction should she need assistance. He was sure she wouldn't have contacted him, but it would assuage some of his guilt. Unfortunately, Pamela refused to tell him anything and he could not bring himself to ask his godmother. It felt too much like prying into her life behind her back.

He never planned to marry. After his parents' disastrous marriage, he'd sworn off the state. Meeting Pamela hadn't really changed that. But to rectify a wrong he considered himself responsible for, he could put aside his aversion. Although he knew he'd never love her—love was for fools and poets—he could provide her with a home of her own and children, if she wanted them. That should be enough.

"So, what do you think we should do? Her mother wants Pamela to have a chance at a Season. She has even sent me the wherewithal to do it."

Kitt's eyebrow raised in inquiry.

"Just some jewelry. She wants me to sell it to finance Pamela's Season."

Kitt couldn't see his godmother haggling with a jeweler over the price of some baubles. "And have you?"

"Of course not, but Pamela needn't know. Clyde and I may not always see eye to eye, but he's not tightfisted. I have more than enough blunt to finance one small Season. I'll give the jewelry to Pamela once she marries."

"Your charitable nature amazes me."

His godmother responded with a noise that sounded suspiciously like a snort just as Pamela entered with Pearl.

"Why are you encouraging her, my lord?" Pamela asked him a short time later.

She was seated beside him in his curricle admiring his expertise as he guided his bays effortlessly through traffic. They were headed for the lending library while Lady Parkington napped. Pamela would have been happy to take a hack and a maid, but saw no way to gracefully refuse his offer in front of his godmother. Especially since she suggested the errand in the first place.

"Encouraging her to what?"

"Don't pretend to misunderstand. I had not thought you a slow top."

He glanced over at her, one eyebrow raised, and she blushed. Turning her face forward, she was thankful for the light, cooling breeze. She should not, she knew, let him fluster her. He was merely being polite.

He looked back to the team, steering it around a cart full of produce, before he asked her another question.

"Have you given my proposal more thought?"

Conscious of the tiger behind them, she said, "I do not think it will work. No one will believe it."

"People will believe a notice in *The Times*."

Swinging around to face him, she stared at his profile. "Surely you do not want to...to..." She swallowed convulsively. "So publicly? No one will believe it. What if...?"

His broad shoulders lifted in a shrug. "There is no need to worry about the 'what if' until it happens."

Pamela's lips firmed at his trivialization of the possible outcome of his scheme. He didn't want to marry her. Guilt was a powerful motivator, but she did not want, or need, his pity.

"I am, justifiably I think, concerned about what the *ton* will think when you appear in public with my godmother."

"You should have thought about that before you fell in with this ridiculous scheme."

Pamela knew her petulance was unwarranted. Lady Parkington was being genuinely kind and Pamela was a little ashamed at herself for being stubborn. But although Lady Parkington knew of the circumstances of Pamela's birth, Kitt did not, and Pamela could not bear for him to know. He would turn away in disgust. If he put a notice in *The Times*, he'd be trapped. She refused to snare him that way.

They arrived at the building housing the lending library and he helped her down while his tiger took charge of the horses. Since she only needed to return some books, their stay was relatively short and soon they were returning the same way they had come—or so she thought.

Pamela was very conscious of the warm thigh brushing against her light blue skirts and the strength of the shoulders so very near to hers. Watching his hands controlling the reins with an ease born of long practice, she recalled distinctly what it felt like when those long fingers brushed her cheek. She trembled at the direction of her thoughts. The day was pleasantly warm, but her warmth had little to do with the sun.

Watching him from beneath her lashes, she was unaware they had reached the outskirts of the city until Kitt slowed the team. She looked around her.

They stopped near a village. Whitewashed cottages huddled together around a picturesque open green with a tidy little church off to one side. The village was so small, you could see from one end to the other. She noted the obviously busy inn at the other end and wondered why he hadn't stopped there.

Kitt disembarked and came around to help her down as the tiger ran to the horses' heads. Once she was on the ground, Kitt flipped the man a coin, told him to walk the horses back to the inn to let them cool off, and wait for them there. Then he turned and led Pamela in the other direction, along a path that disappeared into a small meadow ending at a copse of trees. Daffodils, daisies, buttercups, violets, and more spread out before them.

"Where are we?"

"Just outside of Town. I thought you might prefer to rip up at me in private." He grinned, and his amusement was infectious.

She smiled in return. "Why would I want to rip up at you?"

"Because I want to know why you think the *ton* won't believe we're betrothed even if they see it in *The Times*?"

She looked away, off across the meadow of colorful flowers. The sky was a brilliant blue, the sun bright and warm. For a moment she allowed herself to imagine what it would be like if she were truly Kitt's betrothed. They could stroll like this in the park or along the riverbank. They would talk with their heads close together, ignoring the world around them. He would smile at her and his eyes would be warm and tender.

She sighed. If only.

"Pamela?"

Startled, her gaze flew upwards to his.

"My godmother wants to give you the Season your mother wants you to have, but it will not be easy."

"Oh?"

"We could save ourselves the worry over your grandparents and sister."

"How so?"

"There would be little reason to question your presence in her household rather than with them."

Pamela considered this. It hadn't occurred to her anyone might wonder why she wasn't with her grandparents. They hadn't paid her much attention when she was growing up. She hadn't considered what others might think to find her living with a person to whom she was not related. Why would it matter, anyway?

"They will have to make excuses to cover up the reason you are not with them, or the *ton* will speculate and who knows what kind of story will emerge."

"What kind of story could come out?" she asked. "It's not as if anyone knows the truth."

His laughter took her by surprise, but she couldn't stop the thrill that went through her as his deep voice rang out.

"Unfortunately, the last thing the *ton* will care about is the truth. They will believe what they will, unless the truth is worse. Then they will gladly sacrifice your reputation and your sister's reputation on the altar of righteous indignation. The only thing worse than making a fool of the *ton* is the *ton* thinking they've been made to look foolish."

They stopped beneath the branches of a large oak tree.

He turned and pulled her into his arms. "But if we were betrothed, we could explain we did not want to burden your grandparents further. And with the knowledge of your mother's acquaintance with my godmother, few will question it."

Pamela knew she should not let him hold her like this, but his arms were strong and comforting. She knew she should not crave the feeling of security she experienced, nor should she wish she was different, and truly eligible to be his wife. But she did. And when his head dipped to hers, she knew she shouldn't lift her face willingly and yield her lips to his. But she did.

A soft brush of his lips against hers was all it took to send her reservations flying. His large hands splayed against the small of her back, burning through the thin layers of material. His mouth was gentle—insistent but not demanding. Silvery sensations washed through her; a sigh escaped and she sank into the kiss. She could not wish for more at this moment. Except that he not stop.

She was floating when he raised his head. Her arms were wound around his neck, her fingers threading through the inky blackness of his hair. The muscles beneath the material of his jacket shifted and she felt it clear to her toes.

"You did not answer my question." His lips traced the sensitive shell-shaped skin of her ear.

Sliding her hands down from his neck and resting them against the broad planes of his chest, she slowly brought her thoughts back to order.

"Very well, but with two conditions." She was thrilled to hear her voice was steady.

He stiffened, but said nothing.

"First, you must break it off at the end of the Season, gracefully or no. I will not trap you into marriage just to save my own reputation."

"Perhaps it won't be a trap."

"Which leads to my second requirement," she continued as if she hadn't heard the softly spoken words. "You must swear never to tell me you love me unless you truly mean it."

His smile nearly caused her heart to stop beating. "That should not be a hardship."

"I count on you being a man of your word, my lord." She was a little breathless. His body, intimately pressed against hers, was still playing havoc with her senses.

"Very well." Dropping his arms and stepping back from her, he bowed and took her hand in his. Raising it to his lips, he brushed the back, then turned it over and placed a kiss in the palm. "You have my word the betrothal will disappear at the end of the Season, regardless of the scandal, and I will never utter those three little words it seems every woman but you wants to hear."

"Unless you mean them." She hoped her voice didn't sound as shaky as she felt.

He acknowledged her with a slight nod of his dark head. "Unless I mean them."

Chapter Five

"No-o-o-o!"

The wail came from the blue and white breakfast parlor of the imposing mansion on St. James Square. Servants passing in the hall glanced at each other, but continued about their duties.

"Grandmama, look at this! I don't believe it! How did it happen? It can't be true! It just can't!"

The Countess of Marscombe looked up from the fashion magazine she was perusing to the distraught face of her granddaughter. The acknowledged beauty was anything but at this moment. Her large blue eyes narrowed to small slits, her flawless porcelain skin flushed red from her distress, and her bow-shaped mouth pressed in a mutinous line.

"What is amiss, dear?"

"Look at this!" Sheila thrust *The Times* beneath her nose, one shaky white finger pointing to a spot midway down the page. The Countess looked. And read.

Christopher Orion Covington, Earl of Kittridge,
announces his engagement to
Miss Pamela Anne Clarkdale

"He was supposed to marry me!" Sheila cried. "I was supposed to be the Countess of Kittridge. Not that—that little nobody! Why, Papa said—"

"That's enough, Sheila!" her grandmother interrupted sharply before she said something the servants would overhear. "Caution. Remember?"

Sheila slumped back in her chair, her lips pressed tightly together.

Silence reigned for a few moments as Lady Marscombe studied her granddaughter. Then she spoke in a normal tone. "Perhaps you should go up and repair your toilette before Lady Monson and her daughter arrive for our shopping trip." Taking in the mulish expression on her granddaughter's face, Lady Marscombe lowered her voice further. "Don't worry about this for now. We will speak about it later."

"But Grandmama, everyone will be laughing at me," she whined and her grandmother flinched. Sheila's eyes filled with tears. "Everyone knew that I..."

"Yes, yes, dear. I know. But there's no real harm done. However, if you cry off from shopping, the Monsons will think you distraught and people will pity you. You must show them you are made of stronger stuff. If someone says anything, you must turn them aside without admitting surprise."

Sheila looked uncertain. "And how am I to do that?"

"I'm sure you'll think of something. Now run along. Lady Monson will be here shortly."

After Sheila left the room, Margery Davens, Countess of Marscombe, looked down at the paper with narrowed eyes. She, too, had trouble believing what she was reading. Her son-in-law promised they'd never hear from that quarter again. She wondered now if he knew of this latest development. It was too much to hope the girl would have had the sense to remain in obscurity, but she would wish she had not ventured forth by the time this was all over.

"I don't know how you did this, my girl, but you will rue the day you thought to foist yourself on the *ton*."

Years of planning had, with a little bit of luck, paid off and she would not allow this new development to jeopardize everything. Maurice had promised to keep the girl in Yorkshire. She didn't know how Pamela came to be in London, and she wouldn't speculate on it. She would, however, ensure she didn't stay, regardless of any repercussions. Too much was at stake to allow one insignificant girl to ruin it.

Then she rose and left the room to prepare herself for the annoying questions she would be subjected to concerning the miraculous appearance of a second granddaughter. A granddaughter who, it seemed, had managed to snare the Season's most eligible bachelor without the *ton* even knowing of her existence.

Across town, another conversation was taking place over the breakfast table.

"We can't say I'm your aunt because it will cause too much speculation and will allow the *ton* to arrive at the exact conclusion we do not wish them to arrive at," Lady Parkington was saying. She, too, had read the notice in *The Times* and pointed it out triumphantly to Pamela. "I suppose I can be *your* godmother, too. Do you know who yours is?"

Pamela shook her head, too bemused by the words before her to answer. Seeing the announcement in print finally impressed on her the magnitude of what she was doing. Doubts intruded. Panic was setting in.

"Lord Kittridge."

She looked up at Carter's announcement and watched through wide unblinking eyes as Kitt strolled into the room. He stopped at his godmother's side and raised her hand to his lips.

"How are you this morning, madam?"

His voice, smooth and dark, rolled through her like a particularly potent wine.

"I'm fine. Sit, and have some breakfast."

He straightened and looked at Pamela, a wicked smile on his lips. "Good morning, Pamela."

Her tongue was glued to the roof of her mouth, preventing her from responding, but he seemed not to notice as Carter prepared a place for him beside her. Taking the seat, he glanced at the paper in front of her, then looked at her. He couldn't have missed the blush she knew stained her cheeks.

"I see *The Times* has already arrived."

Her tongue came unglued. "Good morning, my lord."

Lady Parkington cackled. "I would lay odds that a certain house in St. James Square is in an uproar this morning."

"No doubt."

It occurred to Pamela that Lady Parkington and Kitt seemed inordinately interested in her grandparents' reactions to her presence and the announcement.

Carter set a plate piled high with eggs, ham and sausages in front of Kitt then placed a cup of coffee at his elbow. As he tucked into the food, Pamela wondered how he could eat so heartily when her own stomach was tied in knots. She pushed away her plate, the movement drawing his eyes.

"Not hungry this morning?"

"I suspect it's the jitters, now the cat, so to speak, is out of the bag," Lady Parkington answered for her.

One dark eyebrow rose in inquiry. "You aren't having second thoughts are you?"

"And third, and fourth ones, too."

Kitt visibly stiffened and his eyes darkened.

"But, I pr—"

Lady Parkington's voice interrupted their exchange. "Carter, leave us. And close the door behind you." After the door was firmly shut behind the butler, she turned to Pamela. "Now, what's this?"

"I was about to say, but I promised, and I do not renege on promises. We are betrothed—at least until the end of the Season."

His shoulders relaxed and his gaze softened before he turned back to his plate. Lady Parkington seemed not to notice.

"Well, that's good. Now, before you arrived, Kitt, we were deciding on our story as to why Pamela is with me. We can say that Lady Clarkdale and I know each other, but I think we need more, so we'll say I'm her godmother, too. Unless the family is willing to contradict me and set itself up for ridicule, I think that will suffice. I will write to Anne and ask her who the actual person is and whether they will object to my usurping their place for the next few months." She paused to take a sip of tea, then continued. "It will also provide an explanation of how you

69

two met. The *ton* will just think I've been matchmaking. Are we still on for the opera tonight?"

Her abrupt change of subject startled Pamela.

"Yes and no. I thought the theatre might be better. Den would prefer it, I think Pamela might enjoy it more, and I think the current play has received good reviews."

Lady Parkington nodded. "Good." Rising from her chair, she headed for the door, waving Kitt back into his chair when he would have risen too. "Stay. I'm sure you two have things to talk about. I will be in the parlor." Then the door closed behind her and Pamela and Kitt were very much alone.

"My lord," Pamela began nervously, "I..."

"Kitt."

"Pardon?"

"Call me Kitt. It's what my friends and family call me."

Her eyes widened. "But, I couldn't!"

"You didn't have trouble with it in Yorkshire."

Pamela stared daggers at him. "In Yorkshire, I didn't know who you were."

"And if you had?"

"I would have sent a note to Lord Crandall so you could convalesce in better surroundings." Heat crept up her cheeks as she remembered the small room in the back of the stables. A grimace crossed his face, but was gone so quickly she wondered if she imagined it.

"Which is, perhaps, why I didn't tell you." He took a sip of his coffee. "I think a betrothed qualifies as a friend, if not family."

She remained silent, glancing down at the table as she toyed with her napkin and feeling the weight of his gaze on her. Warmth blossomed in her breast, spreading upwards along her shoulders and neck, and downward into her stomach. It was suddenly stuffy in the room although she had been comfortable moments earlier.

"Look at me, Pamela." His voice was low but strong, its timbre deep and rich.

She raised her eyes to his, surprised at the amusement lurking in their depths. This was definitely not funny! They were about to pull a childish prank on the *ton* for...what? So she could safely enter society without her family's backing? What would he gain from this? Why was he so eager to engage in a pretend betrothal?

"Why are you doing this?"

She knew by the sudden flare in his eyes that her question had caught him off guard.

"Does it matter?"

"Yes. I'm not sure I believe you are willing to hold yourself up to ridicule just to help someone like me. What do you gain from this ruse?"

"Someone like you?" His eyes narrowed. "What is that supposed to mean?"

She dropped her eyes again. Drat! Why had she said that?

Long, tanned fingers reached out and tilted her chin up, forcing her eyes to meet his. She kept her expression carefully blank so as not to give away the feeling of shame she felt every time she remembered what her mother had divulged.

"Well?"

"Nothing," she muttered, and setting her napkin down beside her plate, she turned her face away from him and prepared to rise from the table.

His hand on her arm stopped her.

"Stay for a moment. I have something for you."

He pulled a small box from his pocket, opening it to reveal an elegant emerald and diamond engagement ring. When he picked up her hand and slid the ring on her finger, she imagined for a moment the engagement was a real one; that he loved her and truly wanted her for his wife.

What would it be like? To be loved by Kitt. To be protected and cherished. To live with him and bear his children. It would be heaven on earth.

"It's lovely."

He smiled. "I'm glad you like it." When he bent his head and brushed his lips gently against hers, she wanted nothing more than to melt into his arms and kiss him back. There was no time, however, because he rose to his feet in a lithe movement and helped her to hers.

All of London must be here tonight!

Pamela looked out the carriage window at the large building before them and the crowd between them and the doors. Carriages lined the street, and people from all walks of life milled around outside the building. It wasn't until Kitt helped her from the vehicle and whisked her straight through the crowd and into the lobby that she realized not everyone outside was trying to get in. Lord Denton and Lady Parkington followed.

Pamela tried not to stare at the lavishly decorated foyer as Kitt ushered her through and up a curving, red-carpeted staircase. They entered a box and she looked around in fascination. Kitt took her cloak and passed it to a waiting servant, then helped her into her seat at the front. Denny did the same for Lady Parkington, seating her on Pamela's left as Kitt took the seat on Pamela's right. As she continued to take in the extravagantly decorated interior, she was suddenly aware their party had become the focus of nearly every eye in the place. It was not a comfortable feeling, and a small shiver worked its way down her spine.

"You are very lovely tonight." Kitt's voice distracted her from the grand display.

The words brought a flush to Pamela's cheeks, but the smile she bestowed upon him was serene. "Thank you, my lord. But it's only the dress."

"I thought we agreed you were to call me Kitt."

"Did we?"

"Most definitely."

Kitt took in the pale blue silk gown trimmed in white, his eyes skimming over the single strand of pearls and the tops of her breasts mounded above the low décolletage. It was all he could do not to reach out and stroke the creamy skin. He frowned. He didn't want anyone else looking at her like he was. Perhaps he should have suggested a shawl.

"I haven't had a chance to thank you for the pearls." She would have said more, but Lady Parkington's voice sounded beside her.

"Well, I'll be. Never thought Susannah was such a goose."

Pamela turned. "Who is Susannah?"

Lady Parkington looked up in surprise, as if she hadn't realized she'd spoken aloud. "Just an old acquaintance. No one you need worry about."

The chuckle from her other side caused her to turn back to Kitt.

"You will find soon enough that my...uh...our godmother knows more of the *ton* and its members than you would think, considering she does not go out much."

"How does she know?"

"Haven't you noticed she is an avid correspondent?"

Lady Parkington spent literally hours each day writing and responding to letters. There were many responsibilities Pamela helped her with, but dealing with her correspondence wasn't one of them. Perhaps she should not have been surprised to discover her own mother had joined the ranks of those correspondents.

Turning to look out over the theatre, Pamela saw a number of heads still turned in their direction and wondered what everyone found so interesting. As she continued to look around in wonder, she could not stop feeling she did not belong here. All the ladies were dressed in beautiful gowns in brilliant colors, jewels flashing about their necks and in their ears. The richness of the decor was pale in comparison, and for a moment, she gripped her fan tightly in panic. It suddenly occurred to her she was on display; all those eyes turned in their direction were looking at her. A strong, warm hand covered hers and she turned to Kitt.

"Pay no attention to them." His voice was lowered, and she wondered if he could read her mind. "Enjoy the play."

She relaxed and some of the worry fled. *Enjoy the play,* he'd said. She could do that. She would ignore the questioning looks and prying eyes and delight in her first visit to a theatre—and Kitt's company. When the curtain went up and the play began, she turned her attention to the stage and did just that.

"I suppose if I tell you two not to act like lovebirds in public, you'll tell me to mind my own business."

Kitt chuckled and glanced past Pamela to his godmother. "Very astute, madam."

The curtain had just fallen for intermission and despite the words, an unspoken conversation took place between Kitt and his godmother. Kitt rose to his feet.

"Would you like some refreshment or an opportunity to stretch your legs a bit?"

Pamela looked to Lady Parkington, who responded with a shooing motion. "Go, go. Denny will keep me company."

When Pamela looked at Denny, she noted a look of resignation on his face.

Outside the box, she noticed there were many others milling about, some talking in small groups, others entering and leaving boxes. She was relieved to realize Kitt had not removed her from the box for the purpose of being alone with her. Conscious of the looks being sent her way, she walked sedately beside him, aware of little except his tall, very male form next to her.

They reached the foyer at the top of the stairs and Kitt suddenly put his hand over hers as it rested on his arm. Tilting his head toward hers, he spoke in a low aside.

"Courage, my dear. It is time to face the first dragon."

Before she could reply, or ask what he meant, a woman stepped into their path and looked at Kitt.

"Good evening, my lord."

Kitt stopped. "Good evening, Lady Monson."

The woman was obviously trying not to stare at Pamela as she spoke to Kitt.

"I am surprised to see you tonight, my lord. It has been some time since you graced the theatre with your presence."

"My godmother wished an evening out."

Pamela just stopped herself from grinning at the smooth reply.

"I have not had a chance to greet Lady Parkington this evening."

Kitt pointedly ignored the woman's obvious interest in Pamela. "I left her in the box. Lord Denton kindly agreed to keep her company while we were sent for refreshment."

"I see." The woman looked at Pamela, then at the hand on his arm.

The amusement in his voice helped Pamela to relax when he finally deigned to satisfy the woman's blatant curiosity.

"Lady Monson, may I present my betrothed, Miss Clarkdale. Pamela, this is Lady Monson."

While Pamela curtsied, the woman inclined her head in acknowledgment. "Clarkdale? Not related to Miss Sheila Clarkdale, are you?"

"Yes, ma'am, I am."

When Pamela refused to further elaborate, she asked, "How?"

"She's my sister."

Again, the woman waited for more information, but had to ask for it in the end.

"My daughter and I are often visitors to the Marscombe residence, yet we have not seen you before. In fact we visited just this morning."

"That is because I am not living with my grandparents. Grandmama and I do not rub along well together."

"I see."

Pamela knew what the woman wanted to ask, but could not. Remembering what Kitt told her about the *ton* making up what it did not know, she decided to provide at least some of the information she and Lady Parkington had decided upon.

"I prefer the company of my godmother, Lady Parkington."

The woman's eyes nearly goggled. "Your...?" She looked from Kitt to Pamela and back.

"I believe my godmother has a number of godchildren. And how is Lord Monson these days?"

Lady Monson recovered from the abrupt change of subject. "Very well, thank you. I shall tell him you asked after him. If you'll excuse me, my lord."

"Very well done, my dear." Kitt purred in her ear after Lady Monson left. "The story will be all over London by tomorrow noon."

Pamela shivered deliciously as his lips brushed her ear. "I'm sure she thinks our engagement must somehow be incestuous."

He laughed. "Has anyone ever told you that you have an interesting way with words?"

She glanced up at him through her lashes. "No, my lord."

"Minx."

When they returned to the box, Lady Parkington was speaking with another woman.

"I do not have any control over Clyde, Charlotte," Lady Parkington was saying. "Perhaps you or Nicky ought to speak to Gerald."

"As if Gerald will listen to me," the woman complained.

"They are both grown men after all."

"Harumph! Gerald is still a boy compared to Clyde."

"Perhaps you ought to cut the strings. Oh, here are my wonderful godchildren now!"

The woman turned as Lady Parkington greeted Kitt and Pamela as if she hadn't seen them a mere fifteen minutes before.

"Kitt, you are acquainted with my sister-in-law, the Countess of Fallmerton, are you not? And here is my niece, Louisa."

"Of course." Kitt bowed over her hand then turned to Louisa, who had been conversing with Denny, and did the same. "How lovely to see both of you. You are enjoying your Season, my lady?"

Louisa giggled and blushed as she curtseyed. "I have already answered that question from Lord Denton, but yes, I am, thank you, my lord."

"Allow me to introduce you to my betrothed, Miss Pamela Clarkdale."

Louisa's brown eyes matched her mother's, but her brown hair had a tint of red in it, and where Lady Fallmerton's mouth pinched into a disagreeable line, Louisa's smile held genuine warmth. Pamela often lamented that she was taller than nearly everyone in her family, but Louisa stood even taller than her.

Dressed in a white gown trimmed with pale green ribbon, Louisa was a strikingly lovely young woman.

"It's very nice to meet you. May I call you Pamela?"

"Of course, my lady."

"And you must call me Lisa." She ignored her mother's gasp. "Almost no one calls me Louisa." Moments later she rolled her eyes as her mother did just that.

"Come along, Louisa." The countess's tone was decidedly cool. "We must return to our box. Good evening Claire, Miss Clarkdale, my lords." Then she sailed through the curtained doorway. Lisa hesitated for a moment, glancing around the box, then smiled and followed in her mother's wake.

Kitt turned to Pamela. "You have made a friend."

She looked up. "Have I?"

"Of course, you have," Lady Parkington said. "Lisa is a wonderful child. One wonders how she became so with Charlotte as her mother, but there you are. Blood doesn't always tell."

"Hmm. Well, I daresay you might be right." Kitt's remark had an edge to it as he escorted Pamela to her seat. "I take it she is not happy to discover Gerald and Clyde are hobnobbing about together?"

"No. But one cannot seriously blame her. If I had any influence over Clyde, I would do my best to remove Gerald from his orbit, but I do not. I fear she will have to get Nicky to interfere, and Gerald may not like it one bit."

"You may be right, but as I remember it, Gerald has always looked up to his cousin. It might not hurt for him to discover Clyde isn't perfect."

The second half of the play was as fascinating as the first, and Pamela never took her eyes from the stage. When the final curtain went down, she was disappointed the evening was over.

On the way home in the carriage, Lady Parkington asked, "Did you meet anyone interesting during intermission?"

Kitt's eyes gleamed with mischief. "Only Lady Monson. But she was enough."

"Ahhh."

"Pamela held her own under fire. I was quite proud of her."

Warmth spread through Pamela at Kitt's words and she turned away from the window to glance at his profile in the shadows of the coach.

"She was not *that* bad. Although I'm sure only good manners kept her from asking more questions."

Denny ventured his opinion. "Harumph. Never known good manners to stop her before."

Kitt was nearly laughing as he informed them, "It probably had something to do with Pamela's very short answers to her direct questioning."

"I only answered the questions she asked."

"True, but I would bet my last groat she expected more than succinct replies."

Denny had the last word. "And that's a bet I wouldn't touch."

When the carriage reached Arden Street, Kitt and Denny escorted the ladies inside. Bowing over her hand, Kitt asked Pamela, "Would you like to go driving tomorrow afternoon?"

"That sounds lovely."

"Until then." He brushed his lips over her knuckles and followed Denny out the door.

"Well, that was an enjoyable evening. Wouldn't you say so?" Lady Parkington said as they entered the parlor.

"Yes, ma'am, I suppose it was."

"You didn't enjoy the play?"

"Of course I did. But I did not enjoy being on display." Pamela seated herself on a sofa upholstered in deep green while Lady Parkington sank into her favorite chair. "That was the purpose of tonight, was it not?"

Pamela heard her chuckle. "I should have known you would reason it out for yourself. But yes, that was part of it. It was fortunate Lady Monson was there. She is the biggest gossip in London."

"She informed me that she and her daughter are frequent visitors to my grandparents' home."

"I believe your sister and her daughter have formed a friendship."

"Oh."

Mrs. Diggs entered to ask if either of them wished for anything.

"Nothing for me," Pamela said and looked at Lady Parkington.

"Me neither. I think I'm for bed."

Once Pamela helped Lady Parkington up, the two of them climbed the stairs together, wishing each other goodnight as they entered their rooms.

Tilly was waiting to help her out of her dress. After the maid left, Pamela picked up her brush and stood before the window brushing her hair. The nights were still cool, so she did not open the casement.

As she replayed the evening's events in her head, she wondered if Lady Monson would repeat their conversation to her grandmother and what her grandmother's reaction would be. She might have understood if Sheila's father's family ignored her, but she could not fathom her mother's parents' actions.

Was it truly shame or something else keeping them distant?

The parlor was cool with a small fire burning in the grate. Dressed in a pale peach gown trimmed with touches of white and blue, Pamela paced before the large windows overlooking the garden and admitted to herself she was nervous.

Last night had been pleasant. She enjoyed going to the theatre, once she realized everyone was watching her. The best thing about the entire evening was that she'd spent it with Kitt.

He had been everything proper. Escorting her for refreshments and playing the part of the attentive betrothed. She could almost believe their engagement was real—almost.

She stopped to look out over the garden. Lady Parkington had finally hired a gardener and he and his helper were working industriously around the rosebushes. They had already cleared encroaching weeds from the gravel path and trimmed the climbing ivy and wisteria against the house. In less than a week, the garden had become a very pleasant place to spend time in the afternoons.

She jumped as the sound of the front door knocker echoed down the hall. Turning, she forced herself to project a calm she did not feel as she heard Kitt's footsteps approach.

Why was she anxious? It probably had something to do with Lady Parkington's assumption that Kitt was once again merely showing her off. Would he have bothered to take her driving if not for the sham engagement? She doubted it.

They were headed to the park at the fashionable hour, that time of the day when the *ton* turned out *en masse* to see and be seen. While she was interested in seeing the sights, she probably could have done without the added stress of worrying what everyone else might think of Kitt's selection of her as his future countess.

Kitt entered the room and she had to stop herself from staring at his broad-shouldered frame. He was dressed in a jacket of deep royal blue, his shirt and cravat blindingly white, and his buff-colored formfitting trousers were tucked into highly polished boots. She was aware of the hitch in her breathing as he stopped before her.

"Lovely," was all he said, then added, "Shall we go?"

She nodded dumbly and allowed him to escort her out to his waiting curricle.

"I don't suppose you've had much of an opportunity to ride since you've been with my godmother?"

She turned to look at him, admiring the way he handled the reins.

"And when would I have had the time?"

He chuckled at the defensive tone. "Would you like the opportunity to ride here in Town?"

"I suppose I would. I do miss Midas."

Kitt slanted a glance in her direction and their eyes met before he turned back to the traffic. Negotiating an intersection helped him to regain his concentration, but he was acutely aware of the woman beside him.

Her light floral fragrance wafted around him. Not heavy or cloying, it teased his senses delightfully. He was surprised to find her nervous, a hint of worry in the wooded depths of her eyes. Did she regret their bargain?

Her dress made her look younger than her twenty-three years. But no one would mistake her for a debutante after a few minutes of conversation. She was too intelligent to be taken in by the games played by many in the *ton.* And he would swear she hadn't a flirtatious bone in her body.

They reached the park and he completed the turn through the gates and on to the prescribed path. Barely twenty yards beyond, carriages were lined along the grassy verge.

He tilted his head toward her. "Courage, my dear. Remember we are engaged."

Her gaze sought his. "And what does that mean?"

Pamela's eyes warmed as he smiled at her. "It means that, as far as they are concerned," he nodded toward the many equipages in view, "you will someday be the Countess of Kittridge. So smile your brightest, most self-assured smile and enjoy yourself."

She smothered a giggle. "Yes, my lord."

He was still chuckling when they reached the first barouche in which sat a woman near his godmother's age, swathed from head to toe in a garish shade of pink.

"Well, Kittridge, what have you to say for yourself?"

"Nothing, ma'am. But let me make known to you my betrothed. Lady Trane, Miss Clarkdale."

The woman raised a lorgnette and peered at Pamela through it. "Looks nothing like her sister. Pity."

He felt Pamela stiffen. "I'm delighted to meet you, too."

The woman's dark eyes widened. Taken aback, she sniffed. "I daresay you picked the wrong sister, Kittridge."

He bristled at her tone and allowed his displeasure to show. "I beg to differ, madam. Good afternoon."

The next carriage held two women only a little older than Kitt. Each one remarked that Pamela did not resemble Sheila. By the time they had spoken to another matron who made the same observation, he couldn't tell whether Pamela was indignant or amused.

"She looks nothing like her sister," Lady Stilton remarked.

"For which I am extremely thankful," Pamela snapped.

Definitely not amused. He should have warned her that the *ton* was essentially superficial, so the differences in their appearance would be commented upon.

Lady Stilton raised a delicately arched brow, but Pamela ignored it. He was tempted to laugh but resisted. He didn't want Pamela to think he was laughing at her.

"Your sister is quite beautiful."

"I know."

Lady Stilton, who herself was quite stunning, stared at Pamela as if she had grown two heads. He took the opportunity to make their farewells and move on while Lady Stilton tried to think of something to say. He dismissed her with a nod. "It's been a pleasure, my lady."

Pamela turned to say something to Kitt, but stopped as her gaze met a menacing gray stare. Although the day was warm, she suddenly felt chilled.

"Good afternoon, my lord." The modulated tone belied the anger evident just below the surface.

Without thought, she put her hand on Kitt's arm. His solid warmth gave her the courage to greet her grandmother without flinching.

"Good afternoon, Lady Marscombe. Miss Sheila." Kitt's voice was slightly strained as he covered her hand with his larger one.

"We didn't know you were in Town, Pammy," Sheila said innocently, her large blue eyes narrowing as they took in Kitt's hand covering Pamela's.

Pamela grimaced at the nickname Sheila insisted on using, despite Pamela's dislike of it. "Mama knew."

That bit of information gave both ladies pause. Pamela took the opportunity to study her sister. Dressed in the first stare of fashion in a pale pink gown decorated with darker pink roses, her golden blond hair swept up in a fashionable style, there was no doubt Sheila was very pretty. The addition of the slightly distant look in her blue eyes made her seem unattainable—a prize to be won to the young bucks and marriage-minded peers of the *ton.*

"Papa said you..."

"I know what Papa said," Pamela cut her off. "But it's not important." Her grandmother stiffened at her abrupt reply. Sheila didn't seem to notice.

"Where are you staying?" Sheila asked.

"With my godmother," Pamela replied.

Lady Marscombe gasped. "But you don't..."

"I don't what?" Pamela asked sweetly, daring her grandmother to finish the thought. It wouldn't have mattered, she had answered one of Pamela's questions.

Pamela had never known whether she had godparents, but she knew Sheila and Stephen both had them. Those worthy ladies and gentlemen dutifully sent gifts on birthdays and holidays, but she received none. Now she wondered if she'd even been baptized.

At least she could tell Lady Parkington she was not usurping anyone's place.

"I wasn't aware you knew my granddaughter, my lord." Lady Marscombe turned to Kitt.

"I wasn't aware she was your granddaughter," was the smooth reply. "I would not have thought to find a relation of yours where I found her."

The insinuation hit home and Pamela watched her grandmother stiffen her spine even further. One more unwelcome comment and she would snap in two.

Sheila, obviously unaware of the undercurrents, asked, "And where was that, my lord?"

"With my godmother."

Sheila's blue eyes widened in surprise. "You have the same godmother?"

"Apparently so." Kitt's lips tilted in a benign smile. "She introduced us."

A puzzled frown marred Sheila's perfect features.

Another curricle approached as she was about to say something. Kitt gathered the reins, ending the conversation. "Perhaps we should move on." Nodding toward the two women, he said, "Good day, ladies," then snapped the reins.

Moving away from the barouche, Pamela resisted the impulse to turn back to see if they were watching. Letting out a slow breath, she relaxed a little.

"That was not too difficult," Kitt murmured.

"I suppose not." Her reply conveyed no emotion. How long would it be before either Sheila or her grandmother told Kitt her secret?

Another carriage with another exquisitely beautiful woman approached. Her voice was low and seductive as she regarded Kitt hungrily through golden eyes. "It has been a long time, my lord."

Kitt turned to address the dark-haired beauty, but Pamela sensed his reluctance to do so. "Three years, my lady."

The woman glanced over at Pamela, and Kitt hesitated before making the introductions. "Pamela my dear, allow me to introduce you to Lady Wilmot. Lady Wilmot, my betrothed, Miss Clarkdale."

The woman's eyes flared just slightly, but she inclined her head and replied with all the correct pleasantries. Once they moved away, Pamela let out another sigh of relief.

"Have I performed well enough to go home now?"

His eyes crinkled in the corner as he grinned down at her and she had to consciously fold her hands in her lap to keep from reaching up to smooth away the wrinkles.

"You have not enjoyed yourself?"

She sighed. "Not particularly, but it has little to do with the company."

"And much to do with the notoriety."

"I do not like being on display."

They arrived at the house on Arden Street to find Lady Parkington entertaining visitors.

Chapter Six

A man lounged against the marble of the fireplace. Dark hair, dark eyes, a sharp nose and thin mouth made him less than memorable, but Pamela smiled and greeted Lady Parkington's son, Clyde, Lord Parkington, as she was introduced.

The other visitor was younger. Lady Parkington's nephew, Viscount Tinsley, was tall and lanky with auburn hair and hazel eyes. He had a boyish charm that reminded Pamela of her brother, Stephen. She felt a moment of unease when he looked at her intently for a few moments before turning to reply to a question from his aunt.

The tea trolley was brought in and Lady Parkington directed Pamela to pour. Once they were settled with their cups, she sat quietly beside Kitt and listened to the conversation as the four talked of family, friends, and acquaintances.

Revisiting their time in the park, Pamela wondered if Kitt regretted their charade. Obviously her sister and grandmother had been less than thrilled at seeing her. The look in her grandmother's eyes had bordered on hatred, and Pamela wondered what she'd done to earn such enmity. Perhaps she should write her mother and ask. It had been too long since she'd last written, and she made a mental note to do so this evening. The Hallorans' ball was only a few days away, and while she looked forward to her first social event, she was already tired of being the curiosity of the moment.

"...talking to Lady Jersey and Countess Lieven," she heard Lord Parkington say. She'd heard those names before. Lady Parkington had written to one of them about vouchers for

Almack's, telling Pamela with a grin that vouchers were a "necessary evil" of the Season.

"Probably up to no good." Lady Parkington snorted. "And what were you doing in the park this afternoon?"

"Just passin' through," Clyde answered his mother.

"We saw his lordship and Miss Clarkdale, and decided to come and get acquainted." This information came from Viscount Tinsley. "Would've stopped to pick up Lisa, but she was out driving, too."

"Don't tell me little Lisa has a beau?" Kitt asked in mock horror.

The viscount grinned. "Ain't so little anymore."

Pamela thought they were acting silly considering she and Kitt had met "little Lisa" last evening at the theatre.

"Your sister seemed a charming young lady," she put in. "But then again, I suppose you know that."

"Lisa is charming when she wants to be—sometimes only to annoy Mama."

Lady Parkington chuckled. "You've got the right of it there."

Kitt put down his cup and slid his arm along the back of the sofa. This seemed to go unnoticed by everyone except Pamela, who suddenly felt a tingling awareness along her nape.

"Why don't you bring her by tomorrow?" suggested Lady Parkington. "I'm sure she'd love a chance to get out."

The viscount laughed. "Without Mama, you mean? Really, Aunt Claire. Mama will know you are behind the outing, so why not just issue a written invitation? Or, better yet, call during calling hours."

Pamela hid a smile. The viscount might be young, but he did not have air in his head. She wondered whether he truly needed saving from Lord Parkington, or if it was just a normal reaction from the others in the room because he was young.

Lady Parkington pursed her lips thoughtfully, as if the notion hadn't occurred to her before. "Perhaps we will."

"Oh, Lud, what a pickle! This is a disaster!"

Pamela looked up from her reading to find Lady Parkington perusing a missive that had arrived only moments before, shaking her head.

"What has happened?"

"I never expected this!" Dropping her hands, still clutching the letter, to her lap, Lady Parkington looked up at Pamela. "This letter is from Lady Jersey."

Puzzled, Pamela waited for her to continue.

"We have been refused vouchers to Almack's."

"Refused?" Pamela frowned in confusion. "And that is a disaster?"

"Yes, yes, of course it is."

"Why?"

"Because no one who is anyone is refused vouchers to Almack's."

"Well, that just proves I'm nobody." Pamela tried to interject nonchalance into her voice. It wouldn't do to upset Lady Parkington further.

"But—but you don't understand. This will ruin you."

Pamela put down her book and crossed to her benefactor's side. Dropping to her knees beside the chair, she rested her hands on the arm and asked, "How?"

"How what?"

"How will it ruin me?"

Lady Parkington absently patted Pamela's hand "You will not be invited anywhere else. You will not be included in invitations to the theatre, breakfasts, outings in the country, house parties, balls, soirees. You will be shunned, ostracized!" Lady Parkington's voice rose toward the end of her speech. "The *ton* will assume there is something wrong with you, with your background."

Pamela wasn't sure she saw the problem. There *was* something wrong with her background. Even if the *ton* did not know what it was, she knew. The only things that could make her background unimportant would be the approbation of her family and a large dowry. She had neither.

"I've heard of Almack's, of course, but what makes it so important?"

Lady Parkington sighed. "Almack's Assembly Rooms is an exclusive establishment on King Street. Balls are held every Wednesday evening during the Season. Admission is by voucher only, and those are distributed exclusively by the patronesses. It is a necessary evil of the Season. Any young woman who desires to make a good match must be seen at Almack's. It is social homicide not to be admitted."

"So the purpose of attending Almack's is to see, be seen, and snare a good husband?"

"In so many words, yes."

"Then I don't understand the problem for me."

"Of course, you don't. Never having had a Season, or been part of the *ton*, you wouldn't understand the importance of Almack's."

Pamela grimaced at this pointed reference to her lack of social polish.

"But if the purpose is to snare a husband, then why should I care?"

This statement caused Lady Parkington to hesitate before she answered. "It is true the *ton* understands you have no need for a husband, but we both know how untrue that is. How do you expect to meet eligible men if you are not invited anywhere?"

Pamela sighed. Although she knew and approved of the ruse, Lady Parkington still insisted Pamela needed to meet young men.

"If you are not to marry Kitt, then you must meet others for whom you might develop a fondness. If you decide to cry off at the end of the Season and end the betrothal, you will then have other options."

"And if Lord Kittridge cries off?"

Lady Parkington shook her head. "Oh, no, no, no. He won't. If he does, it will put you completely beyond the pale. He would marry you first."

Pamela did not like the sound of that, but remembering the promise she'd extracted from Kitt, she let it pass.

"At least we already have a few invitations. And we will receive one to Lisa's coming-out ball in a few weeks."

Pamela didn't know how that was possible since it was obvious Lady Fallmerton wasn't convinced she was good *ton.* If her background leaked out before then, she doubted she would receive an invitation. But perhaps being related by marriage meant Lady Fallmerton could not refuse Lady Parkington and, by association, Pamela. It was obvious by the way she spoke that Lady Parkington was close to her brother, so maybe he would force an invitation if she assumed wrongly and one did not arrive.

"Regardless of all that, this...this is not good. The patronesses can make or break you, gel. We'll need to rectify this. I'll have to write back to Sally."

Arriving for tea, Kitt had a much different reaction to the voucher refusal.

"Wonderful! Now you needn't worry about an escort. And you will not miss out on anything except a horrible crush and worse refreshments."

Lady Parkington gaped at him. "Kitt, you cannot possibly mean to be so accepting of this!"

"Why not?" He glanced over at her again. "It's not as if I have any fondness for the place, and Pamela doesn't need the approval of the *ton.* She will be the Countess of Kittridge. Soon they will all be following her!"

His godmother opened her mouth to say something then thought the better of it, but Pamela could see the calculating look she gave Kitt as she took in the two of them seated on the sofa.

The room was suddenly warm, and Pamela was conscious of how close Kitt sat to her. His thigh was just inches from her own, his broad burgundy-clad shoulder so close, the ringlets framing her face brushed against him when she turned. He smelled of soap and outdoors, fresh and clean. She wondered at his attentiveness today since only Lady Parkington was present.

"So, what reason did Lady Jersey give for the refusal?"

"That's just it," his godmother replied. "She didn't. But I can't believe there isn't one."

"You mean other than wanting to snub you...or me?"

"Snub me...oh, that!" She waved her hand expressively. "That happened years ago, and should have no bearing."

"Nevertheless, it is a possibility."

Lady Parkington snorted, but said no more, leaving Kitt to his thoughts.

It hadn't occurred to him before, but something Clyde said a few days ago came back to him. He mentioned that after Kitt and Pamela had spoken to her grandmother and sister, Lady Marscombe had sought out and spoken to Lady Jersey and Countess Lieven. Kitt had thrown up a red herring to his godmother, reminding her of an incident a few years back when she and Lady Jersey were rivals.

There was his own history with Lady Jersey to consider as well. It was no secret they could not abide one another, but he wondered now if Pamela's grandmother hadn't done the damage. Lady Jersey was well known for her inability to keep a secret—hence the improbable nickname of "Silence". He was sure the gossip mill would be chewing on something soon. He hoped he learned of it before Pamela or his godmother did.

Pamela checked her reflection one last time in the mirror and was satisfied she would not disgrace Kitt and Lady Parkington. Her dress of white silk shimmered in the candlelight. Emerald green trim adorned the tiny puffed sleeves, the color echoed in the wide ribbon band beneath her breasts that tied in the back, the ends fluttering gracefully along the smooth fall of the gown. She picked up her green silk shawl and matching reticule and left the room to hurry downstairs.

Kitt waited at the bottom. Taking her hand, he raised it and brushed his lips across her knuckles, sending a tingling sensation up her arm.

"Perhaps I should have worn a short sword." There was a wicked gleam in his eyes. When she looked up at him in confusion, he chuckled. "Merely to ensure no one takes liberties."

Pamela blushed as he tucked her arm in his and led her outside to his carriage.

Once on their way, Lady Parkington reached over and patted her hand. "You are quite lovely, my dear. Your mother would be proud of you."

The mention of her mother reminded Pamela of the letter she'd received earlier today. Her mother had written that there was no one to challenge Lady Parkington's role as her godmother and encouraged her to allow the ruse to stand. Another lie.

Would they never stop? Would she live the rest of her life trapped in a lie?

Lord and Lady Halloran were delighted to see Lady Parkington and Kitt, cordially welcoming Pamela once introduced. Lady Halloran was a small sparse woman with graying hair and sparkling dark eyes. She did not remark on Pamela's non-resemblance to Sheila and for that, Pamela warmed to her instantly. Lord Halloran was a jovial man with salt-and-pepper hair and a booming voice. He pumped Kitt's hand vigorously while telling him how lucky he was to have such a lovely betrothed.

Pamela knew she was still blushing once they moved away from their hosts and entered the brightly lit ballroom. For a moment, she could only stare in amazement at the enormous room nearly filled to capacity with the cream of society. A veritable rainbow of silks, satins, and muslins draped the women while the majority of the men were dressed as Kitt—in stark black and white. The room was warm, but not close owing to the open French doors at its far end. The hum of conversation and occasional trill of laughter competed with the strains of music for the country dance in progress.

A number of heads turned their way as they descended the wide staircase and, once again, Pamela felt as if she was on display. The hand on Kitt's arm tightened as insecurities threatened.

"Relax." Kitt tilted his head toward hers. "No one will bite—and tonight you are here to enjoy yourself."

She glanced up at him and was surprised at the warmth in his eyes. "That's easy for you to say." She pasted a smile on her face as she spoke.

He grinned at her nervousness. "Pretend you are the luckiest woman in the world."

She relaxed and smiled genuinely at him as some imp of mischief prompted her to ask, "You mean I'm not?"

91

His laughter had more heads turning in their direction.

Finding a comfortable spot for Lady Parkington to sit, Kitt scanned the room before speaking to her again. "Save me the waltzes." At Pamela's questioning glance, he elaborated. "I don't want anyone but me to hold you that close."

The possessive note in his voice settled somewhere in her chest and the look in his eyes caused her a moment of doubt. Did he really mean it, or was it all part of the act?

Denny arrived. Bowing to Lady Parkington, he spoke briefly to her before turning to Pamela. "Don't suppose you could save me a waltz?"

Kitt clapped him on the back. "Sorry, old chum. Not even for my best friend."

A pair of young men came by, obviously looking for an introduction. Kitt obliged, but remained close until his godmother sent him and Denny off in search of something to drink. Pamela sank into the chair beside her, and smothered a smile at her next remark.

"They would have stood there all evening and scared everyone else off," Lady Parkington grumbled.

Lisa approached on her brother's arm and Pamela stood to greet them.

"I'm so glad to see you," she said to Pamela. She bent and kissed Lady Parkington's cheek. "And you, too, Aunt Claire."

Viscount Tinsley bowed to Pamela as she curtsied to him, then asked for the next set, which Pamela had free. Leaving Lisa and Lady Parkington, she and Lord Tinsley took their places for the forming quadrille.

"You're nothing at all like your sister, are you?"

Speechless, Pamela turned and looked up at him. He was nearly as tall as Kitt. As the dance started and she focused on the beginning steps for a moment, she struggled with how to answer.

"I did not mean offense. I just wondered…"

What he was about to say was lost as the pattern of the dance separated them. Pamela concentrated on the intricacies of the steps, gradually becoming more confident as she remembered long-ago lessons.

"I apologize if I offended you," the viscount said when they were reunited.

"You did not." She heard the chill in her voice. "I was just surprised. But you are not the only one to remark on the difference between Sheila and myself."

"I suppose everyone else has said something about your not resembling one other?"

She smiled at him. "Of course."

"That's not what I meant."

"Oh?"

"I meant that you are more congenial than she is."

"Oh."

As the dance ended, Pamela glanced up at his boyish face. He was certainly handsome, and someday his features would mature into aristocratic lines like Kitt's, but to her he fell into the same category as her younger brother.

"She is very beautiful, but on the surface. People are not always what they seem."

"Ah, a philosopher."

He grinned. "A little, but I prefer history."

"Are you studying any time period in particular?"

"Actually, I'm helping my father put together a family history. We can trace the current line back to William the Conqueror, but beyond that it's a little murky."

She hoped he didn't hear her mumbled words as they reached Lisa and Lady Parkington. "At least you have that much."

Lord Parkington had joined them, greeting his mother and soliciting Lisa's hand for the next dance. She laughed at him.

"Mama will be annoyed with me if I only stand up with my brother and cousin. I'm afraid you will have to dance with Pamela as I have promised the next dance to Lord Severton."

Pamela, however, had promised the next set to another gentleman, and she and Lisa went off with their partners, leaving the maligned cousin with his mother as Lisa's brother also disappeared into the crowd.

She was in the middle of a country dance being partnered by Denny when she spied Sheila. In a stunning gown of pale blue trimmed in silver, her golden tresses piled artfully on her head and a necklace of pearls about her throat, she looked the perfect picture of innocence. Pamela would not have given her more thought, except Sheila was speaking with Kitt, one slim white hand resting possessively on the sleeve of his tailored black evening coat. Pain sliced through her at the striking pair they made, and she missed a step.

Recovering quickly, she smiled up at Denny. "Sorry. I was distracted for a moment."

He glanced over his shoulder.

"Wouldn't worry about that." His no-nonsense way of speaking bolstered her spirits. "Kitt won't let himself get caught."

"What?"

The dance came to an end and Denny led her off the floor toward the couple.

"Kitt's been ignoring her lures since the beginning of the Season. No competition there."

Pamela remembered that one of the reasons Kitt betrothed himself to her was to divert Sheila's interest. She slowed noticeably and Denny glanced down at her.

"I do not need to meet my sister tonight." She did not want to be reminded of all her deficiencies, or made to feel like a giantess next to her petite sister.

His eyes narrowed in concentration for a moment. "Not afraid of the comparisons, are you?"

"Should I be?"

"'Course not. Your sister can't hold a candle to you."

She blinked in surprise, nearly stumbling over the unexpected compliment, then smiled. "Denny, you truly are a treasure."

"That's what I keep trying to tell my mother." His broad grin was infectious, and she had to smother the urge to laugh as they reached Kitt and Sheila.

Sheila's eyes hardened as they approached and Pamela noticed her hand tightened on Kitt's arm. A troubling sensation slid through her at that small gesture, but she shook it off, pasting a calm smile in place as they reached the pair.

"Ah, Kitt. I have brought your lovely betrothed to you." Denny's comment earned him a glare from Sheila. "I believe the next set is yours."

"Your consideration is appreciated."

Pamela noted the laughter in Kitt's eyes when he took her hand in his, smoothly removing Sheila's hand from his arm by the simple action of turning toward Pamela.

Denny inserted himself between them and raised Sheila's hand to his lips. "Your servant, Miss Clarkdale," he said, before placing it on his own arm.

Sheila's eyes slid over Pamela. "Goodness! I would not have recognized you, Pammy." Fluttering her lashes at Kitt, she said, "At home she spent so much time in the stables she often looked as if she'd been rolling in the hay."

Pamela's smile didn't waver, but she could feel her courage faltering.

Kitt slanted a glance in her direction and covered the hand on his arm with his large warm one. "Interesting. I should be as lucky as the hay," he drawled and she heard Denny's muffled laughter. Color rose in her cheeks as Sheila looked daggers at the three of them.

"Has your sister always been like that?"

Pamela roused herself from the haze of contentment she had been floating in ever since Kitt had taken her in his arms and began to whirl her about the floor. "Like what?"

"Do you really want me to say it?"

"Say what?"

Kitt leaned closer and his fresh, clean scent enveloped her. She breathed it in, wondering if she could become intoxicated on the spicy aroma of soap and bay rum. "Has she always been such a bitch?"

Shocked, she missed a step. Then, as his words sank in, she began to giggle. Unable to stop herself, the giggle became full-fledged laughter. When she missed another step, Kitt swung her off the floor and into a small alcove, shielding her from the rest of the room with his body.

Try as she might, Pamela could not stop the laughter that shook her. She wasn't even sure why his comment was so funny. Sheila behaved as if Kitt was hers, but he was betrothed to Pamela. The irony was not lost on Pamela and perhaps that was why she found it so amusing. That she, Pamela, had something her sister coveted but couldn't be forced to relinquish was so far beyond the scope of her imagination it could only be laughable.

When a handkerchief appeared before her eyes, she took it, wiping away the tears of mirth trickling down her cheeks.

Kitt's deep voice intruded on her glee. "I hope I will be let in on the joke."

She looked up at his face. It was in shadow, but the twinkling in his eyes told her he shared her sense of the ridiculous, although he didn't understand her laughter at this moment.

"I was just caught off guard. I don't think anyone has ever thought of Sheila like that before. I was imagining her face should anyone ever say such a thing directly to her."

Kitt was entranced. The sheen of moisture added a luster to her eyes drawing him into the depths of a forest after a summer shower. Sunlight streamed through the emerald green canopy overhead, sparkling on the drops of moisture still clinging to the leaves and brightening the brown of the tree trunks. Woodland eyes—they reminded him that he hadn't been to Covington Manor or Kitt Ridge in a very long time. He had the feeling she would love them.

A booming voice nearby brought him out of his reverie to find Pamela staring up at him with a puzzled look. He shook himself mentally. "You may be right, but I don't expect anyone would say anything so rude directly to her."

Pamela thoroughly enjoyed herself for the rest of the evening. Even catching the eye of her grandmother at one point and having that lady turn away did not depress her spirits. She never lacked for partners, and Denny, Kitt and Lisa ensured she was thoroughly entertained during supper.

"They make a lovely couple," she remarked to Kitt during their second waltz of the evening.

"Who?"

"Lisa and Denny, of course."

Kitt glanced over to where the two people in question were standing beside his godmother's chair, deep in conversation. He had not noticed before how well they looked together. Denny's taller and larger-than-average frame did not seem to dwarf Lisa as it did so many others. Why hadn't he noticed before?

"It would never be allowed."

"What would never be allowed?"

"A match between them."

"Why not?"

"Because Lady Fallmerton wants a title for Lisa, and Denny's is only a courtesy title because he's the second son of a duke."

"And his older brother is already married and has a son or two?"

Kitt shook his head. "Married, but no children. His sister-in-law is increasing, though."

"He told me he had nephews."

"His sister, Muriel, is Lady Avondale. She has two boys."

The waltz came to an end and they returned to Lady Parkington.

"Mama is being difficult, but I will see that you receive an invitation." Lisa was addressing Lady Parkington, obviously out of sorts. "Papa is interrupting his research to come up from the country just for this, and I will tell him Mama has treated you so shabbily."

Lady Parkington's voice was soothing. "No need, child. Do not go against your Mama on this one. It has already been solved. There will be other more important things in the future for you to butt heads over."

Pamela noticed that Lisa's glance slid to Denny before it returned. Then she sighed. "Very well, Aunt Claire. I will say nothing for now."

"Lisa has a tendre for Denny, does she not?"

Pamela and Lady Parkington were in the carriage on their way home. Kitt and Denny had seen them off, then headed in another direction.

"How did you know?" Lady Parkington asked. "I didn't notice it myself until tonight."

"It struck me the night at the theatre, but I did not think much of it until tonight when I saw them standing together. They make a striking couple."

Lady Parkington nodded. "Lisa is self-conscious about her height. She has sworn not to marry anyone shorter than she, but Charlotte is pushing the Marquis of Severton on her, who is even shorter than you."

"There are not many who fill that qualification beyond Kitt and Denny, and her brother, of course. Your brother must be quite tall, for Lady Fallmerton is not."

"Most of the men in my family are. The women are often short, like myself, but Lisa did not take after her mother in that regard. She has often lamented it. Although I was the oldest, my father teased me unmercifully about being the runt of the litter."

"I understand. Until my mother told me Sheila's father was not mine, I wondered why I was so much taller than everyone else. I am nearly as tall as Stephen and, upon close inspection, you would find I am actually taller than my stepfather. But since our grandfather is tall, I have always assumed Stephen and I took after him."

"Did your mother never reveal your real father's name?"

Pamela shook her head. "No. All she would say was that it did not matter because he was dead."

"Did she tell you anything else about him?"

"Only that they had been neighbors and had grown up together."

"I see."

"He was obviously poor, because I know my stepfather paid my grandparents handsomely to marry my mother. Mama said they were in debt because of Grandfather's gambling."

Lady Parkington huffed. "Unfortunately, a not unheard-of situation," she said as the carriage came to a stop. "Your grandfather must have mended his ways—they are more than flush these days."

Chapter Seven

Two mornings later, Pamela was just finishing a letter to her mother when Carter announced Lisa.

"I'm so glad I found you at home. I need a last fitting for my coming-out gown and Mama is down with a megrim. Do say you will come with me?"

In a pale yellow morning gown decorated with blue and green flowers, Lisa was quite lovely, her enthusiasm infectious.

"Of course you must go," Lady Parkington said when Pamela looked to her for permission. "And spend some time shopping for yourself as well. A new bonnet would not go amiss."

"But don't you want to come, too?"

"No, not today. I need my rest after last night. It's been a while since I attended more than one ball in a week."

"But..."

Lady Parkington made a shooing motion with her hand. "Go on and get your bonnet. I'm sure you and Lisa can manage on your own."

Pamela suspected her benefactor was up to something, but didn't dwell on it once she and Lisa were on their way.

After the young women left, Lady Parkington returned to her desk in the study and wrote a short note. Humming to herself as she worked, she was pleased when it was done and called for her butler.

"Have this delivered to Lord Kittridge immediately."

Lady Parkington handed the missive to Carter. Pearl came into the room, and she reached down to scoop up the small dog.

After Carter left, she smiled to herself and went back to the letter she was writing to Pamela's mother detailing Pamela's first forays into the Season. She had to admit, she felt like a new mother describing her child's exploits to distant grandparents as she wrote. It was unfortunate Anne could not see her daughters through their Season, but Lady Parkington was happy to have this time with Pamela and share it as much as possible with her mother.

She came to the end of a paragraph and looked up, her thoughts straying briefly from Pamela to Lisa. She hoped her brother would speak to his wife about Lisa. Severton might be a plum catch, but not for Lisa. Lady Fallmerton might think she was acting in Lisa's best interests, but the girl had a mind of her own and was not afraid to use it. She and Severton would make each other miserable, with Lisa receiving the shorter end of the stick.

"I'm so glad you came," Lisa said once the carriage was moving. "I have wanted to talk to you, but Mama has been making things difficult, especially after the latest gossip." Abruptly, she turned to look at the maid sitting primly across from them. "I count on you not to breathe a word of anything you hear in this carriage, Molly."

The woman, who looked to be in her late twenties, drew herself up stiffly. "You know you can count on me not to say a thing, my lady."

Lisa grinned at the woman. "I know. That's why I brought you instead of Daisy." Then she turned back to Pamela. "The latest gossip is that you have been refused vouchers to Almack's. Is it true?"

"Yes." Pamela shrugged. "But Kitt says it doesn't matter. Your aunt, however, seems to think it a disaster of major proportions."

"It is to some. But more importantly, it is to my mother. Fortunately, there is no way Papa will allow her to keep Aunt Claire away from my coming-out ball."

"Is the gossip mill saying why we were refused vouchers?"

Lisa looked away for a moment. She seemed to be weighing her thoughts before she turned back to Pamela. "I will tell you, but only if you do not assume I believe any of it."

"You have been a very good friend to me. Why would I think that?"

"Very well." Lisa's voice was solemn. "It is being said your mother cuckolded your father and when he found out, he turned you out. That you have no home, no name, and no dowry. And you are in reality my Aunt Claire's companion."

Pamela sat back against the padded squabs. Well at least the gossip was fairly close to accurate. Unless...

"Are they speculating on the identity of my real father?"

Lisa's eyes widened. "It's true?"

"For the most part, yes. Although there is more."

For the first time since embarking on the charade, Pamela truly felt shame. She was bringing disgrace upon Lady Parkington and soon would become an embarrassment to Kitt. She should get out of the betrothal now, before it was too late. They had only been to two balls so far, and the theatre. If she disappeared now before they were seen at too many more, perhaps the damage would not be so bad.

"I will understand if you decide you can no longer associate with me."

"And what kind of friend would that make me?" Lisa looked almost offended.

"But but your mother will not..."

A smile blossomed on Lisa's face. "I will handle my mother. Gerald and I both like you, so Papa will, too. The three of us will simply override her."

Pamela gaped at Lisa in amazement.

"Do not be so surprised. I felt a connection between us that first night at the theatre. Besides, if you marry Kitt, *you* will have the last laugh—and I want to be there when it happens."

The carriage came to a stop in front of one of the most exclusive shops on Bond Street. Once inside, Lisa was ushered into the back with much scraping and bowing. Pamela chose to remain out front, perusing the fashion plates and magazines laid out for waiting customers.

Lisa was not gone long before the bell over the door tinkled, announcing the arrival of another customer. Looking up, Pamela froze at the sight of Sheila and her grandmother entering.

The proprietress hurried through the curtain from the back. A small, thin woman with dark brown hair wound into a tight bun at the nape of her neck, she struck Pamela as a woman who had been hardened by life.

"Ahh, Lady Marscombe. Miss Clarkdale. I have a room made ready for your fitting. If you'll come this way."

"One moment, Madame," the countess said in a superior voice. "I thought this was an exclusive establishment."

"But of course it is, my lady. Is there a problem?"

The countess sniffed, looking daggers at Pamela. Her eyes were like shards of ice, and in that moment, Pamela knew her own grandmother had contrived to ruin her. Worse, now she was about to harangue a poor shop owner because of Pamela's presence.

"Yes, Grandmama, is there a problem?"

Goodness! Had she really spoken? And to her grandmother no less.

The countess's eyes narrowed dangerously. Until recently, that look would have sent Pamela looking for a place to hide. Now she met it fearlessly.

"How dare you speak to me!"

"Oh, did I?" Pamela replied innocently. "How positively horrid of me. I beg your pardon. I shall endeavor *never* to do it again." Then she looked back down at the magazine in her lap, pointedly ignoring the countess's furious sputtering, and what sounded suspiciously like a giggle coming from Sheila.

"Come, Sheila!" Her skirts rustled as she moved.

"But—but, my lady, what about the young miss's fitting?" the shop owner gasped.

"We will come back tomorrow," the countess replied imperiously, "but whether we will continue to patronize an establishment which caters to the lower orders, I cannot say."

And with that, Pamela heard the sound of the bell as the door was opened, the rustle of clothing as the two ladies left, and the bell once again as the door shut firmly behind them.

Staring down at the drawing in her lap, Pamela was overwhelmed with the urge to laugh and cry at the same time. Why did her grandmother hate her so? Her stepfather's hatred she thought she understood. Her mother said he married her knowing she carried another man's bastard—a bastard he promised to raise as his own. She understood his inability to keep his promise when it came to choosing between her and his own children. Her grandmother, however, she didn't understand. Was she that much of an embarrassment? Did they know who her father was, and was that the reason?

A dark skirt moved into her line of vision and looking up, Pamela found herself staring into the very unfriendly face of the proprietress.

"I don't know who you are, missy, but you've just possibly lost me one of my best customers." The woman's voice was so low it was almost a hiss.

"I did no such thing," Pamela replied, her voice clipped.

"You will leave, please."

Pamela sat up straight, staring up at the woman in disbelief. "I will not! I am waiting for Lady Lisa and will not quit the premises without her. But you may concern yourself no more." Injecting every bit of haughtiness into her voice that she could, she continued. "After today you may be sure I will never darken the door of this establishment again."

Uncertainty flickered in the woman's eyes. Pamela wondered if the reference to Lisa or her own tone of voice caused her to think twice.

The bell sounded again, announcing another patron, and Pamela glanced toward the door. The woman, however, also turned and moved toward the newcomer, blocking Pamela's view.

"My lord! It has been sometime since you required my services," the woman positively gushed. "May I be of service today?"

"No," came Kitt's deep tones. "I have only come to find my betrothed. I understand she came in with Lady Lisa DeWare."

He glanced around the woman as he spoke, spying Pamela. "Ahh, there you are, my sweet. Is Lisa not finished yet?"

The woman spun around, her mouth dropping open as Kitt stepped toward Pamela. He lowered himself into the chair beside her and raised her hand to his lips. He noticed nothing, but Pamela took immense satisfaction from the look on the woman's face, and she smiled warmly at Kitt. "No. I suspect it won't be much longer."

The woman scurried through the curtain into the back of the shop, leaving Pamela and Kitt alone.

Conscious of the curtain leading to the back of the shop, she kept her voice low. "How did you know I was here?"

He winked and her heart bumped in her chest. "How do you think?"

"I suppose our dear godmother told you."

He grinned, his lips parting to show a white smile in a sun-browned face. Her fingers itched to stroke along that firm jaw and sift through his midnight locks. For now, however, she kept her hands folded primly in her lap.

Should she say something? Had he seen her grandmother and Sheila leave the shop? What would his reaction be if she attempted to end the betrothal? Just for a moment, she wondered what she would do if he refused to let her go.

"I need to speak to you, my lord."

The hesitation in her voice must have warned him because the grin disappeared and he straightened just a bit. A dark eyebrow arched, but the expression in the blue depths remained neutral.

She took a deep breath, uncaring that he might notice, but glanced down at her lap, unable to look him in the face. "I think we should end..."

"No!"

Startled, Pamela jumped as her head snapped up. The force of his exclamation should have warned her, but she was unprepared for the blazing anger she encountered.

"You will not allow your grandmother to do this to you! I never thought you a coward."

Striving to keep her voice down, she struggled for words. "But you do not understand..."

"I understand enough." He, too, lowered his voice.

"You cannot possibly want..."

"How do you know what I want?"

She stood, unable to keep her agitation in check. "I know you should not want to be associated with me." Pacing across the floor to the counter and back, her head down, she wouldn't allow herself to look at him. If she did, she knew all would be lost.

"And why is that?"

She stopped before him. "First of all there is the situation with Almack's."

"That is not important. Whether or not a person receives vouchers to the assemblies should not affect the rest of his life. I, personally, will never step in that place again."

"But only the right people are—"

"Is that what concerns you? I thought you were different."

She dropped back into the chair beside him, her fleeting annoyance gone.

"Different? How?"

He shifted in the chair, stretching his legs out before him and crossing them at the ankles. The movement drew her eyes and she blushed as they traveled up the long length, raising them quickly to his face to find him watching her.

"I never marked you as a social butterfly."

"You know I'm not. In fact, I'm a social nothing."

"That's the most ridiculous..."

The bell jingled again as the door opened. Pamela stiffened, preparing herself for the disdain of another society matron, and was pleasantly surprised to see Denny enter. The curtain parted at nearly the same moment and Lisa stepped into the room.

There was a worried look on her face before it disappeared as she spied Denny. "Have you come to play escort?"

Denny reddened. "Actually, uh, I came looking for Kitt, but—" he recovered quickly, "—the opportunity to escort a lovely lady is never to be passed up."

And with that, he offered Lisa his arm and the two moved to the door, followed by Pamela on Kitt's arm.

As they moved out into the brilliant mid-morning sunshine, Kitt made a note to thank Denny for his impeccable timing. If not for that, Kitt knew he would now be in the uncomfortable position of trying to talk Pamela out of ending their betrothal.

He wondered if her grandmother and sister, whom he noticed exiting the shop as he approached, had anything to do with her newfound doubts. There was also the distinct possibility the current round of gossip had something to do with it. He had to admit, it had caught him by surprise. And shaken him, too.

Always know who you are dealing with. His father stressed that particular maxim repeatedly. *Blood will tell in the end. If the mother is free with her favors, so will the daughter be.* Kitt vowed never to become involved with the daughter of a woman who could be enticed into an affair. Over the years, he'd eliminated many on the marriage mart through that very method. It sickened him that some of the so-called "ladies" of the *ton* would be willing to have an affair with him while pushing their daughters at him at the same time.

He glanced sideways at Pamela as she walked beside him. The sunshine glinted off the curls peeping from beneath her bonnet, turning it the color of a fiery sunset. The flowery fragrance he associated with her wafted around him, tickling his nose. Her voice, as she answered a question thrown back their way by Lisa, was light but not the high-pitched simpering which made him want to cover his ears. The effect her voice had on him was exceedingly pleasant. Even her skin beckoned wayward fingers. He wished they were someplace where he could pull her into his arms and taste those luscious full lips again.

He did not want to believe she could be free with her favors. The kisses they shared were wondrous, but she never allowed him further liberties. And he was positive he was the only one to have ever kissed her. Didn't that prove she wasn't loose?

On the other hand, many of the ladies of the *ton* would never have allowed men to take liberties with them before they were married. They understood the possibility of ruination. But after marriage... It was the reason one had to be careful with one's choice in the first place. He did not intend to have a mistress if he married, and he would not sit idly by and allow his wife to take a lover.

Look at what happened to his parents.

Pamela slipped away from the Laverlys' ballroom and ascended the stairs to the withdrawing room.

"Drat! Drat! And drat again!" she muttered to herself. Why did Lord Severton have to step on *her* dress? Looking down at the torn flounce, she hoped the maid would be able to repair it quickly. She wanted to be back down in time for her waltz with Kitt.

Pamela was grateful for the solitude of the empty room. Too many people downstairs were ignoring or avoiding her. Thankfully, Kitt and Denny were being vigilant. Lady Parkington and Lisa, much to Lady Fallmerton's displeasure, were also making it clear they disdained the gossip flowing through the *ton*. Even Lord Parkington had danced with her, then remained to chat.

A maid seated her behind a screen in the corner, then knelt to work on the torn flounce, leaving Pamela to her thoughts.

The door opened. "Mama says it will be over before the end of the Season," said a high, whiny voice. "She says no man will have used goods."

"Of course not," chimed in another voice. "Besides, if one cannot attend Almack's, what's the point of being in Town for the Season at all?"

Pamela stiffened, her eyes going to the screen as if she could look beyond it to see who had entered.

"I heard she was banished for having an affair with a stableboy," said a third voice in a breathless stage whisper. "Her sister said she saw them."

"I heard my brother telling one of his friends there are bets all over Town as to whether she's breeding."

"No!" Scandalized shock reverberated through the room.

"Yes! And they say it's not Lord Kittridge's."

"It's not surprising her own grandparents won't acknowledge her. It's positively shameful that she is allowed into society at all."

"Well my Mama says we won't attend any more functions where she's invited. She doesn't want my delicate sensibilities upset." This came from Miss Whiny-voice.

"And to think she has duped poor Lady Parkington into believing her."

The door opened again and the three voices faded.

Pamela resisted the impulse to bury her face in her hands and have a good cry. She needed to be strong. If that was merely a sample of what was making the rounds, Kitt and Lady Parkington were doomed. So were Lisa, Gerald, Clyde, and Denny for that matter. Her hands began to shake and she gripped them tightly to keep her composure. She could not let that happen! She could not allow them to commit social suicide on her behalf.

When the betrothal was little more than a ruse to give her a Season, she'd allowed it. Even when she understood that it was also a way for Kitt to avoid her sister, she agreed. But it was no longer acceptable. She needed to leave, and leave quickly. But where could she go?

The maid finished mending her skirt. Pamela thanked her for her skill and gave her a coin from her reticule. As she headed back, cringing inwardly at the overheard conversation, her steps were slow. Nearing the ballroom, the hum of voices and bursts of laughter grated on her ears. Knowing much of the conversation centered on her, she hesitated at the top of the stairs. Why hadn't she noticed the accusing stares before? A slow pounding started in her temple as she descended. It would be best if she left. Could she find Lady Parkington and convince her to leave?

Couples were taking their places on the floor for the next set. She hadn't missed the waltz, but it was no longer important.

All too aware of the scathing looks cast in her direction, she threaded her way through the crowd. A matron in a sea green gown swept her skirts out of Pamela's way. Another drew her daughter from Pamela's path as if she carried contagion. An aging roué smirked at her as she went by. Lady Draley, who she'd only met once, looked right at her, then turned her back. Another dandy tried to stop her, but she was beyond listening to anyone or anything.

Kitt appeared before her. She could have wept with joy at his arrival. Her knight in shining armor. She wanted nothing more than to throw herself into his arms. But she couldn't. She could no longer allow him to be tainted by their relationship.

She meant to step around him, but he halted her by the simple expedient of catching her arm and threading it through his. She knew she couldn't pull away. It would just provide more fodder for the gossip mill and all the people who were watching them too closely tonight.

"I was wondering where you went," he said in a low voice. "Are you all right?"

She looked up at him. Something was wrong. His voice was gentle, but there was a faint accusatory tone. My God, did he believe it all, too? Tears threatened as pain tightened her chest, cutting off her breath.

"No, I'm not." Her tone was clipped. "I would like to leave."

"Why?"

She did not answer as they reached Lady Parkington, who was deep in conversation. Sinking gratefully into a nearby chair, she said nothing because she didn't want to interrupt. Lady Parkington was speaking with a woman on her other side, a matron dressed in a stylish burgundy gown with diamonds flashing at her throat and in her blond hair. Kitt said no more when it was obvious she would not answer his question, but he remained by her side.

She took a slow breath, trying desperately to keep the tears at bay. He couldn't possibly believe everything that was circulating. Could he? A throbbing began at her temples and she reached up to massage the pain away. Still, nothing hurt as much as her heart.

Kitt was worried. She did not look like someone returning from a tryst as he'd been led to believe. Or, if she was, the encounter hadn't been to her liking. Perhaps he'd been too hasty; too ready to believe anything that might prove his assumptions about women true. His heart refused to believe it, but he'd never allowed that fickle organ to sway him before.

With her face drawn and pinched, her eyes appeared enormous in her face. She looked like she'd been assaulted. He wondered what had really occurred, and whether she would tell him.

The gossip flying about Town had developed a life of its own. He knew her grandmother and sister were the genesis of it, but their motives puzzled him. Was it truly selfishness on her sister's part? Or something else? And the countess? Why did Pamela's very presence seem to upset her? Was Pamela a threat, or just an embarrassment? And had his presence been the reason—or the catalyst—for Pamela's banishment? He wanted to know, to help, but there was little he could do if she wouldn't let him. He was thankful she hadn't broached the subject of breaking the betrothal again, but he suspected he hadn't heard the last of that either.

He and Denny were slowly building a wall about her. Denny's mother had arrived tonight and was speaking to Lady Parkington. If Pamela received the duchess's approval, it would be another brick in the wall.

Movement caught his eye and he glanced down at Pamela again. She was white as a sheet, and massaging her temples. She needed to leave, but he didn't know if she could walk out on her own. If he had to carry her out, that would only provide more fuel to the nastiest of the rumors currently circulating.

Bending low, he said, "Would you like to take some fresh air for a few moments?"

She looked up and the pain in her eyes clutched at his heart. She did not deserve to suffer like this. She had done nothing to deserve the *ton's* enmity. Even if the story of her parentage was true, that was a sin to be laid at her mother's door, not hers. The sins of the fathers...or in this case, mothers, should not be attributed to the child.

But isn't that what you did earlier? The small voice inside his head mocked him for a hypocrite. For a short time, he, too, believed she might have gone off with Lord Severton. And when she reappeared, he'd accused her in his own way. Regret was an unfamiliar feeling for him, but he felt it now.

"Perhaps a moment of fresh air would help." Her voice was lifeless, dull.

She rose and swayed momentarily. "Careful," he said. "Slowly." He pulled her hand through the crook of his elbow and they strolled the short distance to the terrace doors. Once outside, he glanced around, noting no one in sight, then lifted her in his arms and swiftly carried her further into the darkened garden. Finding a secluded bench, he set her down and sat beside her. He slid his arm around her waist as she leaned her head against his shoulder.

The evening was warm. A half moon graced the darkened sky. Stars twinkled overhead like diamonds on velvet, their meager light not reaching into the arbor. A floral scent reached him and he breathed it in. The profusion of flowers beginning to bloom around them could not disguise Pamela's distinctive fragrance. A peculiar sensation invaded his soul; a peaceful feeling having little to do with the quiet garden around them and everything to do with the woman who leaned against him so trustingly. He refused to name that particular sensation—afraid if he gave it a name, it would become all too real.

He lost track of how much time passed before he heard the crunch of shoes on gravel as someone approached their refuge. Thankfully, Pamela was not wearing white tonight, but someone might see his own shirt and cravat if they looked closely enough.

A tall figure rounded the side of the arbor, bright hair silvered by the moon.

"Den!" he called in an urgent whisper. "Over here!"

"Kitt?" Lord Denton entered the small arbor. "Lady P has been wondering where you got off to." He glanced down at Pamela, who hadn't moved.

"Pamela is not feeling well, but I cannot get her back through the ballroom and outside to my carriage without attracting undue attention. Any suggestions?"

He knew he could count on Denny. Between the two of them, they had slipped in and out of nearly every noble residence in London. If there was a way out without being detected, they could find—or create—it.

"Are you feeling better?" Lady Parkington asked as she entered the parlor where Pamela was curled up on a settee reading.

Pamela looked up from the newspaper. Sun shone brightly through the windows, casting its warm glow about the cozy room. Taking her usual chair before the fire, Lady Parkington allowed Pearl to leap up and settle in her gray silk-covered lap. Stroking the dog lovingly, she took the time to study Pamela.

She was still a little pale, and there was more than sadness in her eyes as she lowered the paper. There was deep sorrow. And, in that moment, Lady Parkington knew two things: Pamela had fallen in love with Kitt, and she was about to make a totally needless sacrifice. Knowing there was little she could do about the former, she settled for determining how to discourage the latter.

"I think, perhaps, it is time for me to release Kitt from the betrothal and leave."

"Whatever for?"

Pamela folded the paper and set it on the small table before the sofa.

"I have brought entirely too much notoriety to both you and Lord Kittridge. In addition, there is Lisa to consider. I cannot, in all conscience, continue to act as if nothing has occurred."

"I see. And where will you go?"

Surprise flickered in the brown-green depths. "I...I don't know."

"Then why leave?"

"You know as well as I do what is being bandied about. I cannot allow my presence to tarnish you..."

Lady Parkington smiled to herself. Oh, to have such an unblemished conscience. "Do I look tarnished?"

"Um...no."

"Then why should you think so?"

Pamela's mouth fell open, but was quickly snapped shut. "But the talk...the gossip..."

"Talk! Gossip! That's all there is." She waved her hand when Pamela would have spoken. "Yes, yes, I know some of it is true. But the vast majority of it is the figment of someone else's spiteful imagination, so it doesn't signify."

Pamela stared at Lady Parkington in shock. *It didn't signify?* How could she say that? Last night had been the worst night of her life. She closed her eyes, remembering the moment when she felt as if her heart shattered. Not when she heard the gossip in the withdrawing room, but when Kitt greeted her afterwards, accusation in his eyes.

Even so, he'd whisked her away and brought her home, entrusting her to the care of Mrs. Diggs. His concern was genuine, but doubts intruded. Perhaps there was something there. He hadn't acted on his doubts, but probably hadn't discarded them either.

"If you leave, everyone will believe all the gossip is true," Lady Parkington said now. "Not only that, it will do much more damage than if you stay to face them."

Pamela toyed with a ribbon on her dress. "You can't possibly have heard everything currently making the rounds."

"I've heard enough."

"But...but..." Was that panic beginning to rear its head?

"I tell you what—" Lady Parkington leaned forward in her chair, "—we won't attend any parties for at least a week. Lisa's ball is in two weeks. By then some of the gossip will have died down—and the most outlandish of it will have gone by the wayside."

"But that's just it!" Pamela burst out, agitated. "I can't attend any more events—especially Lisa's ball."

"Why not?"

"Because others won't attend." Pamela's voice sounded a little desperate. "Don't you see? They won't come because I will be there. I do not wish to be the reason Lisa's ball is a failure."

"Oh, pooh. Lisa's ball will be a success regardless. Despite her mother, the Fallmertons are important enough that no one will risk their displeasure. Especially once my brother arrives."

Pamela didn't see how this could be, but kept silent in the face of her patron's confident tones.

Chapter Eight

Pamela kept to the house for an entire two days before Kitt appeared and all but forced her to go driving with him.

It was an agonizing two days. Pamela lost count of how many times she changed her mind concerning whether or not she should end the betrothal and slip away to lick her wounds in obscurity. She went over every conversation she'd heard, tried to match it with everything that happened since the day she convinced Kitt to leave Yorkshire without her, and tried to put it all in the best light possible. That last endeavor gave her another headache. There was no "best light".

She knew Sheila had seen her and Kitt together in Yorkshire. Running off to tattle was nothing new. Sheila had been doing that ever since she could string two words together. She also realized Sheila assumed Kitt was one of the stable hands.

What she gleaned from overhearing her stepfather's comments to her mother haunted her. Unaware of her presence in her mother's dressing room, he'd told his wife of the plan he'd rashly blown, uncaring how much it upset her. He'd never planned to acknowledge or dower her. Never planned to allow her to leave Clark Hall. She knew she could not blame her stepfather for her mother's illness, but it fell in perfectly with his plans nevertheless.

Mrs. Creal, the housekeeper, was quite old. When Lady Clarkdale fell ill, Pamela took over her responsibilities. As Mrs. Creal slowed down, more of her duties fell to Pamela as well, until Pamela kept the household together. Pamela became in fact, if not name, the chatelaine and housekeeper. Despite that, she could not have been more shocked at her stepfather's intentions.

The scene in the library with her stepfather had confused her. Distracted by his accusations, she'd told him about Kitt without thinking. His subsequent violent fit of rage was uncharacteristic, but it was "the plan" he devised that horrified and sickened her.

He wanted to force her to marry the unknown "stable lad" and then, due to her newly-reduced circumstances, force her into the position of housekeeper. She would forfeit her place in the household due to the *mesalliance*, but he would come through the affair looking like a paragon. Anyone knowing of her disgrace would have said he'd treated her fairly.

Kitt saved her from that. Just by not being one of the stable hands her stepfather could bully into marrying her, he'd freed her from the life of near servitude her stepfather planned for her.

Not for the first time, she wondered at the whim of fate that placed Kitt in her path. If she had not slipped away down to the stream for a little solitude, she would not have found him. If she had not brought him back and hidden him in the stables, he would not have kissed her, and Sheila would not have seen them.

If they had never met...she would not have fallen in love.

A gust of wind tugged at her bonnet and she instinctively reached up to hold it down, bringing her out of her thoughts. Glancing around her, she realized she'd been woolgathering instead of enjoying the drive. Looking over at Kitt, she found him staring at her, one dark eyebrow arched. Her face heated.

"I hope," his deep voice drawled, "your thoughts were not as bad as all that."

The wind settled and she dropped her hand to her lap.

"I'm afraid they were, but I apologize for my rudeness in ignoring you." To prove her contrition, she asked, "Where are we going?"

He smiled and his eyes twinkled. "It's a secret."

"You have not abducted me, have you?"

"That would assume you have no wish to be with me."

Well, she couldn't answer that. Other than the house on Arden Street, the only place she currently felt safe was in Kitt's presence.

They left the city behind and she noted the fields as they passed, brown but starting to reveal the results of earlier plantings. The air was warm and the pleasant smell of earth, horse and Kitt wrapped her in a protective blanket. For a while, the only sounds were those of the horses and curricle moving down the road at a steady pace.

Kitt turned back to the road for a few moments, negotiating a sharp curve to turn the vehicle off onto a small country lane. They drove with a high hedge beside Kitt for a short distance before turning into an opening and onto a well-kept driveway that ended at a small manor house.

Of dark red brick, the three story dwelling sat amidst extensive, well-manicured parkland, shaded by tall oaks. The portico over the front door was a large balcony on which she could see a small table and some chairs. As they came to a stop, the front door opened to reveal a woman in a dark dress with a white collar and cuffs. She was frowning and Pamela's heart plummeted. Had the Town gossip reached all the way out here?

Kitt hopped down as a young boy came around the house to take the reins from him. Lifting Pamela down, Kitt turned toward the woman who now stood arms akimbo with hands on her substantial hips.

"Don't look at me like that, Dorie." He drew Pamela forward.

"And how should I look, my lord?"

"You should look happy to see me and be pleased to meet my betrothed, Miss Clarkdale."

At that, the woman's face broke out into a broad smile and her dark eyes lit up. "Well, it's about time!" She turned to look at Pamela. "Should a knowed you'd pick a beauty. Welcome to Covington Manor, miss."

"Thank you."

Kitt ushered her into the cool interior.

The dark wood floor was polished to a brilliant shine, reflecting the large chandelier hanging in the entryway.

Mahogany wainscoting and white, silk-covered walls gave the interior a dignified look. A wide staircase rose up to their left, its banisters gleaming in the light, the stairs carpeted in forest green. Two niches beside the door held hooks and an umbrella stand, and a small table beneath a landscape painting held candles and flint. The ceiling had been painted to resemble a nearly cloudless summer sky.

Relieving her of her cloak and bonnet, Kitt handed them to Dorie. Pamela was still staring about her in wonder when Kitt spoke. "Would you like to refresh yourself before we have luncheon?"

Flustered, she responded, "Oh, oh yes, that would be nice."

Kitt relinquished Pamela into Dorie's care and headed toward the rear of the house while she followed the housekeeper up the stairs.

"'Tis happy I am Master Kitt has finally decided to take a bride. Frisky would have been happy for him, too." She showed Pamela into a room decorated in blue and cream. Sumptuous sky blue velvet was pulled back from the large windows, the same color echoed in the bed hangings and dried flower arrangements on the fireplace mantle. The walls were painted a soft cream color, but the ceiling, as the one in the main foyer, was painted to resemble a brilliant blue sky.

A young maid entered on their heels carrying towels and a pitcher. She dipped a curtsy in their general direction, then went over to the washstand and poured water from the pitcher into a basin. Once the housekeeper left, Pamela washed her face and hands, then sat at the dressing table and allowed the maid to repair her hair. Fifteen minutes later, she was descending the wide staircase feeling refreshed.

She found Kitt in the drawing room standing near a row of floor-to-ceiling windows. As she crossed the room, she took note of its bright and airy atmosphere. Painted a sunny yellow with white and green accents, it was a very feminine drawing room. When she reached him, she realized the window before him was actually a door opening onto a terrace.

"It's lovely." He turned to face her, a smile tilting the corners of his mouth.

"I thought you might think so. I have not been here in a while."

He escorted her onto the terrace, where she noticed a table set for two. Dorie appeared, followed by two young men pushing trolleys loaded with covered dishes. As he seated her and she picked up her napkin, he turned to Dorie. "Thank you. We will serve ourselves."

Dorie ushered the two young men back into the house, leaving them alone.

The garden below them was a profusion of late spring flowers, their scents subtle but pleasing. The uplifting notes of a lark trilled from above them and in the distance she could hear water splashing.

"Why bother to live in the city when you have such a beautiful home this close?"

He grinned as he served her some poached salmon from one of the dishes.

"Until six months ago it was occupied."

"By who?"

"My old governess." He poured them each a glass of wine, the pale liquid translucent in the light.

"Frisky?"

His boyish grin was infectious. "Miss Frisk never approved of the nickname I saddled her with. I spent much of my early childhood here. When my parents went to London, my mother would send me here with my governess so she could slip away and visit."

"So this is not your family seat?"

He shook his head. "No. Kitt Ridge is a sprawling estate on the west coast. The house sits on a particularly high ridge overlooking Bristol Channel, hence its name. On many days, you can see Wales from there."

"And your father?"

"He never cared for this place. My mother completely redecorated it, but as far as I know, my father rarely came here—unless he was looking for her."

Kitt watched her eat, satisfied with her appetite. His godmother confided in him that she hadn't eaten much over the last two days. A change of scenery was just what she needed. Although, why he'd brought her here, he didn't know.

To be sure, he loved this place—as long as he didn't allow memories of his mother to intrude on his enjoyment. He tried not to think of his mother very often; her defection still hurt despite her death nearly a decade ago. His memories of this place were of wandering the parkland, swimming in the pond and fishing in the stream. By the time he went off to school at nine, he was closer to his governess than either of his parents. Three years later, his mother deserted her husband and son.

"I think my father would have sold it, but he didn't want to displace his sister."

"His sister?"

"My Aunt Lydia came here to live shortly before I was sent off to school. She was an invalid due to a riding accident some years before. I believe she and my mother got along quite well, but once I went off to school, I did not see her much. Frisky stayed on as her companion because she had no other family and would have looked for another position once I no longer needed her. When my aunt died three years ago, Frisky was too old to go anywhere else."

As they finished lunch, Kitt asked Pamela if she'd like to stroll around the grounds. Dorie was summoned and sent for Pamela's bonnet, then the two of them set off. As landscaping went, it was very simple. The gardens boasted all manner of flowers, climbing vines, small trees, and two fountains. Once beyond the formal terraces, the parkland spread out before them in stretches of grass dotted with wildflowers and clusters of trees. All it needed, Kitt mused, was a woodland nymph or two.

He nearly laughed out loud. When had he become so fanciful? Glancing down at Pamela beside him, he couldn't see her face because of the brim of her bonnet, but he knew she was taking in everything around them.

"Do you hunt here?"

He shook his head. "No. It was once a hunting lodge, but some ancestor put a stop to it and no one has ever restarted the practice. Why do you ask?"

"I have seen a few deer and wondered if they were here because they felt safe."

"Possibly."

They came to the stream. An arched stone footbridge spanned the flowing water. Kitt's tread was firm over the uneven stones as he assisted Pamela onto the bridge. At its center, they stopped and looked down.

"It's so peaceful here." There was a wistfulness in Pamela's voice. "I could stay here forever."

Kitt slipped his arms around her, turning her toward him and anchoring her against his body.

"You could," he said, his fingers coming up to stroke her cheek. "You could come here to live if you wished."

Pamela raised her eyes to him, reminding him why he felt she belonged here. Her eyes blended with this place. The woodland, parkland and meadows were all reflected in the brown and green of her eyes. She was the nymph this place lacked.

"I could?"

"If I get a special license, we could be married by the end of the week."

Joy such as she had never known blossomed in Pamela's chest. Her heart soared on eagle's wings. Warmth raced through her veins, filling her with happiness.

Yes! Yes! Oh, yes!

The words were on the tip of her tongue but remained unspoken as Kitt continued. "You would no longer have to worry about gossip, or your sister and grandparents. No one would ever snub you again. You would have everything you ever wanted."

She crashed to earth with a jolt. *But what about love?*

The question went unasked. For she knew the answer. Kitt felt responsible for her. He felt sorry for her. But he did not love her. He would marry her out of a sense of responsibility, and to protect her. He would throw away his entire future on a misguided notion of honor. She could not let him do it.

"No." She dropped her eyes to his chest as she spoke, blinking furiously to keep back the tears.

Kitt stiffened. "Why not?" She couldn't tell from the sharpness of his voice whether he was angry or disappointed.

When she remained silent, he asked, "Are you worried about what everyone will think?"

"No! Yes! Oh, I don't know!" She broke away, turning to stare off down the course of the stream. Kitt moved behind her and his hands slid up her arms, leaving gooseflesh in their wake.

"You shouldn't care." His voice was gentle, his breath stirred the tiny wisps of hair at her temple. "I don't."

She closed her eyes and leaned back against him. Oh, how she wanted to believe him. She wanted to believe the *ton* didn't matter. She wanted to believe his declaration that he didn't care meant he cared for her enough to brave society's censure.

But she couldn't. The *ton* was a world of its own. If you didn't play by its rules, regardless of your rank, you were shunned. That was the world Kitt had been born into, the only world he knew. She could not allow him to walk away from it because of her. He would never be happy, and he would eventually come to resent her. It would destroy him.

"It doesn't matter. I can't let you make such a sacrifice for me. I'm not worth it."

She was not prepared for his anger. His hands tightened on her shoulders and he spun her around to face him. "Not worth it?" he thundered. "What the hell is that supposed to mean?"

Pamela would have backed away from him had the bridge wall not been behind her, forcing her to stand her ground. Blue fire blazed from his eyes. Inside, she cringed. Drawing on the courage she had used to face her stepfather, she confronted him bravely. "I will not be a charity case. I might consider your proposal if you loved me, but—"

"Love!" he spat with such vehemence she winced. "What in the name of all that's holy does love have to do with this?"

"Very little to you, obviously." Her anger rose to match his. "Nevertheless, I refuse to marry without it."

Kitt's mouth worked for a moment, as if he would say something more. Then, with a last blast from searing blue eyes, he spun on his heel and stalked away.

"You won't believe what's happened now!" Lisa blurted as she entered the parlor in a flurry of yellow and blue. Pamela and Lady Parkington were just sitting down to tea. Pearl jumped up from the hearth and directed two sharp barks at Lisa before settling back down before the fire.

"You did not come here alone, did you?" Lady Parkington asked her.

"Of course not, Aunt. Molly is probably settled in the kitchen with a cup of tea by now. And I left Mama a note. I cried off from making afternoon calls with her." Clad in a high-waisted robin-egg blue muslin gown, yellow and blue ribbons threaded through her dark curls, Lisa brought sunshine into the room with her.

The rain of the last three days had done nothing for Pamela's already depressed mood. Lisa's arrival with an interesting bit of gossip garnered her reluctant interest.

Mrs. Diggs entered with another cup and saucer, placing them before Lisa. Once she left, Lady Parkington turned to her niece. "Well now, what's so exciting?"

"Yesterday was Wednesday, was it not?"

Lady Parkington nodded.

"Which meant we had to go to Almack's."

Pamela noticed Lady Parkington frowned. She was still of the mind that what actually ruined Pamela was the denial of vouchers to Almack's, not the subsequent gossip.

"Well," Lisa continued as if she hadn't noticed, "Gerald wouldn't go. Mama was furious with him, but he said he wouldn't ever darken their doors again. Mama threatened, but he merely left the house."

Lady Parkington sat up at this. "He refused?"

Lisa nodded.

"But, but I've never known Gerald not to give in."

Lisa's eyes were dancing. "Exactly! I thought Mama would have a fit of the vapors. But then..."

Pamela watched Lisa deliberately take a bite of cake, then sip her tea delicately. There was more and Lisa was stalling. Pamela nearly smiled at her friend's barely suppressed excitement.

"There were no gentlemen at Almack's!"

"None?" Lady Parkington was stunned. "What do you mean, none?"

Lisa took another sip of her tea. "Well, there were very few eligibles. Nearly all the gentlemen present were married or already betrothed. Even all those annoying dandies and coxcombs were not present. It was a veritable crush—of young ladies."

Lady Parkington sat back in her chair, the delicate gold-rimmed cup forgotten for a moment. Suddenly, a smile broke out on her face and she leaned forward again. "So, Lisa, tell us the rest. How does Gerald's refusal to attend fit?"

Lisa's laughter echoed around the small room.

"I should have known you would discern the connection. You are right, of course. Gerald and Den—uh—Lord Denton merely convinced a few friends to convince a few friends it would be a lark not to have any young men show up at Almack's last evening. He and I had a great laugh about it this morning, but needless to say, Mama was not amused." Lisa's sigh was decidedly theatrical. "She is rather put out with the both of us right now."

Pamela admitted to herself the whole business *was* rather funny.

"I wish I could have seen Sally's face." Lady Parkington was laughing along with Lisa.

"I told Gerald he should do it again next week, but he says he's not sure he can convince his friends to go along two weeks in a row. But he is telling anyone who asks that the reason he won't be back is because you've been denied vouchers. He says he considers it an insult to his family. And Mama is worried Papa will agree with him."

And with that, Lisa sat back on the sofa, a satisfied smile on her face.

"Aren't you worried, too?" Pamela spoke for the first time.

Lisa shook her auburn curls. "I hope Papa does agree with Gerald, then I can cry off, too. I considered pleading a headache last evening as it was, but I was glad to have seen the results of Gerald's efforts. I haven't enjoyed myself so much since the

Season started—and I only danced twice the whole evening. There were just not enough gentlemen to go around."

Lady Parkington was still chuckling over the "Almack's Incident", as she and Lisa had labeled it, when Lisa left.

"Well, well, it looks as if you have made a conquest in my nephew."

Pamela looked at her in horror. "Oh, no! Don't say that! Lord Tinsley is close in age to my brother, Stephen. In fact, he reminds me of my brother."

"Tut, tut. No need to fly up in the boughs. He's not for you, anyway. And not just because he's too young."

"Of course." Pamela's voice was flat. "He is a viscount, after all."

"Oh, don't be a widgeon! That has nothing to do with it," Lady Parkington snapped. She set down her cup and saucer and regarded Pamela silently for a few moments. "There are other reasons why he wouldn't do for you, the first of which is you're already in love with Kitt."

Pamela stared at the old woman in amazement, her cup halfway to her mouth. "How...how...?"

"How did I know?"

Pamela nodded, unable to speak. She set the cup and saucer down on the table beside her perch.

"It's written all over your face. Now I don't know what happened when you went for that drive a few days ago, and I haven't wanted to pry. You have not been yourself for the last week, but more so the last three days."

Silence fell between them. What could she say? She wanted to talk to someone, but she was afraid Lady Parkington would think she was being a goose. No one in the *ton* married for love. Why should Kitt be any different? She would have the protection of his name, children to raise, a home of her own. Wasn't that enough?

"He asked me to marry him."

The admission slipped out before she could stop it. Absently, she picked up a scone and crumbled it on to the small plate.

"Well, of course he did. You're betrothed."

125

"No, you don't understand. He wanted to get a special license."

"And this has you in the doldrums?"

A wobbly smile emerged. "Not truly."

"But..."

"But he doesn't believe in love and I refuse to marry without it."

There. It was out. She steeled herself for the snort of disbelief. When it didn't come, she looked over at Lady Parkington and found her staring across the room, a sad expression on her face. Finally, she sighed and turned back to meet Pamela's gaze.

"Love destroyed Kitt's parents." Her words were tinged with sadness. "Marianne was so completely in love with John that she was blind to his faults. She couldn't see his jealousy was irrational. It never occurred to her he wouldn't believe her avowals of fidelity. He just couldn't believe she wouldn't respond to every lure thrown her way."

As if sensing her mistress's needs, Pearl jumped into Lady Parkington's lap and nestled there.

"I think John loved her as well, but his way of showing it was...well, it was unnatural."

"What do you mean, unnatural?"

"It was a vicious circle. They'd argue, he'd get drunk and hit her—sometimes worse. They'd make up, and it would start all over again. She lost two babes, one before Kitt and one after, due to his violence. He couldn't help himself. All she had to do was smile at another man and he'd lose his wits."

"Why didn't they stay in the country?"

"She tried. But he was very conscientious when it came to his seat in Parliament, and he refused to leave her at Kitt Ridge. So, year after year, she came to Town, knowing what would happen. It was worse after Kitt went off to school because she couldn't use him as an excuse to stay close to home. She often brought him along, installed him and his governess in the Manor, then slipped away as much as she could to visit him.

"After she disappeared, she wrote to Kitt at school. As far as I know she never told Kitt why she left. And it's obvious Kitt's knowledge of the state of his parents' marriage differs from mine. There is no way he could have idolized his father had he known.

"But for all that, he raised Kitt well. Except for his views on marriage, you could not find a finer, more honorable, man in all of England than Kitt." She smiled, a mischievous sparkle appearing in her eyes. "Besides my brother, of course."

Chapter Nine

The next morning a missive arrived from Lady Fallmerton, inviting them to make up a party to Vauxhall Gardens. Pamela was suspicious, but Lady Parkington took it in good humor.

"It is probably Lisa and Gerald's doing, and Charlotte is not so sure of herself when it comes to me. I would never come between her and Nicky, but she does not understand that, so she does not deliberately snub me because she's not sure what Nicky might do."

"And why is that?"

"Because Nicky and I have always been close. I was a mother hen to all my brothers: James, Anthony, and Nicky. But Nicky was the youngest, so he had to tolerate more." She laughed before she continued. "He went off to school the same year I married, and although we did not see much of each other, we kept in touch. When he bought a commission and joined York's forces in Northern France, we all worried about him, but there was little we could do. He was back a year later—but not before we first thought him dead. And it was another year before he could walk again."

Pamela was surprised at her response to Lady Parkington's revelations. It was easy to see how much she loved her brother, and Pamela knew how she felt.

There was not the same number of years' difference in age between them, but she and Stephen also shared a special bond, albeit not one forged through an almost parent-child relationship. With only three years difference between them, they had been companions. Until Stephen went off to school, the two of them had been nearly inseparable.

"Lud! Look at me!" Lady Parkington's self-derisive snort cut into Pamela's thoughts. "Becoming maudlin over a baby brother who is near fifty years old. Nicky would laugh heartily at me if he knew."

Vauxhall Gardens was like a fairyland. Pamela stared around her in delight as they alighted from the carriage. In the distance, she could hear music, but just barely over the noise of the crowd. And what a crowd it was.

People from every walk of life who could afford the entrance fee crowded the avenues beneath trees strung with brightly colored lanterns. There were footmen, butlers, maids, cits, shopkeepers, upper classes, members of the *ton* and more, all mingling along the pathways and in the secluded walks branching away from the brightly lit thoroughfares. The night air was warm, the scent of the trees, flowers, and the damp of the nearby river filling the air. As they reached their reserved supper box, Pamela noticed a space had been cleared before the tiered pavilion holding the orchestra. Lady Parkington told her there would probably be fireworks later in the evening, but she said nothing about dancing.

Lisa sat beside her, pointing out people and curiosities here and there.

"There's Lady Bellingham. She likes everyone to think she's an old tartar." Lisa pointed out a large woman, heavily swathed in chartreuse silk with diamonds and pearls draping her voluminous figure. "But don't let her fool you. She's a dear."

A svelte beauty in cerulean blue went by, her dark hair piled high and decorated with dyed-to-match ostrich feathers. She was on the arm of a gentleman who must have weighed twenty stone. "And there's Lady Martinson. Don't get in her way. She's been chasing Kitt for years according to gossip, but he's never paid her any attention. Oh, there's Lord Montgomery. He's a nice young man. He went to school with Gerald. He's always staring at me. I hope he doesn't come over here." The young man in question was a perfect dandy. His white shirt points were so high he could barely turn his head, and his cravat was tied in an exceedingly intricate knot. His bright green waistcoat was covered by a darker green evening coat, topping yellow pantaloons. He looked like he should be adorning a garden.

Pamela continued scanning the crowd as it passed by their box, only giving cursory attention to Lisa's comments.

"Oh, look, there's your sister. And is that...no, it couldn't be...but it looks like she's with Kitt. I don't believe it."

Pamela's eyes snapped in the direction of Lisa's stare. To be sure, it was Sheila, elegantly clad in a gown of blush pink, strolling along on the arm of a gentleman, but they were so far away Pamela could only just barely make out her escort's profile. But he did look like Kitt. His head tilted in just the right way, his dark hair falling over his forehead. He was dressed in stark black and white and when he smiled at Sheila, even from this distance Pamela's heart skipped a beat. She could not tear her eyes away, and watched the couple until they disappeared.

The night was no longer magical. The lights were no longer as bright as they had been mere moments before, the music not as lively. Pamela's interest in the crowd around her and the food set before her waned.

She had not seen Kitt since their trip to Covington Manor. Their ride back to the city had been accomplished in almost complete silence. Beyond inquiring as to her comfort, he had not spoken to her at all. And she, a little ashamed of her outburst, had been too embarrassed to try to bridge the chasm. Now it looked as though he had turned to Sheila for comfort.

Not that she blamed him. Sheila was a diamond—a beauty who could be bright, witty and charming when she wanted to be. While Pamela, well, she was no beauty—she was too tall and nearly on the shelf. Why would Kitt bother with her when he could have Sheila?

Lord Denton came by, accompanied by Lord Tinsley.

Bowing over his mother's hand, Lord Tinsley exchanged pleasantries then took a seat beside his sister. Lord Denton joined Pamela.

"Are you enjoying yourself?"

"Yes." She tried to inject the right amount of enthusiasm into her voice. "It is all quite lovely."

He chuckled. "You mean, what you can see of it, that is?"

She smiled genuinely. "Of course."

"Would you like to see more? We could take a stroll."

She was about to refuse when she caught Lisa's eye. There was no mistaking the expression. Lisa was imploring her to agree.

"I...yes...that would be nice."

A few minutes later, Gerald and Lisa left the box arm in arm. Pamela and Lord Denton followed.

"I understand Kitt took you out to the Manor?"

"Yes, he did. It is quite beautiful."

"It is lovely, but I'm surprised he took you there."

She turned to look up at him. His green eyes nearly danced in the muted light. "Why is that?"

"Because he has taken no one else there, nor allowed anyone else to go there in the past. He always used his old governess's presence to keep people away, but even since she died, he has never entertained visitors. He always goes alone. It is a very special place for him."

Lisa and Gerald were arguing over something, but suddenly stopped and turned to Pamela and Denny. Lisa glanced around, then casually said, "Do you mind if I steal Lord Denton, Pamela?"

Pamela looked from Lisa to Gerald to Denny, and suddenly all was clear.

"No," she replied, "not at all." Taking the arm Gerald offered, she glanced back and said, "Now just don't get lost. I don't want to have to explain your disappearance to your Mama."

Lisa pouted, her dark eyes twinkling. "Now you are starting to sound like an older sister. I've always wanted one, but you don't need to become one."

Gerald laughed at his sister's expression. "You can't have it both ways, Lisa. But I will acquit Miss Clarkdale of that role by reminding Lord Denton I enjoy sleeping in."

"Your wishes are so noted." Denny's grin contradicted the solemnity of his words.

As they turned to continue their stroll, Gerald said, "I'd be delighted to welcome you as a cousin, perhaps, but I do *not* need an older sister."

She laughed—and it felt good to do so. "You and Lisa are both incorrigible."

"I know, but I promised to get Lisa out of the box before Lord Severton made his appearance. Mama has all but announced the match, but I'm afraid she's doomed to disappointment."

"Because Lisa won't have him?"

"Partially. I suspect she doesn't think Papa will agree with Lisa. Some days Mama is blind to Papa's faults. And one of his big faults is spoiling Lisa. He will not force the match, no matter how advantageous."

Pamela was glad to hear the earl would not just agree with his wife's assessment of whom Lisa should marry.

"Would he allow a match between Lisa and Denny?"

Gerald glanced back at the two for a moment before answering. "I don't know. Being a second son is a difficult position these days. Especially if it is likely you will never inherit." He looked ahead and sighed. "Mama, like most of our class, is only interested in seeing Lisa well set-up. Papa will be interested in her happiness, but he will also expect Lord Denton to be able to keep her in style."

"I see."

"Papa is not a Methodist, but Denton's reputation is not spotless, either. He and Lord Kittridge are two peas in a pod. It will be interesting to see what Papa thinks next week when he arrives."

They talked about the family history he and his father were compiling, Gerald regaling her with a few interesting stories from the past. By the time they turned to make their way back to the box, Pamela had put Kitt's indiscretion behind her and was enjoying herself. Or she was until they stopped so Lisa could rejoin her, and Pamela thought she caught sight of Sheila and Kitt in the shadows of one of the pathways, locked in a passionate kiss. The woman's back was to her, but she was sure it was the same pale pink dress she'd noticed on Sheila earlier. All she could see of the man was his dark hair, but her senses told her it was the same person she'd seen strolling with Sheila.

"Thank you for not complaining," Lisa said. "I needed the opportunity to talk to Den...uh...Lord Denton without Mama being suspicious."

"It was no trouble. Your brother is easy to talk to," Pamela responded absently. She was thankful Lisa had her back to the couple in the shadows, and hoped neither Denny nor Gerald saw them either. "But I certainly hope you know what you're doing."

Lisa glanced back at Lord Denton and Pamela could see the uncertainty in her eyes. It brought her back to the present and she shoved the picture of Sheila in Kitt's arms to the back of her mind.

"So do I."

Lord Severton was speaking with Lady Fallmerton when they arrived. He glanced suspiciously at Lord Denton and Lord Tinsley following behind the ladies, and Pamela understood why Lisa had insisted on returning in her company. Lord Severton would not have believed Lisa had walked with her own brother the entire time, but he might believe Lisa and Pamela walked together with the men nearby for protection.

"I thought Lord Kittridge might grace us with his presence," Lady Fallmerton said as Pamela took her seat beside Lady Parkington.

Pamela remained quiet.

"Thought I saw him earlier," Lord Severton said, "speaking with Marscombe's chit."

"I'm sure you must have been mistaken," Lady Parkington sniffed.

"Don't think so..."

"Ooh, it must be time for the fireworks," Lisa interjected.

Pamela noticed the crowd had become denser. From their vantage point, however, they did not need to leave their box in order to watch the display.

It was spectacular. Even Pamela, who was not at her best, was awed by the explosions lighting up the night sky in bright splashes of color. The crowd was also suitably appreciative, its "oohs", "aahs", and thundering applause lengthy and loud.

As the four women made their way home in the carriage, Lisa was full of admiration for the display and went on at length about how much fun it would be to see it again.

By the time Pamela and Lady Parkington entered the house, the sound of the wheels of the Fallmerton coach fading in the distance, Pamela couldn't wait to get inside and away from Lady Parkington's too observant gaze. It had been nearly more than she could bear to pretend interest and delight when her heart was breaking.

She'd always expected Kitt might eventually turn to Sheila. After all, Sheila always got what she wanted, and the gossip was that she wanted Kitt. As she climbed the staircase, Pamela wondered to what lengths Sheila might go to get what she wanted. The answer only depressed her more.

"Are you sure you don't want me to accompany you?"

Pamela watched Lady Parkington tie a bonnet trimmed in purple flowers over her silvered coiffeur.

"No. Letitia and I have been friends since long before you were born—neither of us needs chaperoning."

Pamela colored at the remark. "I wasn't suggesting you did, ma'am."

Her employer chuckled. "I know you weren't, but Letitia and I want to gossip without listening ears. She gives her companion the morning off whenever I come to visit, so you may as well have some time, too." She approached Pamela and looked up into her face, concern creasing her brow. "Besides, you look as if you could use some rest. You are looking peaked. Go out in the sun for a bit."

Pamela forced herself to smile. "I am fine."

Carter cleared his throat and Pamela was grateful for the interruption. Once Lady Parkington was on her way, Pamela went back into the parlor, where she found Pearl curled up in her mistress's favorite chair.

"Come along, lazybones. I suppose we could both do with some air."

As she set out for Hyde Park a short time later, Pamela felt her spirits lifting. For the last two days, she had often revisited the times she'd seen Kitt and Sheila at Vauxhall. She tried not to jump to conclusions, but his continuing absence made it difficult. If he had chosen Sheila, why hadn't he said something? And, why had no one else said anything? Was he waiting for her to do something? Without warning, pieces of a conversation she'd had with Lady Parkington floated through her head.

"And if Lord Kittridge cries off?"

Lady Parkington had shaken her head. "Oh, no, no, no. He won't. If he does, it will put you completely beyond the pale. He would marry you first."

Was he waiting for her to end it? How would she know?

She sighed as she turned into the gates of Hyde Park. Allowing Pearl to run free was not possible as the small dog would dash off and possibly get lost, so Pamela kept her leash firmly in hand.

The park was not crowded at this time of day—the fashionables would not make an appearance for many hours yet. Pamela was thankful for the time alone. The rain the night before had washed away the normal stench of the city, leaving a freshness in its wake. Pamela breathed deeply as she walked. The light fog hanging over the city when she first awakened was lifting, the gray giving way to patches of blue and sunshine. Birdsong trilled from the trees. Pearl tugged on her leash, attempting to pull Pamela faster along the graveled pathway, but she was not to be hurried. She needed this time.

A woman walked by holding an infant in one arm and a small child by the hand. A flower seller offered her a nosegay, which she declined, but gave the girl a penny anyway. Two young boys dashed by, causing Pearl to bark sharply at them and try to give chase, only to be pulled back.

Her thoughts in turmoil, Pamela walked on. It had now been almost an entire week since she'd last seen Kitt—if she didn't count the Vauxhall sightings two nights ago. Five days since the trip to Covington Manor. Five days since she'd told him categorically she would not marry without love.

She found an unoccupied stone bench overlooking the river and sat down. Pearl collapsed into the grass at her feet, resting her head on her front paws.

Another conversation from her past ran through her head.

"I know this sounds odd coming from me," she heard her mother's voice, "but if you cannot marry for love, then you are best not marrying at all."

Once before, she'd thought herself in love, but that emotion, whatever it was, paled in comparison to what she felt for Kitt. Because of that, she could not clearly recall Lord Crandall's face without Kitt's features overlaying the image.

Her mother would have liked the match with Lord Crandall and Pamela would have been content. But her mother knew nothing about Sheila's part in killing that hope.

The sun glinting off the water became a hazy image of blue and gold, reminding her of the look in Sheila's eyes when they'd met on the stairs. She closed her eyes and was back at Clark Hall, standing on the middle landing in the front hall as Sheila came through the door.

The early March sunlight streaming through the window above the front hall door was not enough to brighten the gloomy entryway. The dark wood paneling, although polished and gleaming, always made the hall seem smaller than it was. The door opened and Sheila entered, followed by a gentleman. Her maid scurried in behind the couple and, after relieving Sheila of her cloak and muff, disappeared into the back of the house.

"It was a lovely drive, my lord." Sheila's voice floated up to her.

"I'm glad you enjoyed it," was the rumbled response, and Pamela froze as she recognized Lord Crandall's voice. "Perhaps when the days are warmer we could take a picnic."

"That would be splendid," Sheila tittered.

Once Lord Crandall left, Sheila turned toward the stairs, noticing Pamela for the first time.

"Oh, I didn't realize you were there." Her cheeks were flushed from the cold outside.

"No, I don't suppose you did."

Sheila climbed the stairs until she stood beside Pamela.

"Wyatt took me for a drive." Sheila's voice was neutral, but Pamela saw the excitement mixed with triumph in her eyes. Even if Sheila had no use for Lord Crandall, she would have still entertained him in order to have something she perceived as belonging to Pamela. And until that moment, Pamela had considered him her suitor.

"I see."

"You don't mind, do you?"

Pamela shrugged. "Why should I?"

And she hadn't. Sheila hadn't believed her, but it hadn't mattered—because she'd already fallen in love with Kitt.

Pamela's eyes popped open. The water of the Serpentine continued to slip silently by, the sun still glinting off its surface. Pearl lay in the grass at her feet.

Was it true? Had she been in love with Kitt even then, when she knew absolutely nothing about him? Was that why Wyatt's defection hadn't hurt? Was that why, when she left Clark Hall nearly a month later, she had been able to walk away?

She hadn't left her heart behind as she thought—it had already been gone.

After the scene in the stables, she had hidden in the house for nearly three weeks while she and her mother determined what she should do. Thankfully, her stepfather rarely visited his wife's sickroom, so it had not been difficult. Her mother surprised her. Although weak and ill, she was determined to help Pamela leave with more than the clothing on her back, in spite of her husband.

Finding Lady Parkington's advertisement in *The Times* seemed like fate. Correspondence had been quick due to the Parkington estate being just north of York.

Shaking off the unpleasant memories, Pamela stood and retraced her steps. The sun had burned off the remainder of the fog and felt good on her face. She still had no idea what she was going to do about Kitt, but she would not jump to conclusions until she spoke to him first. Lady Parkington might have realized that Pamela was in love with Kitt, but she was just beginning to realize it fully. For now, she'd do nothing. She knew she'd see Kitt at Lisa's ball in three days, unless he put in an appearance before then. That would be soon enough to talk.

Fate, unfortunately, had other plans and when she arrived back at the house on Arden Street, Sheila was waiting for her.

"Oh, thank goodness you're back!" Sheila exclaimed when she entered the parlor. "I've been waiting hours!"

Pamela knew that wasn't true—she hadn't been gone hours, and Carter told her that her sister had only been there for a quarter hour.

"You didn't come here alone, did you? Does Grandmama know where you are?"

Sheila pouted. "Of course not, she would never have allowed me, and I brought Bess along."

Pamela grimaced. Bess was Sheila's overworked and underpaid maid. The one who received all the blame when Sheila misplaced a shawl or reticule, but never received any thanks for turning her mistress out in fine style. The one who was expected to resurrect a ruined gown, or create elaborate coiffeurs while Sheila paced her room. In Pamela's estimation, Bess was a saint.

Tea was brought and once they were alone, Pamela eyed her sister nervously. Despite the forced cheerfulness, this was not a social call.

Sheila perched uneasily on the edge of the sofa, her blue muslin dress pale against the dark green pattern of the cushions. Her face was pale, too, and Pamela wondered if she was sick. But no, Sheila was never sick.

Sheila's hands shook as she replaced her cup in the saucer, then set both down on the low table before her. Clasping her hands together in her lap, she looked up at Pamela. When she still didn't speak, Pamela's patience ended.

"What do you want, Sheila?" She didn't mean to sound waspish, but she could not shake the feeling that something was very wrong.

"I need your help." Sheila's eyes darted around the room as she spoke, refusing to make eye contact. "I don't know what to do and...and...I can't tell Grandmama."

"How?"

"You must break your betrothal to Kitt...I mean, Lord Kittridge."

Pamela's guard went up. She stared at Sheila as if she had just asked for the moon, trying to determine if she was serious.

"Why?"

Sheila's gaze shifted again. Her lashes swept down to rest against porcelain cheeks. "Be...because I...I'm carrying his heir."

The world stopped turning. Pamela felt the blood drain from her face, and her heart drop to her shoes. This could not be happening.

Sheila had to be lying.

"I don't believe you."

Sheila lifted incredulous eyes to Pamela's face. She obviously hadn't expected Pamela to challenge her. "It's true!" she insisted, her cheeks paling further. "I...I didn't mean to let things go so far...but...but..." She burst into noisy tears.

Pamela frowned. It was not like Sheila to be so distressed. Mayhap there was some truth to her claim. Picking up one of the napkins from the tray, she handed it to Sheila.

"What happened?"

"It...it was only the second time I met him." Sheila sniffed. "He...he said I was beautiful. We went out into the garden after dancing."

Pamela still wasn't sure she believed her, but pressed on. "And?"

"And...and...he kissed me. It was so different...I...I didn't realize what was happening until it was all over." Sheila blew her nose noisily into the napkin.

"Just a kiss?"

"No...no, not just a kiss. We...we went into a gazebo...and..." Sheila's face reddened and she looked away.

"Have you told him this?"

Sheila's scandalized look told Pamela all she wanted to know. "How...how could I? Especially after that announcement."

"Why did you wait this long to say anything at all?"

"I...I decided to wait...to see if...if...anything came...of it. No one else knew, so I...I thought ...if..."

Pamela could well imagine Sheila thought she could escape such an indiscretion with no consequences. After all, she'd never had to answer for anything else for most of her life. Why not this?

Pamela's shoulders slumped and she looked down at her hands. When she raised her head again, Sheila was dabbing at her eyes.

"Are you sure?" She wouldn't put it past Sheila to jump to outlandish conclusions.

"Of course I'm sure."

Pamela bit her lip. "I will speak to Kitt."

"But you mustn't tell him," Sheila insisted, agitated. "If you just release him from the betrothal, I will tell him myself."

"Then what do you suppose I should say?"

Sheila seemed to be thinking. Then she brightened. "You could say you don't think you would suit after all." She took a bite of an almond biscuit and chewed thoughtfully. "Maybe you could say you prefer someone else?"

"And what makes you think he will believe that? No one has paid me any attention. In fact, thanks to you and Grandmama, very few even speak to me." Pamela tried to hide her bitterness, but it was difficult. The knowledge that her difficulties had been instigated by her own family, and now that same family was conspiring to destroy what little happiness she had garnered for herself, grated.

Sheila dismissed her concerns. "Oh, well, I'm sure you'll think of something. As long as you say nothing about my...my condition. I would wish to tell him myself."

Pamela stiffened at Sheila's insinuation. "I do not bear tales," she snapped. "Your secret is not mine to tell."

She wondered why Sheila had not said anything to Kitt already. Perhaps she knew the consequences of Kitt breaking the betrothal as opposed to Pamela, but it was not like her to be so concerned about someone else. Maybe she was worried instead about the gossip that would flow if Kitt broke the betrothal in order to marry his former betrothed's sister. It would put Sheila in a bad light, and goodness knew she would not want to be seen in a bad light. She'd stay on the sidelines until the betrothal was broken, then suddenly be there to console Kitt. She would walk away with everyone's approval—again.

Sheila had the grace to look chagrined, and Pamela wondered if she was remembering all the times she'd run bearing tales to her father. Pamela, however, would not lower herself to do the same. She might—and it was a very big "might" because she had some thinking to do first—end the betrothal to Kitt, but she would keep Sheila's secret.

Pamela was still sitting in the parlor when Lady Parkington returned. The walk had refreshed her, but Sheila's visit left her despondent. Consequently, she was not surprised when her employer took one look at her and said, "You look like someone died. I thought I told you to get some sun?"

Pamela roused herself and looked at Lady Parkington. "You did, and I did. I think I tired both Pearl and myself out." She glanced over at the terrier curled up before the fire and said with a wan smile, "Neither of us has moved since we returned."

Lady Parkington looked over at the little dog and smiled. Pamela wasn't sure if she believed her or not, but she said nothing more. Thankfully, Mrs. Diggs had already removed the tea service.

After lunch, they settled in the parlor to discuss the newest gossip Lady Parkington learned from her friend when a visitor was announced.

"The Earl of Fallmerton, my lady."

Pamela looked up as a man walked into the room, promptly shrinking it to dollhouse size. Well over six feet, with burnished, dark red hair turning silver at the temples and hazel eyes, he towered over his sister, who moved with more speed than Pamela had ever seen her move and flung her arms around him.

"Nicky!" she squealed delightedly. "This is a wonderful surprise."

Pamela barely noticed Lisa enter the room behind her father, so astounded was she by this unexpected display of affection by Lady Parkington.

"And why is it so surprising that I would visit my only sister?" he asked with a chuckle as he hugged her back.

"It is not the visit that is surprising, it is the day," she retorted. "I would have expected you not to arrive until the day of Lisa's ball so as to spend as little time as possible in London at this time of year. But since you are here, come and meet my newest godchild."

Pamela rose as Lady Parkington led him over. Surprise crossed his face and he studied her closely as they were introduced. She wondered if Lady Fallmerton had told him about his sister's scandalous companion.

Lisa announced her presence. "Good afternoon, Aunt Claire. Do you mind if I steal Pamela away for a while? Gerald has promised me a trip to Gunter's."

"That would be fine. It will give your father and me a chance to catch up."

Pamela wasn't sure she was up to an outing to the famous confectioner's, but knew she would be *de trop* if she remained. As she retrieved her cloak and bonnet, she wondered if she could plead a headache and retire to her room.

She did not feel like good company right now, but she couldn't disappoint Lisa. It was likely Lisa had arranged it all and Denny would show up. It was obvious to Pamela that Lisa was using Kitt and Denny's friendship as a smokescreen. With Kitt not available, the rest of the *ton* did not seem to think it odd his best friend was his betrothed's escort on occasion. And since Pamela had not attended any events since the Laverlys' ball, it didn't happen often.

Hurrying back down the stairs, she gave herself a mental shake. She would not let Sheila ruin her afternoon's enjoyment. She could mope over Kitt's betrayal when she was alone, but she would not dampen Lisa's enthusiasm this afternoon.

As the front door closed behind Pamela and Lisa, Lady Parkington turned and slipped her arm through her brother's. Once the two were back in the parlor with the door shut, she turned to him, a mischievous smile on her face.

"Well, Nicky," she began, seating herself in her favorite chair, "which one of our dearly departed brothers do you think was the father of that lovely child?"

A smile lit the lean, aristocratic features of the Earl of Fallmerton as he glanced down at his sister. Seating himself in a matching chair and stretching his long legs out before him, he contemplated her and her question for a long moment before he replied.

"I don't know, Pamela Claire. Why don't *you* tell *me*?"

And she did.

Chapter Ten

Nicholas James Adam DeWare, Earl of Fallmerton, was the current holder of a very old and venerable title. A formidable man, his tall, whipcord-lean figure was still fit as he neared a half-century, and he was known in society circles as not only a leader, but one many wanted to follow. He was fair in his dealings, generous with his praise and favor, and known to be faithful in his marriage. His tenacity for a cause brought him admiration, and he was a war hero, having been wounded at Hondschoote in Northern France under the Duke of York in 1793. Like the distant monarch whose sobriquet of "Longshanks" was applied to him, too, he was concerned with the people of his country and took his duties in Parliament seriously. Few crossed him.

But someone had crossed him. It was there for all to see in the grim lines of his face and the closed expression in his hazel eyes. Sprawled in a chair in one of the small, dimly lit parlors at White's, a half-empty decanter of port at his elbow, none dared to approach him. None except the Earl of Kittridge, with whom he was now engaged in a low-voiced conversation.

The curiosity of the other patrons was palpable, but no one made the slightest attempt to get close enough to eavesdrop. Whatever was the matter, it was not worth invoking the displeasure of Nicholas DeWare, the same man whose oldest brother had once earned the nickname "Beware" due to his explosive temper.

Yet for all their inability to learn what set the earl on edge, the patrons discovered that if they remained quiet, a word or two of the conversation would reach their ears.

Words such as *dead*. And *married*. And *sold*. And *lying scoundrel*. And *Gerald*. And *family tradition*. And, last of all, punctuated with a groan, *Charlotte*, leaving all to wonder if the earl had had a falling out with his wife.

Kittridge didn't seem exceptionally put out by whatever revelations Fallmerton poured into his willing ears. In fact, he seemed quite pleased. At one point even throwing back his head and laughing while Fallmerton continued to scowl.

Just before the two left, however, the patrons were rewarded for their patience when Kittridge made a comment concerning Almack's, to which Fallmerton replied with a laugh of his own.

"Charlotte is vexed with Lisa and Gerald for their refusal to enter that place again, but more so with me because I am in agreement with them. I think Gerald has the right of it when he says Almack's is little more than a second-rate assembly hall whose importance is extremely overrated."

Kitt sat at the rosewood desk in his spacious library and stared at the letter before him. The dog-eared missive was yellowed with age, the flowing script on the page growing faint from years of being carried around and read again and again. He no longer could read parts of it, but it didn't matter. He knew the whole of the short missive by heart.

December 1795

My darling son:

It is with a heavy heart I write this, for I know you will never understand what has happened. I can no longer live with your father and must seek to preserve my health. It will be difficult not seeing you grow up, but I know your father loves you as I do, so I am content to leave you in his care. Perhaps someday I will return, but if it is not to be so, be ever mindful I love you and always will.

It was signed simply, "Mama".

He'd received it not long before the Christmas holiday. When his father arrived to collect him, he had noted the sadness in his father's eyes. In that moment, he hated his mother.

He'd never told his father about the letter, but kept it as a reminder of the perversity of women. Regardless of their profession of love, they would not hesitate to turn their backs if something better came along.

He had been twelve when he received the letter. When he was seventeen, his father revealed that his mother had gone away with a Frenchman—an exiled *duc*. According to his father, she preferred his lifestyle to the mundane one of wife and mother.

Women are fickle, my boy. He could still hear his father's woeful voice. *Loving them is not enough to ensure they will love you back.*

When he questioned his father about what he meant, he explained Kitt's mother had been the daughter of the Marquis of Haddon. Although the marquis treated her as his own, it was common knowledge in the *ton* that she was the product of one of the marchioness's many affairs.

Remember, my boy, blood will tell in the end.

Blood will tell. His father maintained that was the reason his mother left. At least she hadn't created the scandals her own mother had. He should be thankful for that much.

Kitt roused himself from his gloomy memories. His parents were long gone, but the lessons lingered. He was willing to marry Pamela to thwart her family, but doubts intruded. Knowing her background mirrored his mother's disturbed him, but there were differences. The most obvious one was that his mother had been accepted and well dowered by her family.

Pamela would cherish any children they might have. His own mother had smothered him. She often went out of her way to spend time with him. Despite his insistence on remembering Frisky as the mainstay of his life at Covington Manor, memories of his mother remained. She came often when he and Frisky were in residence, frequently spending the night. When his father came for her, she would return to London with him reluctantly. He'd wondered if it was because she met a lover between London and the manor.

Regardless, he would ensure Pamela never had the opportunity to stray. Perhaps if he hadn't been an only child his mother might have stayed. Keeping Pamela pregnant would not be an arduous task. Just the thought of her swelling with his child gave him a warm feeling he refused to define, but left him content.

Smiling to himself, he rose from his desk and crossed the library to the fireplace. He stared down at the letter in his hand for one long, last, minute, then tossed it into the flames. His mother was gone, but he had learned his lesson.

Turning, he left the library to dress for the evening. As he climbed the staircase, he wondered what Pamela would be wearing tonight.

"You look like an angel."

"A very tall angel, no doubt," Lisa responded dryly to Pamela's comment, and the two laughed.

Lisa was indeed stunning in a white silk gown tied high beneath her bosom with a wide gold ribbon, from which fell a gossamer-thin gold overskirt. Because of her height, the skirt fell like a waterfall, its fullness flowing around her gold embroidered white slippers in a swirl of white and gold. White flowers adorned her rich dark hair and a single strand of perfectly matched pearls marched around the slim column of her throat. The sparkle in her eyes reflected the glow of the hundreds of candles overhead.

"You look happy tonight. Dare I ask why?"

The twinkle in Lisa's eyes deepened, and a blush covered her cheeks.

"It is because Papa has told Mama Lord Severton will not suit." She leaned closer and Pamela could smell her jasmine fragrance as she continued in a low voice. "And he told me, but not Mama, he would listen if Lord Denton came to call."

Pamela nearly hugged her right there in the middle of the ballroom. "Oh, Lisa, how wonderful!"

"I suppose it is a victory of sorts, but I don't know if he will approach Papa."

"Perhaps you ought to say something."

"Oh, no! I couldn't!" Horror colored Lisa's words. "He would think me too forward."

Pamela sighed. "Very well. I suppose I'll just have to drop a hint or two."

Lisa's laughter caused Kitt and Denny, who stood not far from the two women, to turn and look at them.

"Oh, Pamela, I vow you are as good as a sister any day."

She grinned at Lisa's enthusiasm, touched anew by her generous acceptance.

The whole evening had been something of a revelation for her. First, she and Lady Parkington arrived to dine with the family, to discover Kitt present as well. Understanding she had been invited because she was being sponsored by Lady Parkington, she did not understand Kitt's presence but thought maybe it was because he and Lord Fallmerton were obviously good friends.

As Lady Parkington predicted, the worst of the gossip had blown over. There were some who still looked at her askance, but none treated her as if she were a particularly nasty disease. She wondered if it had anything to do with the fact that Gerald had partnered her for the first dance of the evening and Lisa's father had partnered her for the second. Lord Parkington claimed her after the earl. Even Lisa's mother had spoken kindly to her in front of some of the guests.

They were treating her almost like family. She wondered if Lady Parkington had convinced her brother she needed the support.

A dandy came by and solicited Lisa's hand for the next set. Pamela waved the two of them off. As they disappeared into the crowd, she allowed her eyes to wander about the ballroom. Lisa's mother had created a wonderful setting for her daughter.

Large banners in autumn colors hung from the ceiling. The brown, gold, red, orange, and burgundy drapes swayed in the light breeze allowed in by the open windows set high above the floor. At the ground level, the colors were repeated in swags adorning the white walls. The decor was cleverly designed not to clash with many of the pastel colors that were the required uniform among the debutantes, but at the same time to flatter Lisa's coloring.

As might be expected, the event was veritable crush. Even though the *ton* had to have known Pamela would be present, few, if any, stayed away. Except perhaps her grandmother and Sheila. She had yet to encounter either of them this evening, or even glimpse Sheila's perfect countenance among the clumps of young misses scattered about the room. She should be relieved she hadn't encountered them, but couldn't shake the feeling that there was still time for something to go wrong.

As for Sheila's claim that she carried Kitt's babe, Pamela was still trying to confirm it. A lifetime of Sheila's half-truths and lies had cured her of taking Sheila's word for anything. No, she would confirm the story herself before she said anything to Kitt. Even if she found out Sheila was indeed pregnant, she still wasn't sure she would believe Sheila's claim of Kitt being responsible, but she would decide what to do when she possessed more information.

For that reason, she asked Tilly to try to discover when Sheila's maid, Bess, had time off. It might take a few days to ascertain the information, but she did not want to question Bess with Sheila's knowledge. The maid would not tell her the truth if she thought Sheila might learn of it.

"Woolgathering?" Kitt's voice jolted her out of her thoughts and she spun around to face him. Dressed for the evening in his usual stark black and white, her heart did a curious flip-flop at the look in his eyes.

"I suppose so," she confessed, resisting the urge to breathe deeply of his spicy scent.

"Something important?"

"Not particularly."

He took her hand and drew it through the crook of his elbow, leading her toward the floor. "I believe the next set is my first waltz of the evening."

The possessive note in his voice left a warm trail as it entered her ears and wormed its way to her heart. If only he loved her as she loved him. She would not have refused his offer at the Manor. She would not have spent almost a fortnight wondering if she had driven him away. Instead she would already be his wife, and away from London.

And it would be too late to do anything about Sheila. Would she have wanted that? How would she have felt had she married Kitt, then learned of Sheila's condition? If Sheila was lying, it wouldn't have come up at all.

"You have not yet told me where you've been." Goodness! Was that a touch of reproof in her voice?

The corner of his mouth quirked and amusement lit his eyes. Overhead, the colors blurred as they whirled down the floor.

"Let's just say I was intelligence gathering."

"Intelligence gathering?" Her eyes narrowed. "What kind of intelligence?"

"Actually it was a family matter. I will tell you about it someday."

"I thought you had no other family."

One dark eyebrow rose. "I do have an heir, so it stands to reason I must have some family—however distant."

"I hadn't thought of it quite that way." Chagrined, she cast about for another topic. "Lisa says her father might not be adverse to Denny's suit."

"I know."

She nearly missed a step. "You know? How?"

"Because I was the one who made the suggestion to him."

"You? But I thought you said Denny was not acceptable?"

He frowned. "That was not what I said. I'm fairly certain what I said was that it wouldn't be allowed because Lady Fallmerton wants a title for Lisa and Denny's is only a courtesy title."

"And that has changed?"

"Not entirely, but Lisa's father has ruled out Severton. I know Lady Fallmerton still has hopes, but at least Denny would not be ruled out for lack of a title."

"Does he know that?"

"Does who know what?"

"Does Denny know he can now speak to Lisa's father without fear?"

Kitt chuckled. "I don't think Denny was ever afraid to speak with Lord Fallmerton. But he wants what's best for Lisa, and he's not convinced he's it."

She sputtered. The dance came to an end and Kitt led her off the floor. "How could he not be convinced he's best for Lisa? Has he *looked* at her lately?"

"I assure you, he has more than looked at her lately, but it doesn't signify. If he doesn't feel he's worthy, nothing will change his mind."

Pamela didn't understand why she was so outraged on Lisa's behalf. Why was it that Denny not pursuing Lisa for her own good rankled while Kitt doing the same for her seemed wrong? If Kitt was willing to marry her to ensure her well-being and she refused to consider it because it sounded too much like sacrificing himself, why did the same sacrifice on Denny's part for Lisa make her see red? She had no explanation. Indeed, she wasn't sure she wanted one.

Kitt led her out the French doors to the terrace. A variety of flowery scents greeted her and she breathed deeply of the cool-scented night air.

"I hope you didn't think my absence was due to our little disagreement," he said as they descended the short flight of steps to the garden path.

"I didn't—" she began, but stopped. In fact she had, and she refused to lie about it. "Well..."

His amusement was obvious in his voice. "I rather thought you might think that. I apologize for not telling you I was leaving."

"There was no need. You are not accountable to me."

"I suppose that's true, but in this case, common courtesy would have dictated I not just up and disappear."

Pamela had no answer to that as they moved further into the darkened garden. Turning off the graveled path, Kitt led her along a more narrow path.

"I missed you, you know," he confessed. "All the while I was away, I kept thinking you believed I agreed you were not worth the sacrifice."

How could he so easily read her?

"But you are, you know." His voice softened as he stopped and turned toward her, drawing her into his arms.

She looked up at features thrown in shadow. The moon gave off the meagerest of light, but his eyes glittered in the darkness.

"What? I am...what?" She wanted to know, but didn't want to know.

"You are worth the sacrifice." One long finger came up and stroked her cheek.

Her heart stuttered and the shiver that slipped down her spine had nothing to do with the coolness of the night. When he lowered his head, there was no thought for anything other than the warm lips that covered her own.

The kiss was brief, but long enough for Pamela to discover that, despite Sheila's claims of Kitt's betrayal, she still loved him. She opened her mouth to say something, but footsteps and muted voices intruded. Swiftly Kitt led her down another path, then doubled back. Moments later they were ascending the steps to the terrace where a shock awaited her.

Another couple exited the brightly lit ballroom, the woman laughing up at her companion as the door closed behind them. Pamela stiffened as she recognized her sister, superbly dressed in a sea-green gown with yellow ribbon trim around the neckline and on the tiny puffed sleeves. She took no notice of Sheila's escort until Kitt stopped, then her eyes widened in shock and disbelief.

"Hello, Pammy." Sheila's voice was stilted and formal, despite her use of the hated nickname.

"Sheila, Wyatt," she acknowledged past the lump in her throat. She rarely thought of Wyatt as "my lord" even though she knew he was Lord Crandall.

Once upon a time he had courted her; had led her to believe he might offer for her. But now here he stood with Sheila, watching her with a curious expression on his handsome face.

"I should have known." Kitt's voice was almost a groan, tinged with resignation. "How are you, Wyatt? I did not realize you were in Town."

"I only arrived a few days ago," was the reply. "I called at the house, but you were away, so I put up at the club until you returned."

Pamela looked from one to the other. They knew each other? How? Sheila was watching them both with a distinct gleam in her eyes. What was she thinking?

"I don't understand." She looked up at Kitt. "How do you know Wyatt?"

"We are distant cousins," Kitt replied. "In fact we are often mistaken for one other—from a distance."

It was then that she noticed the similarities between the two. Wyatt was a toned down version of Kitt. Where Kitt's features were sharp and defined, Wyatt's were softer, as if blurred around the edges. Both had dark hair and were taller than average, although Kitt was the taller of the two. Wyatt had dark eyes rather than Kitt's blue, but the nose and mouth were shaped similarly.

No wonder Kitt's face had so easily replaced Wyatt's in her head. The leap had been little more than a hop.

"Distant cousins?" She looked from one to the other again. Suddenly pieces began falling into place, although the picture her mind created was by no means complete.

I do have an heir...however distant.

"Wyatt is your heir?" She barely got the words out.

He grinned down at her. "For now."

"How?" Wyatt's last name was not Covington. It was Crandall.

"A very long and involved story that reaches back at least three generations."

"I see."

Sheila shifted on Wyatt's arm, drawing everyone's attention.

"I believe I've had enough air, my lord."

Her simpering grated on Pamela's ears.

Wyatt turned to look down at her, patting the hand that rested on his arm. "Then I shall return you to your grandmother. I would not wish you to catch ill."

Curtsies and bows were exchanged, then Wyatt turned and led Sheila back inside.

Pamela paced back and forth before the banked fire in her room. Her footsteps were muffled by the thick rug which also served to keep her feet from the cold hardwood floor. There was a chill in the room, but she ignored it. Her thoughts were in a whirl.

Cousins! Kitt and Wyatt were cousins! Wyatt was Kitt's heir! She had been too stunned to do much except pass the rest of the evening like an automaton. She smiled and responded when spoken to. Danced with a number of gentlemen. Even spoke with Lisa, Gerald and Denny at different times. But she remembered little after the meeting on the terrace.

She closed her eyes and recalled the scene. There was something there she should have caught. Something changed tonight. But what?

Now that she knew Kitt and Wyatt were cousins, a whole host of new questions raised their heads. Was that what Kitt was doing in Yorkshire? Had he visited Wyatt? Had Sheila known? Had she met him there? And why hadn't Kitt wanted Wyatt to know he'd been injured?

She stopped and shivered in the deepening chill. This was getting her nowhere. All she had were questions. She'd have to wait until she next saw Kitt to get some answers. Sighing, she crossed the room and climbed into the large bed.

A number of thoughts struck her all at once. She groaned as she rolled over and punched the pillow. Why hadn't she seen it before now?

Wyatt and Sheila's father were partners in a number of ventures. Before Maurice had been knighted for service to the Crown during the war with Napoleon, he had been a very prosperous cit. He still owned several factories and other concerns, although they were now overseen by stewards.

Two years ago, Wyatt had been a frequent visitor at Clark Hall. At first, he was there to speak to Maurice. Then he began to invite Pamela on drives and escort her to various assemblies. Even her mother thought he was on the verge of asking for her.

Then, without warning, he stopped coming around. There were no more drives, teas, or assemblies. It was as if he had dropped from the face of the earth.

Just before last Christmas, he appeared again. Why hadn't she figured it out? She was happy to see him, but he seemed to take no notice of her. Oh, he hadn't overtly courted Sheila in front of her, but that scene in the front hall had not been the first time Sheila had been out with Wyatt. How could she have been such a fool?

Sheila wanted a title. Wyatt was the best catch in their area without going to the expense of a Season, something her father felt was a waste of money.

Then their grandparents had offered to sponsor Sheila for a Season. Had she grown tired of Wyatt? Perhaps she thought she could aspire to a higher title in London, which would explain setting her sights on Kitt. An earl was definitely a better catch than a baron. Her dowry was, in all likelihood, quite generous. Probably tempting enough to turn the heads even of those who disdained fortunes made "in trade".

How much did Wyatt know? Had Maurice told him about Pamela's background two years ago? Was that why he stopped visiting? His sudden reappearance just before Christmas was no longer surprising—Sheila turned eighteen in November.

Life was not fair. Pamela had heard it before, but never had she felt it as keenly as she did now. Everything she'd ever wanted ended up Sheila's. She was tired of forever being the loser.

Tears sprang to her eyes as she pictured Sheila on Kitt's arm. Pamela was too often the victim of her sister's greed and spite to believe her claim outright.

"I will not cry," she sniffed. "I won't!" She flipped over on to her back and stared up into the darkness above the bed. "I won't let her win this time."

Sheila was lying. She had to be.

A thought occurred to her that suddenly made sense. Perhaps what she was missing was Wyatt's obvious interest in Sheila. If Sheila was truly pregnant, perhaps it happened before she arrived in Town.

I'm carrying his heir. It wouldn't take much for Sheila to manipulate the words to make Pamela think the child was Kitt's when in fact it was Wyatt's. Any son of Wyatt's would also be Kitt's heir—if Kitt never married.

Settling into the bed, she was relieved she'd seen through Sheila's lie. She would still talk to Bess, but she was confident she'd figured it out.

Regardless, she would not give Kitt up without a fight.

The damp, gray fog did nothing for Pamela's spirits the next morning as she and Pearl set off for the park again. Tilly had informed her the night before that Sheila's maid, Bess, agreed to meet her in the early morning before Sheila needed her. It was the best time to talk without being discovered.

Bess waited for her at the agreed upon spot near the river, looking about uneasily until she spotted Pamela with Pearl. The little dog barked fiercely as the maid approached, but quieted when Pamela reached down and scooped the small animal into her arms.

"Such a ferocious beast!" Pamela laughed at her antics. "How are you, Bess?" She smiled fondly at the woman.

"Very well, miss. And you?"

"I'm well enough."

"You're looking very grand," Bess ventured. "'Tis glad I am that you are, too."

Pamela smiled. At Clark Hall, Bess had been assigned to both her and Sheila, but Sheila took up so much of her time Pamela most often did for herself. Not that Bess minded doing for her, it was just that Sheila was so demanding Bess had time for little else.

"Well, you haven't changed much. I hope Sheila isn't keeping you too busy."

Bess smiled at that, revealing straight but discolored teeth. "You know Miss Sheila is jest herself. Always losin' stuff or damagin' it. An' wantin' more an' more. She ain't never gonna change. Her Ladyship insisted Miss Sheila have some fancy lady's maid when we got here, so's I'se jest s'posed to look after her wardrobe."

"Is she happy, Bess?"

"I suppose so." The maid's reply was cautious. "But I don't rightly know for sure 'cause you ain't there for her to make miserable."

Pamela's shock must have shown on her face.

"I don't let on, but I'm glad to hear you done good for yourself. I heared you got yourself betrothed to an earl. Good for you, I'm thinkin'."

"Well, as for that—Sheila claims that same earl has gotten her with child."

"No!" Bess's eyes widened in outrage and dismay.

"I need to know, Bess, if she's telling the truth." Pamela hated to hear the pleading note in her voice, but she couldn't help herself.

Bess shook her head. "I don't know if'n it was your earl, mind you, but she's telling the truth about the other."

Pamela's shoulders slumped. She had convinced herself Sheila lied. That Sheila would not have allowed herself to be ruined.

"Are you sure?"

Bess nodded. "She's been sick in the mornings. Mind you, I'm the only one who knows, but I'm sure."

"When did it start?"

"When did what start? The sickness?"

Pamela nodded, unable to speak past the burning lump in her throat.

"A fortnight ago, maybe a little longer."

Pamela absently tightened her arms and Pearl began to squirm in protest at being squeezed. Pamela put her down.

"Could...could it have happened before...before she came to Town?"

"I don't rightly know. You know she ain't never been real reg'lar like." Bess pursed her lips as she thought. "She was a little sick on the way here, but you know she ain't never traveled well neither."

Pamela closed her eyes. Yes, she knew. Not only had Sheila never been regular, but she was also unpredictable.

Bess cut into her thoughts. "She also had her time afore we come to Town. But it was light, and only a day."

Chapter Eleven

Pamela returned to Arden Street trying desperately to reconcile Bess's confirmation of Sheila's condition with what she knew of Kitt. She didn't want to believe Sheila, but the weight of the evidence was tipping the scales in her favor.

"I've missed something. I know it! But what?" she mumbled to herself as she walked.

Pain rose in her chest and she blinked to hold back tears. Breaking her betrothal to Kitt went against everything she wanted. Yet, how could she consider marrying him if what Sheila said was true? Pamela knew Lady Parkington expected the engagement to bear fruit. It was the reason she hadn't pushed to introduce Pamela to other eligible gentlemen. And it was the reason she said nothing more about the refused vouchers to Almack's. Since Kitt refused to attend, she was satisfied that in the end the loss of the vouchers hadn't hurt.

Despite their argument at Covington Manor, Kitt's attentiveness hadn't wavered, although she continued to wonder if it was for appearance's sake. More importantly, he didn't seem to be interested in Sheila. Had that been a ploy as well?

If she cried off, how would she explain herself to Lisa and Denny? And her mother? Lady Parkington had written to her mother about the engagement as if it were real. How would she explain if Kitt married Sheila instead? She laughed bitterly to herself. She wouldn't have to explain anything. Everyone would know soon enough.

It was ironic that she had been disowned because her stepfather declared her to be "no better than her mother" when

159

it was Sheila who had followed in her mother's footsteps. She was not surprised, however. Sheila had been playing fast and loose since she was old enough to flirt with anything in long pants.

Yet she would never have expected Sheila to allow anyone to go that far. Why had she? Or had she? Hadn't Lisa's brother told her Kitt and Denny were experienced rakes? Sheila was, at heart, a simple country girl. A spoiled, greedy, country girl, but no match for the skillful seduction of a sophisticated rake. If that's indeed what happened.

She shook her head to clear it of her circular thoughts. Believing Kitt would take advantage of someone of Sheila's obvious ignorance and inexperience did not match what she knew of his character. There had to be another explanation.

She had no answers by the time Kitt arrived to take her for a drive, but her mind was made up. There was no benefit in prolonging the inevitable.

She, therefore, did not completely comprehend her relief when Lisa and Denny joined them and the foursome set off in Lady Parkington's open barouche. The vivid blue of the sky and the golden warmth of the sun lifted her spirits and she found herself smiling at Lisa's obvious joy.

"Papa says you and Kitt must come to Merton for Christmas," Lisa told her as the conveyance entered the park. "Have you set a date yet?"

Pamela turned to look at Kitt. Now what? How were they to get out of this?

"Not a specific date yet," he replied easily, "but after the end of the Season. Perhaps mid-June."

"Have you decided where?"

"No. But definitely not at Pamela's home. Perhaps Kitt Ridge." He glanced in her direction, then continued. "It will be small. Family only."

"Lud! Aunt Claire will be the only one in attendance."

Denny laughed. "Got you there, Kitt."

Pamela sat numbly as Kitt answered Lisa's questions with a glibness that suggested they had given the matter much thought. Though she refused to give into despondency and ruin the outing, her mind would not leave the problem alone.

Lisa's peals of laughter brought Pamela out of her thoughts with a jolt.

"Aunt Claire will have your hide if you try such a thing!"

Kitt was chuckling as well. "Of that I am certain. Especially as she has already talked your father into giving the bride away if Pamela is amenable."

Shooting puzzled looks from one to the other, Pamela interjected a cautious question. "Try what?"

Lisa darted an amused glance her way "Lord Kittridge threatened to spirit you off to Gretna Green and deprive us all of a fine June wedding."

It took all of her willpower not to allow her mouth to drop open at that outrageous boast, and the look she threw at Kitt promised further discussion at a later time. It was bad enough, she thought, Lady Parkington apparently was beginning to plan a wedding, but to joke about the possibility when he knew it wouldn't happen was unconscionable. She could have ground her teeth in frustration.

Instead she tried to smile sweetly. "Oh, no. We couldn't possibly do that." She slid her arm through his and looked up at him in challenge. "But a special license is a distinct possibility."

The flare of awareness in his eyes as he returned her gaze sent heat washing through her. The blue irises darkened nearly to black, and her heart skipped a beat. When the corners of his mouth tilted upwards, she suddenly felt lightheaded. "Name the day. Your wish is my command."

Pamela felt as if the rug had been pulled out from under her. What had she done? And in front of Lisa and Denny, too. Scrambling for an appropriate reply that would not tip the other couple to her intentions, she mumbled, "Perhaps we should discuss this in private."

Kitt's smile became a full-fledged grin. "As you wish, my dear."

Pamela's frown at the endearment was at odds with the feeling of contentment it engendered. How could he be such a cad and still affect her like this?

"Is your brother coming to Town this year?" Lisa turned to Denny, and Pamela was thankful for the change of subject.

"I don't think so. I believe he and Catherine are staying in the country to await the birth of his heir. Or so he hopes."

"How wonderful!" Lisa nearly bounced in her seat. "Do you think they'd let me be the baby's godmother? I've always wanted to be like Aunt Claire."

Denny was very slow to answer, his throat working convulsively before he got out the strangled words. "I don't know."

Pamela smiled to herself. Denny might think not offering for Lisa was in her best interest, but his heart obviously didn't agree. Lisa might have to settle for being an aunt instead of a godmother.

"Has Geoff settled down now that he's about to become a father?" Kitt asked.

"Not particularly." The lighthearted twinkle was back in Denny's eyes. "I think Papa despairs of his recklessness. Unfortunately, Catherine is just as wild. The two of them deserve each other, and Mama visibly shudders when she imagines what their children will be like."

They stopped to speak to an acquaintance of Lisa's, then moved on. A short distance later they came face-to-face with Princess Esterhazy.

"So," she stated unnecessarily once introductions were made, nearly glaring at Pamela, "you're the chit everyone's talking about."

"I suppose so, ma'am," Pamela replied, keeping her eyes downcast. The last thing she wanted to do was to offend the princess. Lady Parkington would be horrified to know that Pamela secretly thought the Patronesses of Almack's simple if they believed all the nonsense making its way through the *ton* about her.

"You have garnered some influential friends," the princess remarked. "One wonders why."

"Perhaps the most important word is 'friends'." Pamela let the statement hang, allowing the woman to make what she would of it.

Stealing a peek at the other three occupants of the barouche, she realized they were all trying *not* to take part in the conversation. Lisa and Denny were speaking to each other in low voices, their heads close together. Kitt was watching her, so also not paying attention to her inquisitor. She pressed her lips together to keep from smiling. The cowards!

"I see." The princess sniffed. She glanced at the other three occupants then lightly tapped Kitt on the sleeve. "And you, my lord. Do *you* think we have made a mistake?"

Kitt dragged his gaze from Pamela's bowed head to look at the princess. "I do not think I'm the right person to answer that," he replied tersely. "But we have not allowed it to hinder our enjoyment."

The princess's brow furrowed and her eyes narrowed at the barb. It had not escaped any of the Patroness's notice that Miss Pamela Clarkdale was still being received in polite circles despite being denied vouchers. The princess would not admit it, but it rankled that their acquiescence to the Countess of Marscombe had made them look foolish. It was common knowledge that Lord Kittridge abhorred Almack's, and he and Lady Jersey had exchanged words in the past. That none of them had considered Lady Parkington's connections was uncharacteristic. Normally they were quite thorough in their consideration of the possible repercussions of their decisions.

The Earl of Fallmerton's comment in White's had been repeated with glee all over Town, and since that Wednesday when nearly no gentlemen were in attendance, Lady Fallmerton and her daughter had not returned. In addition, the Duchess of Mellerton, a staunch supporter of Almack's, had yet to put in an appearance this Season, although she was now in residence.

Perhaps it was time to have a meeting of the Patronesses to discuss this unusual turn of events. If Almack's was to retain its position as the entree into polite society for young women, they must take care not to let something like this happen again.

"Then I must not keep you from enjoying your ride." She smiled graciously. "It has been a pleasure making your acquaintance, Miss Clarkdale."

"And mine as well, ma'am," Pamela responded.

The princess was barely out of earshot before Lisa began to giggle. "Do you think we have made a mistake?" she parroted. "You should have told her 'of course you have'."

Kitt, too, was grinning. "Sheath your claws, minx. There was no need to draw blood."

"Pshaw!" Lisa declared and turned to Pamela. "You were too complaisant."

Pamela smiled. "It was either that or say something which would have put me completely beyond the pale."

Lisa's laughter was irrepressible, and the four of them arrived back at the house on Arden Street in high spirits. Over tea, Lisa described the whole encounter to Lady Parkington in minute detail.

"Thinking twice, are they?" Lady Parkington chortled. "Good. Good."

Before he left, Kitt reminded them he would be back to collect them at eight for the Duchess of Mellerton's dinner party.

The Mellerton mansion in Mayfair was a large, imposing structure with Palladian columns supporting a massive portico. Servants in immaculate green and yellow livery ushered them in and took their cloaks. Pamela looked around in awe.

An enormous chandelier hung in the entryway, its candles casting light over gleaming mahogany paneling and banisters flanking the marble staircase. Landscapes in elaborate gilded frames dotted the walls.

They were shown into the drawing room where a number of guests already congregated. Pamela glanced around the sea of faces for familiar ones and found Lisa and Denny almost immediately. She didn't realize how nervous she had been until she relaxed upon spotting them. The duchess greeted them warmly, drawing Pamela into a fragrant hug as she rose from her curtsy.

"Anyone who can claim this rascal deserves that and more," she explained, a twinkle in eyes the mirror of Denny's. Turning to Kitt she said, "And thank you, my lord, for your last-minute help."

Pamela didn't get a chance to ask what she meant until after they had greeted the duke and moved further into the room.

"What help?" she asked.

"At the last minute Lord Carstairs could not make it and she would have been short. Denny remembered my cousin was staying with me and asked me if he would fill the spot."

She stopped and turned to stare up at him in surprise. "Wyatt is staying with you?"

Kitt's eyes darkened and his mouth firmed into a line. "Of course. He usually does when he comes to Town."

"Oh."

"Might I ask why this is such a surprise?"

"I...I don't know, really. It just never occurred to me. I never thought of Wyatt as frequenting London."

Kitt's displeasure was obvious, but he did not voice it because another couple approached at that moment.

"Lovely, lovely," Lord Wheaton murmured when Kitt introduced her. He was old enough to be her grandfather and still clung to the fashions of his youth. He wore a wig and his coat, although of new fabric, was fashioned in a style popular in the latter part of the previous century.

Lady Wheaton merely looked at her, and Pamela wondered if she had a smudge of something on her face so closely did that lady study her. When she finally spoke, she confused Pamela even more by saying, "You remind me of someone."

"I...I do?"

"Yes, but I can't remember who at the moment." Shaking her gray head, she looked up at her husband and quizzed him. "Who does she look like, Alfred? Surely you remember?"

But he didn't and after a few moments of conversation, they moved on.

Pamela glanced up at Kitt only to find him staring after the couple, a perplexing look on his handsome face.

"What do you suppose they meant by that?"

"I don't know," he replied absently. "Maybe you resemble someone on your father's side and she knew them."

She froze at his words; the blood drained from her face. He knew? How? Unconsciously, the hand on his arm tightened, drawing his attention to her.

"Are you all right?" The concern in his voice shook her out of her daze.

"Y-yes, I think so." She didn't sound convincing, even to her own ears. It was no surprise then, that he found a chair and bade her to sit. Leaving her momentarily, he returned with a glass and handed it to her.

"Drink."

She drank. The sherry was sweet with only a mild bite to it as it warmed its way down her throat.

When had he found out? Why hadn't he said anything? Why hadn't he broken their engagement? Did it not matter after all? For all her worrying, did he truly not care?

Pamela had no answers to these questions and was loath to put them to Kitt. Yet it only now occurred to her he would have heard the gossip. Why hadn't she realized that before now? Of course he would have heard and, therefore, known.

"I've been an idiot," she muttered.

"How?"

She looked up sharply. She hadn't meant for him to hear. Now what?

She was trying to formulate an answer when the majordomo appeared in the door and announced, "Dinner is served, Your Grace."

"I have been informed I am your dinner partner, Miss Clarkdale."

Pamela nearly groaned aloud as she looked up into the face of Wyatt, Lord Crandall. *Why me?* Pasting a smile on her face, she prepared to rise.

Kitt rose to his feet and helped her to hers. Lord Crandall said, "I'll take good care of her." Kitt looked from one to the other, his eyes narrowing, then pivoted on his heel and stalked away without another word. Pamela watched him go, wondering why he seemed angry.

Putting her hand on the proffered arm, she looked up into Lord Crandall's face as they moved toward the door. "Why did you say that?"

She hadn't meant her voice to be so sharp, and Lord Crandall seemed taken aback by the question.

"It was just a comment. To let him know you were in good hands."

She relaxed slightly, but still wondered why Kitt reacted the way he had.

"I'd not poach, you know. I respect my cousin too much for that." She heard the sincerity in his voice and unbent a little more.

After they were seated and the first course was being served, he turned to her. "Besides, I am nearly engaged myself."

"Nearly?"

"It's not official yet, but I feel I can tell you—with the condition you keep it a secret, of course." He waited and she realized he was looking for her agreement to keep his news confidential. Nodding, she was thankful for the intuition that told her to brace herself moments later when he said in a low voice, "Sheila and I have an understanding."

Thoughts reeling, she managed an equally low, "Congratulations," before she turned to apply herself to the soup.

Further along the table, Kitt watched them through narrowed eyes. Pain he refused to acknowledge sliced through him as he noticed the two of them talking in low voices, heads close together. He closed his eyes on the sight, but could not block out the image.

Her familiarity with his cousin irritated him. Why, he wasn't sure, but he knew it had something to do with what happened in Yorkshire.

Hadn't Seth told him Miss Pamela was hoping for an offer from Lord Crandall? How could he have forgotten the one time Wyatt's name had come up—how her eyes shone and a smile brightened her face? Her refusal to talk about what happened after he left Yorkshire rankled. Had she waited for Wyatt to declare himself? Was she still hoping for an offer? Had Wyatt come to London to find her?

Lady Wilmot's sultry voice drifted to him. "You do not look very happy, my lord."

Turning away from the sight of Pamela and Wyatt, he prepared himself to be cordial to the last person he wanted to converse with. He knew the duchess was not aware of his past association with Lady Wilmot and so acquitted her of deliberate meddling. The lady in question, however, took advantage of what she considered to be her good fortune to attempt to reclaim his affections. Unaware she stretched the limits of his patience, she painstakingly pointed out everything about Pamela she considered flawed.

It was the longest dinner of his life. By the time the ladies followed the duchess from the room, leaving the men to their port, he needed a good strong drink.

Pamela could not keep her thoughts straight. One moment she was pitying Wyatt for being taken in by Sheila, then she was convinced Sheila was lying about carrying Kitt's babe. Still later, she was applauding Wyatt for doing the right thing— because the babe was obviously his. There was just the small problem of Bess confirming that Sheila had "her time" before they came to Town.

When she realized she was ignoring her other dinner partner, she shoved it all to the back of her mind to mull over later and turned to the young man seated on her other side.

As the women adjourned to the drawing room after dinner, Lisa joined her.

"Mama is planning a dinner party for next Friday. You and Aunt Claire will receive invitations."

Pamela disguised her surprise by glancing across the room. Lisa's mother had been much warmer toward Lady Parkington and, by association, her, since her husband's arrival in Town. She wondered if that meant the earl had forced the issue, but she could not see that happening. Especially since the countess seemed softer, more approachable than before. It was difficult to befriend someone reluctantly and not have them sense it. No, she was definitely warmer toward them for some other reason.

The two young women sat on a small settee near a window.

"This evening has been nice. Denny's parents are very warm—not at all what one would think of when you envision a duke and duchess."

Pamela hid a small smile. Lisa was so much in love with Denny that Pamela would have been more worried if she hadn't realized Denny had fallen, too. The problem, she knew, was getting him to admit it.

It was the same problem with Kitt. Except she wasn't sure he *had* fallen in love with her. His remark in the park at Covington Manor proved he did not feel the same way she did about love. If only...

"Uh-oh."

Lisa's low exclamation brought her out of her reverie. Looking up, she noticed a woman approaching. Her first thought was, thank goodness it wasn't Lady Wilmot, who'd monopolized Kitt at dinner. She'd ignored the ache she felt as she watched him smile and converse with the dark-haired beauty, reminding herself that she had very little claim upon him. It did nothing for her self-confidence to see the two of them together, talking like old friends.

The woman stopped before them. Dressed in a simple dress of citron silk decorated with emerald ribbon, emeralds flashing around her neck and in her ears, she arrived like a ship under sail. Lisa scrambled to her feet and Pamela followed suit as she studied them through a long-handled jeweled lorgnette.

Lisa greeted her with a curtsy. "Good evening, Lady Cowper."

"Lady Lisa," she acknowledged. "Introduce me," she commanded and turned to Pamela.

Lisa obliged. Pamela felt the woman's eyes on her and wondered at her scrutiny. The urge to ask if Lady Cowper wanted to see her teeth emerged from thin air and she dropped her eyes to conceal her amusement.

"Why have I not seen you before?" Lady Cowper demanded.

"I do not go out much," Pamela responded demurely.

"And you don't live with your grandmother, I understand."

Everyone knew that, but why it was any of their business eluded Pamela. "No, ma'am."

"I see." Her voice was clipped. "And your parents?"

"My parents live in Yorkshire, as I'm sure you are aware."

Pamela bit her tongue against saying more. The whole *ton* was familiar with her background thanks to her grandmother and Sheila. Why she needed to explain it to Lady Cowper was beyond her.

"I understand that Lady Parkington is your godmother."

"Yes, ma'am."

"And how did that come about?"

Pamela was taken aback.

"I imagine in the usual way, Emily," another voice answered and Pamela and Lisa both looked up in astonishment.

Lady Cowper spun around to face Lady Fallmerton, who continued, speaking to Lisa and Pamela, "I believe Lord Kittridge and Lord Denton might be looking for partners as the duchess has ordered the setting up of card tables. Run along, girls."

As she finished speaking, the duke strolled into the room followed by the rest of the men. Lisa and Pamela curtsied to Lady Cowper and headed toward the group.

"You will not believe it," Lisa exclaimed to Denny as she reached him. Lord Tinsley and Lord Crandall joined them as Kitt took Pamela's hand and placed it in the crook of his elbow.

"Believe what?" Denny asked.

"My mother." The wonder in her voice drew her brother's attention.

"What did Mama do now?"

"Lady Cowper was interrogating Pamela, and she intervened." Lisa glanced back over her shoulder to where the two matrons stood conversing by the settee.

"Good for her." Lord Tinsley's approval caused everyone else to look at him curiously, but no one ventured a question. "Papa will be pleased."

Pamela didn't understand any of the conversation. Having no idea who Lady Cowper was, the importance of the exchange eluded her. She was content to stand beside Kitt and allow his strength and warmth envelop her.

Lady Fallmerton's defense however shocked her into speechlessness. Why? And why would Lisa's father be pleased?

The rest of the evening passed in a blur. Pamela partnered Kitt at whist against Lisa and Denny. She spoke to Denny's mother, the duchess, before they left. And Lady Fallmerton pressed her cheek to hers before they left as well. All in all, it had been an extremely confusing evening.

It was no surprise, therefore, that she nearly forgot the plan she and Wyatt hatched over dinner.

The knock on the library door roused Kitt from his perusal of the ledgers before him.

"Enter!"

Tibbs entered with a card on a salver. "There is a Mr. MacTavish to see you, my lord."

Kitt picked up the card and read it. "Show him in."

Darrin MacTavish looked more like a boxer than a solicitor. Large and brawny with a head of bright red hair, he stood tall enough to look Kitt square in the eyes.

"'Tis glad I am to finally meet you, my lord," he said in a thick Scottish accent as he took the seat Kitt offered him.

Kitt resumed his seat behind the desk. "What may I do for you, Mr. MacTavish?"

The solicitor chuckled. "Actually, I'm here to do something for you."

"And what is that?"

"Enlarge your fortune."

A dark eyebrow arched.

"It is with sincere regret that I inform you of the death of the Duc d'Aubert in Edinburgh this past fortnight."

Kitt had no idea who the Duc d'Aubert was, so his passing meant very little to him. If what the solicitor said was true upon entering, however, the *duc* had left him something. But why?

"I am aware you were not acquainted with His Grace. He made it clear you had never met. Regardless, his will indicates you are his sole heir. Upon his death you became the owner of a small holding in the lowlands, a house in Edinburgh, interests in several shipping concerns, and an extremely large bank account. He would have liked to pass his title on to you as well, but with all the recent upheaval in France, felt it was best to allow it to die with him. Per his instructions, I have sent a letter to the French Consul informing them of his death."

Stunned silence greeted this explanation. For the life of him, Kitt could think of no reason why he should be the sole heir of a French *duc*.

"I see you are surprised by this knowledge, however, I can assure you all is in order." Mr. MacTavish opened the case he carried and extracted a single sheet of paper, which he handed to Kitt. "I thought you would want to read His Grace's will for yourself."

Dated October 1808, the simple document was titled *"Last Will and Testament of Henri Christophe Louis Phillipe Dumont, Duc d'Aubert"*. It indicated that, as his sole living heir, Christopher Orion Covington, then Viscount Bowlden, should inherit all of his worldly property and goods. The year was familiar, but Kitt could not remember why. There was a separate notation at the bottom, dated December 1812, changing his title to the Earl of Kittridge.

"I'm afraid you have me at a disadvantage," Kitt finally said. "I have no idea who this person is...was."

MacTavish smiled. "He was your grandfather."

Chapter Twelve

The brightly lit ballroom in the Marquis and Marchioness of Onwyn's residence in Grosvenor Square was filled to overflowing. Pamela stood at Lady Parkington's side watching the quadrille come to an end. Beside her, Lisa chatted with Lord Denton. She caught sight of Sheila and Wyatt across the room. Dressed in another pale pink dress, Sheila looked beautiful, but distant. The image tickled a fleeting memory.

She watched as Wyatt left Sheila standing beside their grandmother and began to make his way across the room. Anticipation hummed through her. The next dance was a reel and she had promised it to him.

Kitt appeared as Wyatt bowed to her. She could sense his displeasure, but did not know what to do about it. Taking to the floor on Wyatt's arm was her only option, but she knew doing so was damaging her relationship with Kitt. She needed to carry out the plan with Wyatt. Kitt would later understand, but for now it was their secret.

"Have you located a small parlor?" she asked Wyatt.

"Yes." The dance parted them momentarily. When they were reunited, he said, "You do not have to do this."

"I know, but it's necessary. For my peace of mind." And possibly, her future.

"Very well."

The dance continued with relative silence between them until just before it ended. Then he gave her instructions on where to go. Returning her to Lady Parkington's side, he bowed over her hand and left.

"So that's the young man your mother thought you would marry?" Lady Parkington's voice intruded into her thoughts. "I must say, he's quite handsome. I understand he and Kitt are cousins."

"Yes, ma'am."

"And wealthy?"

"I would assume so."

"Hmmm."

Pamela scanned the ballroom for Kitt, but found no trace of him. Turning back to Lady Parkington, she made an excuse to seek the withdrawing room and slipped away. Once out of the ballroom, she followed Wyatt's instructions and soon was standing in a small unlit parlor.

Darkness shrouded the corners of the room, but Pamela paid little attention except to note with relief that the room was empty. She had only waited a few minutes when Sheila entered the room.

"Oh, I expected—" Sheila stopped short, her mouth rounding in an "O" of surprise.

"I know who you expected," Pamela replied. "I asked Wyatt to send you here."

"Why?"

"Because I needed to speak to you and I knew I couldn't do so in the ballroom."

"Oh." Sheila wandered over to the window, stopping in a pool of moonlight.

Pamela closed and locked the door. She did not need an audience or anyone else intruding, even accidentally. She was anxious enough as it was.

"Have you spoken to his lordship yet?" Sheila's voice was curious.

"No." The moonlight streaming through the window was the only light in the small room, turning Sheila's hair bright. Her gown shimmered.

"Why not? You said you would speak to him—end the betrothal."

"I know, but I haven't had the chance."

"Why not? It's been nearly a week."

"I've been trying to decide what to do."

Sheila's eyes narrowed. "Decide what to do? You know what to do."

"I'm not so sure I do."

"Sure you do what?"

"Sure I know what to do."

"But all you had to do was—"

"I know. But the thing is..."

Sheila was staring at her like she was a recalcitrant child who had deliberately disobeyed her nanny.

She took a deep breath. "I'm not sure I believe you. No, that's not right. I *don't* believe you."

Outrage crossed Sheila's features. "What? What do you mean?"

"You heard me. I don't believe you." A calmness was beginning to assert itself, and Pamela slowly exhaled.

"How could you not? I told you what happened. Why don't you believe me?"

"Why should I?"

The look on Sheila's face would have been comical if Pamela was concerned about her reaction.

"Why should you?" Sheila repeated, dumbfounded. "But, but—"

"The thing is, Sheila. I don't know why I should take your word that you're breeding. You don't look like it. And it's not as if I can verify it myself."

"But it's true! I told you about being sick."

"I know, but I can't help but remember all the past instances when you have lied to get something you wanted. Usually something that was mine to begin with. You are not very reliable when it comes to veracity."

Sheila's mouth dropped open in astonishment. Her eyes narrowed menacingly. "So, what do you plan to do?"

"Nothing."

For the first time in her life, Pamela felt a confidence she knew she once lacked. She would not let Sheila win this one. Bess might have confirmed Sheila was pregnant, but she would trust her instincts. Right now, they told her Sheila's child was not Kitt's; that Kitt would not have taken advantage of Sheila in such a way.

Loving Kitt meant she trusted him. And trusting him meant she could not believe he was guilty of the kind of behavior Sheila attributed to him. There *had* to be another explanation for Sheila's condition. She wondered if she dared ask Wyatt after tonight if he was the responsible party.

Sheila was watching her closely; studying her. Suddenly she laughed spitefully. "You're in love with him!" Pamela felt the heat wash through her face and was glad of the darkness. "I should have guessed."

Sheila left her pool of moonlight to cross to stand before Pamela.

"He'll never marry you," she said maliciously. "He's only toying with you. After all, what have *you* to offer him? You're just a nobody."

Pamela kept her composure with difficulty. "That may be true, but I refuse to hand him over to you. If you are truly carrying his child as you claim, then you'll have to tell him yourself—without my interference. I refuse to lower myself by accusing him of something I don't believe he did."

"Poor, poor, Pammy. Hopelessly in love with someone who shouldn't even know you exist," Sheila taunted as if Pamela hadn't spoken.

"But he does know I exist." Triumph laced her voice. "*You* might remember that."

Her dart hit home as Sheila's eyes widened.

"I will tell Grandmama."

Pamela was unperturbed. "I suspect you will have to eventually."

"When word gets out, the both of you will be ruined."

Pamela laughed in genuine amusement. "You have been around the *ton* long enough to know it is *you*, and possibly *I*, who might be ruined, but Kitt is likely to walk away with no harm done to his reputation."

Tears trembled on Sheila's lashes and Pamela steeled herself not to be moved.

"You would truly ruin me?" Sheila's voice wobbled. "Your own sister?"

She sighed, all emotion gone save disappointment. "No, Sheila, I would not. I did not ruin you and neither did Kitt. Furthermore, I refuse to see why I should sacrifice my happiness for your indiscretion. It is time for you to take responsibility for yourself and stop expecting me to be your scapegoat. That ended when your father threw me out of the only home I have ever known with nothing but the clothing on my back. If it hadn't been for Mama, who knows what might have happened to me."

"But you're just a nobody. Papa said so. He said you were—"

"I'm not interest in what your father says about me. His opinion no longer matters." She spoke sharper than she intended, but she was tired of Sheila's childish theatrics.

Pamela turned toward the door. It was time to return to the ballroom. They had been gone much longer than she planned. Kitt must be looking for her by now. How would she explain her absence?

"I just wanted you to know I did not intend to end my betrothal."

She unlocked the door and opened it.

"You'll be sorry." The gloves were off. Sheila's animosity was a tangible force in the room. "You'll wish you had never come to London." Then she pushed past Pamela and hurried down the hall.

Sagging against the door for a moment, Pamela let out a sigh. "I suspect I already am," she whispered into the stillness. Then she followed her sister from the room, closing the door softly behind her.

As door clicked shut, two shadows detached themselves from a corner of the room, stepping closer to the pool of moonlight.

"Bedamned!" Wyatt exclaimed. "What a mull."

Kitt strolled over to the window. He stood contemplating the darkness beyond for a long time. *I refuse to lower myself by accusing him of something I don't believe he did.* Pamela's voice echoed in his head. *I did not ruin you and neither did Kitt.*

His life would never be the same again. Her confidence in him was staggering. And heady. He felt a bit guilty eavesdropping, but if he hadn't, he might not have ever known. He went back to the moment during the conversation when his life had changed.

...accusing him of something I don't believe he did. With those words, Christopher Orion Covington, twelfth Earl of Kittridge, tumbled irrevocably in love.

"I'll have a talk with Sheila," Wyatt was saying. "Her grandmother won't like it one bit, but I already have her father's permission. We'll be married as soon as possible."

Kitt spun around to face his cousin. "Are you saying that you...?"

"Of course." Wyatt wasn't the least bit embarrassed. He began to pace back and forth across the small room, his hands clasped behind his back. "Shouldn't have happened, but her father encouraged me. He didn't want her to have a Season in the first place. Was afraid she'd get airs and come back and look down her nose at him."

"But I thought you and Pamela..." Kitt let the thought trail off.

"Considered it at one time. Then Maurice told me she wasn't his. He only agreed to keep her because he wanted Anne." He ran his hand through his dark hair. "Our families have been in business together for a long time. I promised my father when he died that I'd marry Maurice's daughter to keep the ties close. Truth is I've always been attracted to Sheila, but felt I should court Pamela as she was the oldest." He stopped and shrugged as if that finished the explanation.

Relief poured through Kitt at Wyatt's confession. Truth be told, he couldn't see what Wyatt saw in Pamela's sister, but it didn't matter. As long as he wasn't after Pamela, Kitt could afford to be gracious.

"Do you need assistance procuring a special license?"

Wyatt grinned. "Now that would be welcome." He turned toward the door. "I'd better return first." Hand on the doorknob, he turned back to Kitt. "My thanks for coming along. I'm sure Pamela wanted you to know at least some of what we heard, but I'd appreciate it if you waited until I got Sheila out of London before you told her I brought you along." Then he was gone.

Kitt grinned in the darkness. The Season wasn't over yet, but it was time to end his betrothal. He wondered if he could persuade Pamela to agree.

He would get two special licenses—just in case.

But first there was a mystery to clear up and he suspected it was not going to be pleasant.

"What's so important that you had to drag me out instead of coming to see me?"

Lady Parkington's voice was sharp as she entered Kitt's library. Kitt looked up from his seat behind the desk. Her morning gown of forest green with brown ribbon trim reminded him of Pamela's eyes. He rose to greet her.

"Good morning, madam. You do not look as though you've been dragged anywhere."

"Don't try to gammon me."

Kitt smothered a grin as he seated her in a comfortable chair before his desk and took the matching chair across from her. He picked up his grandfather's will off the desk as Tibbs entered with a tea tray and set it on a table near Lady Parkington. Once he was gone and Lady Parkington poured herself a cup of tea, she sat back with her cup and pinned him with her shrewd gaze. "Well?"

"I have a few questions regarding my mother." He tried to keep his tone light. "And I did not want to be rude by blatantly excluding Pamela from the conversation."

"What kind of questions?"

The crinkle of paper drew his attention. His fingers were clenched around the edge of the will. Forcing himself to a calm he didn't feel, he suddenly realized he was nervous.

The paper drew Lady Parkington's attention as well, but she said nothing as he returned it to the polished surface of the desk. For a finite moment, he considered telling his godmother he didn't want to know after all.

"When she left my father, where did she go?"

Surprise crossed her features. "I thought you knew. She went to Scotland."

"Did she leave alone?" He wasn't sure he wanted to know, but what choice did he have? The solicitor's visit had cast doubts over everything he thought he knew about his mother.

Lady Parkington put down her cup and saucer. Sitting back in her chair, she studied him for a long minute before she replied with a question of her own. "Why are you asking me this now?"

Kitt steeled himself not to squirm under her all too-knowing gaze. She was the only woman with whom he'd never had to pretend. The only woman who knew him well.

"You once told me once if I ever wanted to learn the truth all I had to do was ask." He didn't want to sound anxious, but he knew he did.

She nodded. "I did."

He took a deep breath. "I'm asking."

She continued to contemplate him for another few minutes. His anxiety grew. Would she refuse now that he'd asked?

After the solicitor left, he'd remembered why the date on his grandfather's will seemed familiar. It was only two months after his mother's death, and the notation at the bottom had been added less than a month after his father's death.

Lady Parkington sighed. "No, she did not leave alone. She had help. She could not have left on her own."

"Could not...?"

"She was in no condition." She picked up an almond biscuit and took a bite, chewing thoughtfully. "Her injuries were too severe."

"Injuries?" She'd lost him. What did injuries have to do with his mother leaving his father?

She was quiet again, her eyes roaming the elegantly appointed room. Kitt waited. She seemed to be stalling, but he knew she was thinking. Weighing the knowledge and consequences of telling him. Finally, she sighed again and turned solemn eyes on him.

"Do you truly want to know? Are you certain you want to hear the truth?"

Kitt knew, then, that whatever she told him, he would not like it. There was the distinct possibility it would alter everything he thought he knew about his parents. But he'd already decided that was possible. After Mr. MacTavish, he didn't need any more surprises, and he vacillated between wanting and not wanting to know. He was afraid, dreading to discover, his life had been built around a lie, but only his godmother could tell him if his hunch was correct.

"I need to know," he said simply. "And I hope I can count on you to tell me the unvarnished truth." He tried, vainly, to remain in control of the conversation.

She nodded. "Very well."

She refreshed her cup, then took a sip. "I warned your father he ought to tell you the truth. That someday you would want to know and he wouldn't be here to defend himself, but he was too mired in his own guilt to consider it.

"Your mother was one of the loveliest women I have ever known. She was sweet, lovable and very sociable. I was a few years older than her but—I don't even remember how it happened—we became friends and corresponded until she died. Men fell under her spell when she smiled, but it was your father *she* fell for. Her father, the marquis, doted on her. He did not think much of your father, but Marianne was insistent, and they were married."

She took another sip of her tea and when she looked up at him, the look in her eyes was troubling. It was more than just sadness.

"They were blissfully happy for a whole year. Trouble began when Marianne developed a friendship with young Lord Coltrain. He wasn't any older than Gerald is now, but that was much closer to Marianne's age than your father was. Marianne treated Coltrain like a brother, but your father became mad with jealousy, and Coltrain was too stupid to realize what was happening. Fortunately, his father did and shipped him off to

India before things got out of hand. Unfortunately, the damage was done."

"What damage?"

"Your father began to see every man as a threat. Marianne would never have been unfaithful, but he refused to believe it. When they came to Town for the Season, all they did was fight. Marianne began to hate London. But your father was very conscientious about his responsibilities in Parliament and he refused to leave her in the country. It was a vicious cycle. He would accuse her of being too friendly with someone, they would quarrel, then he would storm off somewhere and get drunk. She probably could have lived with that—if that was how it ended."

"But it wasn't?" His heart beat loud in his ears. None of this resembled what he knew of his parents' marriage.

"No." She put her empty cup and saucer down on the table and sat back in the chair. "When he was drunk, he was violent."

Kitt closed his eyes. He swallowed convulsively. Had he known? How could he not have known?

"When she lost the first babe, he swore he'd never hit her again. He kept that promise until you were about two years old. She lost another babe when you were about three and the doctor said she'd never have another. It nearly destroyed her. She'd always wanted a large family."

His heart squeezed in his chest. He'd always wanted siblings.

"More than that, your father's mistrust was what truly killed their marriage. Marianne was very conscious of her mother's scandalous activities. She did not want to be labeled as her mother's daughter. The *ton* suspected she was not the marquis's child, but no one dared voice it.

"You were about eight, I think, when she wrote to tell me she had been contacted by her real father. You might remember your grandfather died only the year before."

"Who was he?" Kitt barely got the question out over the lump in his throat. He knew, but needed the confirmation only she could give.

"An exiled member of the French nobility. A *duc*—I don't remember the name. He escaped France before the peasants began chopping off every aristocratic head they could lay hands on. The rest of his family refused to leave and all eventually were killed. He settled in Edinburgh so as not to interfere with Marianne's life. He knew of her existence, but since the marquis accepted her as his own, he was comfortable leaving well enough alone."

Kitt leaned his head back against the cushion of the chair and closed his eyes. He tried to picture his mother but could not. He'd spent too long trying to forget her—and her faithlessness. He was suddenly ashamed of his disbelief.

As if she read his thoughts, Lady Parkington said, "Don't blame yourself for what you thought. Marianne knew your father would never tell you the truth. You were only a child, after all. And it was clear you worshiped your father, which she said was as it should be. She never doubted your father's love for you. She accepted you might come to hate her, but in truth, she had little choice."

"Little choice?" Kitt's voice was dubious. His conscience still wanted to hold her accountable, yet hesitated.

"I don't know how he found out, but the *duc* discovered your father's violent tendencies. Sometime in the fall of '95 she and your father had a particularly virulent argument and Marianne fell down a flight of stairs. She was unconscious for days, and when she awoke she was in Scotland."

She produced a handkerchief and dabbed at moist eyes. "She had already been in Scotland for three months before she wrote me—or you. Her injuries were so severe they kept her sedated in order to give her time to heal."

Lady Parkington seemed to pull herself together, but he wasn't fooled. There was more, and he steeled himself for the worst. Her next words were like a shot through the heart.

"She never walked again."

Lady Parkington had not been gone above an hour when Denny arrived to find Kitt in the process of giving his secretary last minute instructions.

"Did we have plans?" Kitt asked him.

"No. I just dropped by to see if you wanted to accompany me to Tatt's. I know you've been looking for a mount for Miss Clarkdale and I heard they have new blood in."

Kitt paused for only a moment before he said, "Sorry. Can't. I'm leaving Town for a few days."

"Again?"

Kitt paused at Denny's tone. He hadn't considered how it might appear if he were to disappear again. Especially after the conversation he and Wyatt eavesdropped on two nights ago. Perhaps he should send Pamela a note before he left this time.

"Where are you going?"

"The Ridge. There's something I have to do. I'll only be gone a few days."

Tibbs appeared at the door of the library. "My lord, your horse is out front."

Denny walked outside with him. "I'll explain when I return. In the meantime, keep an eye on Pamela for me."

"Why?"

"It's complicated. Just don't let that sister of hers anywhere near her."

Kitt swung into the saddle of the enormous black stallion. The animal reared when the groom released him, but Kitt easily won the tussle.

Denny shook his head. "Someday that animal will be your death."

Kitt grinned. "I'm not the one who likes to ride half-broken bits of prime." He was referring to Denny's brother's recklessness. "Gabriel is completely tame."

Denny snorted. "The words 'tame' and 'Gabriel' don't belong in the same sentence. But don't let me keep you standing. I'll keep an eye on things until you get back."

Kitt was grateful his friend asked no more questions. At the moment, he wasn't sure he could have answered them. He didn't even know why he felt it imperative he return to Kitt Ridge. He only knew he needed to make peace with himself— and his parents.

She never walked again.

The words pounded through his head. Why hadn't he known? Why had no one said anything? The servants had to have known. What about Frisky? Had she known, too?

He tried to concentrate on the countryside around him as he headed west out of London. The area was in the midst of a glorious spring. The scent of earth and growing things were welcome after the dirt and odors of the city. Blue sky, undimmed by chimney smoke, stretched before him to a distant horizon. But concentration was impossible with his godmother's words ringing in his ears. Attempting to outrun them, he pushed Gabriel hard.

The roads to Bath were good and well-maintained. Once beyond, however, they were unpredictable. The last letter he received from his steward noted there had been quite a bit of rain in the last month, so the roads might be worse than usual. He would know when he got there. Regardless, he knew the area between Bath and Kitt Ridge like the back of his hand.

When the towers of his home came into view late in the afternoon two days later, both he and Gabriel were exhausted. Riding straight through, only stopping to eat and catch short naps along the way, both horse and rider welcomed the sight before their weary eyes. The stallion was strong, his stamina incredible, but Kitt had pushed him nearly to his limit.

"Pamper him well," he told the groom who came running as he reached the front entrance. "He deserves it."

The butler and housekeeper greeted him as he entered the immaculate front hall. He wanted to go visit his parents' graves immediately, but he could barely stand up.

"I'm very tired, Lowers." He started up the staircase. "But while I rest for a bit, could you find my mother's portrait and put it in the library? I'm sure it's in the attics somewhere." He hoped his father hadn't disposed of it.

If the butler thought this a strange request, he kept it to himself.

"And have someone awaken me in a few hours if I'm not already up by then," Kitt threw over his shoulder before he disappeared at the top of the stairs.

Kitt entered the master suite with his jacket and cravat already over his arm, his fingers unbuttoning his shirt. Within minutes, he slipped between cool sheets and was asleep almost before his head touched the pillow.

Chapter Thirteen

"Mama is vexed with me again!"

Lisa's dramatic pronouncement as she burst into Lady Parkington's parlor was accompanied by an unladylike flop onto the settee next to Pamela.

Pamela and Lady Parkington smiled at each other.

"What now?" Lady Parkington asked.

"After I turned down the Earl of Jossend's request for my hand just this morning, she took me to task."

"That's all?"

Lisa sighed. "If only it were. She annoyed me so much I told her I would not consider the suit of anyone who could not at least look me in the eye. She was not amused."

Lady Parkington chuckled. "I imagine not."

"To make matters worse, when she said Lord Kittridge was taken, I blurted out that I didn't want him." Lisa lurched to her feet and began pacing the small room. "I didn't want to let the cat out of the bag, but Mama isn't slow. So I fled."

"At least she acknowledges that he's taken."

Lady Parkington's comment reminded Pamela that in the *ton* some still considered Kitt fair game. Miss Whiny-voice, who she discovered to be none other than Sheila's friend, Agatha Monson, for one. Lady Wilmot for another. Both had attempted to ingratiate themselves with Kitt when she was present, but only Lady Wilmot had been so bold as to try to dismiss her completely. Miss Monson merely batted her eyes and simpered in a nauseating manner. Were she any other person, Pamela would have found their behavior laughable. Being unsure of

Kitt's feelings, however, only left her vulnerable in the face of their spite.

"...arriving as I was leaving. Mama will be down with a megrim for days."

"Stop!" Lady Parkington raised her voice a fraction. "You will give *me* a megrim with all this excess motion. Now sit down and tell me what this is really all about."

Lisa stopped in a swirl of royal blue and pink. She looked from Pamela to her aunt, then back at Pamela again before she sank into the other chair before the fire. Pearl jumped into her lap.

"I told you, Lord Denton was arriving as I was leaving."

"Ahh. Am I to believe you knew he would be arriving and why?" Lady Parkington asked.

Lisa's cheeks turned pink, but her eyes were uncertain. "I...uh...I think so."

"Why are you worried?"

"Because Mama does not want to settle for a second son."

"Do you think your father would turn him away for this reason?"

"No, but..."

"Then you needn't worry. If your father says yes, your mother will come around."

Hope lit her eyes. "Do you truly think so, Aunt? I couldn't bear it if Mama..."

"Your mother wants only what's best for you," Lady Parkington soothed. "You may not necessarily agree on what that is, but know your happiness is indeed her ultimate goal. Your mother and I rarely agree on many things, but I have never doubted she loves you, Gerald, and your father very much."

Lisa wilted into the chair cushions, letting out a long breath.

"Now Pamela, ring the bell. We will have tea until Denny comes looking for Lisa."

Lisa brightened as Pamela rose and crossed to the bell pull.

"Do you think he will come to find me?"

"Most assuredly."

But he didn't. They waited through the afternoon, discussing wedding plans for Lisa, with Pamela reluctantly being pulled in. At one point, as niece and aunt debated the possibility of a double wedding, Carter entered with a note for Lady Parkington. It turned out to be a missive from Lady Fallmerton asking if Lisa was there but not demanding she return home.

As the afternoon crawled by with no sign of a visitor, Lisa's replies became less and less coherent and her eyes darted to the door more and more. Distress etched itself across her features, despair entered her eyes. By the time Carter entered the room to usher in a caller, she had neared the end of her tether.

Viscount Tinsley entered. At the sight of her brother, Lisa's self-control shattered and she burst into tears.

Startled, he halted for a moment before pulling a linen handkerchief from his pocket and dropping to his knees in front of his sister. Pressing it into her hand, he said, "I'm sorry, Lisa. I didn't think it likely you had heard."

"Heard what?" Lady Parkington asked sharply. "What has happened?"

There was a note of alarm in her voice and Pamela felt a chill slither down her spine. The viscount's arms encircled his sister and he patted her back, talking soothing nonsense. He did not answer his aunt.

Pamela watched as he consoled his sister. He didn't seem awkward or embarrassed, just concerned. He'd make some lucky young woman a wonderful husband someday, she thought. As Lisa's sobs lessened, he finally lifted his head and looked at his sister. "Everything will be fine, Lisa. Truly it will."

Lady Parkington picked up the cane that sat beside her chair. In the months Pamela had lived with her, she'd never seen her employer use it. Now she did, but not for what it was designed. Instead she poked the viscount in the back with the end of it and demanded, "What has happened?"

He turned a confused expression on his aunt. "You don't know?" Turning back to Lisa, he regarded her momentarily. "Then why the tears?"

Her cheeks reddened under his stare and she remained silent.

Lady Parkington thumped her cane on the floor.

"Well, we'd know if you'd tell us."

He rose in a fluid motion and crossed the room—out of reach of the cane, Pamela noted.

"A groom arrived earlier from Mellerton Chase. Lord Denton's brother was thrown from his horse. He and his parents are headed to Devon as we speak."

"Oh, no!" Lisa's cry echoed through the room. Pamela watched the blood drain from her face and wondered if she would swoon.

He turned to Lisa. "Mama sent me to collect you. She didn't want you to hear it from someone else."

Kitt brought Gabriel to a halt beside the coach carrying Lady Parkington and Pamela. Scanning the inn yard, he was satisfied with the aura of prosperity surrounding the place. It had been a while since he last stopped here, but it did not look as if it changed much. That meant, he hoped, they would be treated to an excellent luncheon. Swinging down, he reached the coach just as the door opened.

He helped Lady Parkington down first and was assisting Pamela when the second coach rolled into the yard. The Earl of Fallmerton, his countess and Lady Lisa alighted from that one as Viscount Tinsley rode up on his mount.

It had been three days since he received the short note from Denny informing him of his brother's death. The funeral was day after tomorrow, but they would reach Mellerton Chase this evening.

He hadn't had the time to tell Pamela about his mother or his visit home. He wondered what her reaction would be. Would she assume he was like his father? He did have a temper, although he rarely lost it. Violence was an anathema to him. And violence against a woman was not to be borne. Only a coward would strike someone smaller and weaker than himself.

Never raise your hand to a woman. They cannot defend themselves against a man's superior strength.

Before his godmother's revelation, he never questioned his father's instruction. He still did not question its veracity, but the hypocrisy of it infuriated him. He wondered how his father lived with himself after his mother was gone.

A groom approached and he handed over Gabriel's reins, distracted from his thoughts. Following the rest of the party into the inn, he resolved not to think of his parents for now.

As expected, luncheon was superb. After the last dish was cleared, he suggested a short walk to stretch cramped muscles. Pamela, Lisa and Gerald readily agreed. The earl, countess, and Lady Parkington waved them off.

Emerging from the inn, Kitt led them around the side where the sound of rushing water greeted them. They stopped beside the stream, enjoying the sun glinting off the water. A path lined with towering oaks ran beside it. Sunlight filtered through the branches, dappling the waterway and path. A light, cooling breeze fluttered the ribbons on the ladies' bonnets. Birdsong drifted from the trees.

Lisa and Gerald had taken the path, and Pamela and Kitt followed. As they walked a few paces behind, Pamela could hear Lisa and Gerald squabbling, their voices floating back to Kitt and Pamela.

"You know she wouldn't say anything in front of the family, but it's normal to think about it," Gerald was saying.

"I don't care," Lisa retorted angrily. "It's tasteless and coarse. Especially at this time."

"I know, but she isn't the only one. Even you should understand that."

Pamela looked up at Kitt. He was watching the bickering siblings, his brows drawn into a frown.

"What are they arguing about now? It sounds serious."

His gaze swung to hers. He had been deep in thought, she realized, but he answered her question readily enough.

"The countess has pointed out to Lisa the advantages of this misfortune." Despite the graveness of their journey, his lips tilted momentarily. "Lisa is indignant on Denny's behalf."

191

"Advantages?" What could be advantageous about losing one's brother?

"With his brother's death, Denny is no longer a second son. If his sister-in-law delivers a girl, he becomes the Marquis of Rawlings."

Stunned, she could only stare at him as he continued.

"Death is always a shock, always unexpected, and always has bad timing. That Denny finally decided to ask for Lisa's hand despite his circumstances is fortunate. But his brother's death will be seen by many as a boon for Lisa."

Her heart went out to her friend. "How awful for Lisa. No wonder she is angry." Remembering the wait of almost a week ago, Pamela could imagine Lisa's mortification at being told that even though she thought she caught a second son, she might have caught a duke after all. To hear it from her mother, who made no secret she wanted a title for her only daughter, must have been like pouring salt on an open wound.

Kitt's voice interrupted her thoughts. "Gerald is right, however. The rest of the *ton* will not be coy about their speculation. Lisa should understand that. The gossips will chew over every possibility."

"What possibilities?"

"Whether Geoff's widow will have a son or daughter, or whether she will lose the babe in her grief. The less scrupulous will wager on whether Denny will somehow take steps to insure that he will inherit. Some will hint that Denny somehow caused his brother's death. And unfortunately, Lisa will be caught up in the finger-pointing and insinuations."

Pamela's shock must have communicated itself, for he stopped and turned to face her. He reached out and cupped her chin in his hand, stroking her cheek with his thumb. His hand was strong and warm, the light touch sending skittery sensations spiraling through her. Despite the warm day, she shivered in anticipation.

"Wh-why would a-anyone point fingers a-at Lisa?" She managed to get the question out over the lump in her throat.

A genuine smile lit his face. "After all this time and being the subject of so much gossip, you are still such an innocent." Despite his words, his voice did not mock her.

He bent closer. Instinctively she raised her face to his. The air around them shimmered. Her heart beat loudly in her ears. He murmured something beneath his breath that was lost when his lips touched hers.

His hands moved to her waist, warm even through the layers of cotton and muslin, pulling her closer. Her own moved up the smooth material covering his chest to clutch at his shoulders, holding on for dear life as her knees turned to jelly.

"I don't want to hear anymore," Lisa's strident tones intruded.

Kitt raised his head. Pamela could feel the blood rushing to her face. She slid her hands from his shoulders, intending to turn toward the pair. But Kitt held her securely against his lean frame.

Neither sibling showed any surprise at finding them so close together. Lisa marched past, eyes flashing and color high. Kitt released Pamela, who hurried to catch up with her. The men followed a pace behind.

"Lisa! Lisa, wait!"

Lisa slowed, then stopped and turned. Tear-filled eyes greeted Pamela.

"Don't, Lisa." Pamela drew the younger girl into a hug. "Don't let it upset you. Denny will need your support when we get to Mellerton. Don't worry about anyone else."

"I know I shouldn't." Tears clogged Lisa's voice. Pamela released her and the two began strolling back to the inn. "But it makes me so angry. To think that anyone would think Denny..." Her voice trailed off in resignation.

They continued in silence until the inn came into view.

They accomplished the remainder of the journey to Mellerton Chase with no further incident. Lisa rode with Pamela and Lady Parkington, who entertained both young women with stories from her long ago Season.

Hours later the coach rolled down a wide tree-lined avenue and Mellerton Chase came into view. Pamela stared in awe at the Palladian mansion gleaming in the fiery hues of the setting sun—a jewel of breathtaking beauty. Kitt and Gerald arrived ahead of the coaches and were standing on the graveled drive conversing with Denny.

Denny's face was etched with anguish when he moved toward the coach, but Pamela noticed it soften as his eyes alighted on Lisa. There was no objection when he asked Lisa to walk with him while the housekeeper and majordomo took charge of the remainder of their party.

Kitt gave Pamela a brief update in a low voice before escorting them inside. The pall of death could not be masked by the beauty of the house. Black crepe hung everywhere. Servants moved silently along opulent corridors, their long faces mirroring the family's suffering.

Kitt informed her the worst had come to pass. Overwhelmed by her grief, Denny's sister-in-law had gone into early labor the day before and been delivered of a baby girl in the wee hours of the morning. The infant, almost a month early, clung tenaciously to life, but her mother had all but given up.

Kitt and Gerald were taken in one direction by the majordomo while she and Lady Parkington followed the earl and countess and the housekeeper. The earl and countess were directed to a beautifully appointed suite overlooking the rear gardens. Lady Parkington was given a room across the hall. It was connected by a sitting room to Pamela's chamber, a large room lavishly decorated in pale blue, gold, and white.

"His lordship said you wouldn't mind sharing with his betrothed, seeing's how the house is nearly full," the housekeeper said to her. "This here's the Sunrise Suite."

Pamela did not miss the housekeeper's reference to Denny as "his lordship" and Lisa as "his betrothed". She was sure the countess hadn't either, as everyone pronounced themselves satisfied with the arrangements. Pamela knew she would not have merited such a room alone. Her inclusion with the Fallmerton party elevated her status.

Lisa entered the room a half hour later. Her eyes were shining, her lips pink and slightly swollen. She was delighted to discover the arrangements.

"I don't know whether to be happy or sad," Lisa confessed, holding out her hand for Pamela to inspect the sparkling diamond ring. "Denny said we might have to wait until December."

Seated in the middle of the large blue silk draped bed, Lisa absently traced the circular pattern woven into the coverlet. Pamela lounged against one of the posts at the end.

"Not that I mind, but...oh...I do. I thought it might be fun to have a double wedding with you and Lord Kittridge."

Pamela stilled, glad Lisa didn't seem to notice. She didn't want to tell Lisa she wasn't sure she and Kitt would be getting married.

"...but he said Lady Rawlings's condition is worsening. She refuses to eat and doesn't want to see the baby at all."

"Why not?"

"Apparently the baby looks like her father. Denny thinks that's a good thing, but his sister-in-law doesn't. Says she will remind her too much of her dear Geoff. Lady Avondale, Denny's sister, has offered to take her if Lady Rawlings doesn't want her. But I don't understand how she can not want her own child?"

Pamela didn't understand it either. If she and Kitt married and had a child, she'd never let it go. Especially if something happened to Kitt. The child would be her only link—how Lady Rawlings could think otherwise was inconceivable to her.

"I don't know, Lisa."

"Man that is born of a woman hath but a short time to live, and is full of misery. He cometh up, and is cut down, like a flower..."

Denny had never been a figure of envy among the *ton*. Though handsome and eligible, he was still a second son with only a courtesy title. Kitt never gave it much thought. Watching Denny and his family grieving over their loss, however, he found himself envious of the closeness and affection between them. The *ton* might now consider the situation advantageous to Denny, but Kitt knew Denny did not—that he would be content to remain a second son to have his brother back.

Kitt wanted a family like that. It wasn't until recently that he realized he'd not had a model upbringing. He'd always felt there was something missing. And, until last week, he assumed what was missing was his mother's influence.

He'd made peace with himself over his lack of knowledge, but it would be sometime before he reconciled his father's duplicity with the man he idolized.

"Forasmuch as it hath pleased Almighty God in his great mercy to take unto himself the soul of our dear brother, Geoffrey David Richard Avery..."

The archbishop's words floated over the solemn gathering in the churchyard. Despite the dismal atmosphere hovering over the people standing together around the freshly dug grave, birds trilled cheerfully under a brilliantly blue sky. The warm day coaxed flowers into bloom, attracting a variety of insects, while the sun preened from above.

"...commit his body to the ground; earth to earth, ashes to ashes, dust to dust..." In his sister-in-law's absence, Denny laid a rose atop his brother's casket, pausing for a moment with his head bowed as his hand rested against wood warmed by the sun. Once the casket was lowered into the ground, Denny threw the first handful of dirt, then stepped back and reached for Lisa's hand. Kitt expelled a long, slow breath as he noticed Lisa respond by stepping closer to Denny's side.

"It's good he has Lisa," Pamela said beside him, a hitch in her voice. He wondered how many others in the crowd noticed Lisa's inclusion as part of the Mellerton clan. She'd sat beside Denny in the church and stood at his side by the grave. "She will help him get through this—if he lets her."

"That will, of course, depend on her parents."

"How?"

He turned to regard her for a moment before replying. "She can't help him through anything if she's in London and he's here."

"Oh." She chewed her bottom lip thoughtfully. "I hadn't quite thought of it that way."

His hand covered hers resting on his arm, and squeezed in reassurance. Although very little had been said between them, he was glad she was here. He had yet to speak to her about the conversation he'd overheard between her and her sister, but it was never very far from his thoughts.

His gaze roamed over the assembled crowd—the cream of society. The Mellertons were not an especially large family, but the presence of the *ton* made up for the lack in size. No one who felt close enough to offer condolences stayed away, although some merely came to be seen and to pick up any tidbit of gossip to be had.

Denny's engagement had been announced in *The Times* the day after he'd spoken to Lord Fallmerton. Even though he hadn't spoken personally with Lisa, her parents felt confident enough of her acceptance to send off the announcement. Denny was grateful they had. The report of his brother's death hadn't been published until two days later. There would still be some who might cast suspicious glances at Lisa over the sudden betrothal, but there was nothing anyone could say to make it sound havey-cavey. The timing was just unfortunate.

The crowd was moving on, to the house where a meal would be laid out. Many of the guests would leave right after luncheon, the rest in the morning. Kitt, Pamela, Lady Parkington, and the Fallmertons would remain for a few days at Denny's request.

Beside him, Pamela stilled. He glanced down at her. Her gaze was fixed on something in the distance and he followed it. The Earl and Countess of Marscombe were speaking to a man and woman he did not recognize.

"I didn't realize they were here," she said slowly. "I haven't seen Sheila."

"She's not with them," he told her. "I spoke briefly with them this morning." And warned them away. The countess blamed Pamela for Sheila's sudden desire to go home, but he made it clear he knew exactly why Sheila had returned to Yorkshire and he was not averse to using his knowledge should they make Pamela uncomfortable. He wanted to ask why Pamela's very existence was so abhorrent to them, why they could not acknowledge her as their grandchild, but he didn't. Perhaps it had something to do with the identity of her father.

He wanted to tell Pamela what he knew, but his promise to Wyatt when he obtained the special license kept him silent. If he found a missive from Wyatt awaiting him in London, he would explain everything. If not, he'd have to continue to be patient. With an inward sigh, he turned Pamela in the direction of the churchyard gate. He knew too many secrets. Secrets that were not his to tell, but Pamela had a right to know. He would feel better when he could clear the air between them with complete honesty.

They took their time walking back to the house. Pamela, he knew, had no wish to run into her grandparents, and he wanted some time alone with her.

He desperately wanted to speak to her about ending their betrothal, but now was not the right time. With Lisa being drawn into Denny's grief, she needed Pamela for support. Hopefully, the next few days would resolve the issue.

"One month," Lady Fallmerton told her daughter. "And you may not believe it, but it will pass very quickly."

Seated in the sitting room adjoining their room and Lady Parkington's, Pamela and Lisa were enjoying an early afternoon coze when Lisa's mother had entered.

"It seems like such a long time, Mama."

Lady Fallmerton smiled and Pamela could see that, while not a ravishing beauty, she was very attractive.

"It was necessary to prevent the gossip. The only other solution was to wait until Lord Rawlings is out of mourning."

"Why?"

Lady Fallmerton sighed and looked from Lisa to Pamela and back. A hint of color crept up her throat to her face.

"I had not thought to have this talk with you until the day before your wedding, but I feel it is important you understand why we decided on a month's waiting period. The archbishop would have gladly granted a special license and wed you and Lord Rawlings tomorrow, but there is too much at stake."

Lisa looked confused, but Pamela had the uncomfortable feeling Lady Fallmerton was about to have what most referred to as "the talk" with her daughter. She felt decidedly *de trop*. As if she knew what Pamela was thinking, Lady Fallmerton turned to her.

"Has your mother spoken to you about marital relations?"

Pamela was very relieved to answer truthfully in the affirmative. "Yes, ma'am. She felt it was necessary before I left home."

Lady Fallmerton seemed relieved as well and Pamela suddenly realized she might have felt obligated to include her in the conversation had she said "no".

"What's at stake, Mama?"

Turning back to her daughter, she replied, "There must be no question that any child you bear is Lord Rawlings's. The *ton* will be counting the months. Because it is possible you could become pregnant on your wedding night, an early delivery would cause some to question the child's parentage. The month will provide breathing room."

Lisa shook her head. "You are not making sense, Mama. I don't care what the *ton* thinks, and neither does Denny."

Pamela rose to her feet. "I think you will be more comfortable having this discussion without an audience."

"Thank you, Pamela." The countess's smile was warm.

Pamela curtsied and withdrew. The hall was busy with footmen carrying trunks and boxes. There were at least three guest room doors open, voices coming from all. Nearing one, she could hear a couple arguing, but it wasn't until she stopped to let a footman carrying a trunk pass that she realized it was her grandparents.

"It seems to me you have no one but yourself to blame, Margery," her grandfather said. "You've concocted so many tales to cover your own embarrassment, it is not surprising they're coming home to roost."

"So, what do you plan to do about it?"

"Nothing. Just like always."

"And your own part in all this, I suppose, is minimal?"

"You know what's at stake. I would have handled it differently, that's all. But I'll have you know I'm glad the chit has done well for herself. Blood will tell, y'know. It always does."

Pamela backed away from the door as a footman came down the hall. Turning, she asked a footman leaving another room if there was a back way into the garden, then headed in the direction he pointed.

Slipping out into the sunshine a few minutes later, she closed her eyes and raised her face to the sun in worship. The warmth on her skin gradually dispersed the goose bumps that had risen on her arms at her grandfather's words.

I'm glad the chit has done well for herself.

She was sure her grandfather had been talking about her. He was glad for her. She hugged the knowledge to herself, nearly giddy with happiness. The sky was bluer, the sun brighter. The day had turned nearly perfect.

Uncaring that she was bonnetless, she wandered the gardens, soaking up the sun and contemplating her life.

So much had changed since she met Kitt. Had it only been three months? She catalogued the twists and turns.

Lisa's friendship and her family's acceptance went a long way toward negating the hostility she'd encountered. Now that she realized Kitt knew of her background and still hadn't ended the betrothal, and Sheila's attempt to derail it seemed to have failed, she was cautiously beginning to hope Kitt was planning to marry her after all.

Her outburst at Covington Manor might have made him even more hesitant. He obviously didn't believe in love and she, well, she loved him so much that just thinking about breaking the betrothal caused her pain. How would she live without him?

As if her thoughts conjured him up like the scarves a fairground gypsy draws from a hat, Kitt appeared before her. The sun glinted off his dark hair, giving it blue highlights to match his eyes.

"Aren't you concerned about being out without a bonnet?"

"I didn't think of it. I just wanted to give Lisa and her mother some privacy."

He fell into step beside her as she continued to stroll along the pathways between flower beds.

"Lady Fallmerton says Lisa and Denny can marry in a month."

"So Denny tells me. We are invited back for the event."

She stopped and turned to him. "Here?"

He stopped as well. "That hasn't been decided, but it will either be here or Merton Park. Regardless of where it takes place, it will be family only. With Denny still in mourning, there will be enough raised eyebrows as it is." He turned and began walking again. This time she fell into step beside him.

"Lady Fallmerton says it is so there can be no gossip concerning Lisa giving Denny an heir." She felt the blood warm her cheeks.

"True. But it is also because his sister-in-law's situation will hopefully be resolved by then."

"How is she?"

"Denny tells me the doctor has convinced her that dying of starvation is a most painful way to go and she has apparently recovered enough that it's unlikely she'll go any other way. So she has begun to eat again. She is, however, very depressed and still hasn't asked to see the baby."

"And the baby?"

"The doctor says she is still unsteady, but improving. I think he's afraid to say much more."

They continued walking beside a tall hedge, each caught up in their own thoughts. As they rounded the end, a summerhouse built to resemble a Greek temple came into view, its white columns bright in the afternoon sun. The glare caused Pamela to shade her eyes as she inspected it. Kitt led her up the three steps set in the base. The interior was cool, with a brightly colored throw rug, two small occasional tables, and a floral print covered chaise, sofa, and two overstuffed chairs strategically placed to take advantage of the views. An open magazine lay on the chaise, an unfinished game of chess set up on a table. There was even a fireplace, although Pamela doubted its effectiveness since the rest of the structure was open from all sides with no walls between the pillars.

"It's lovely." She spoke without thinking. With the house no longer in view, the remainder of the gardens were spread out around them.

Kitt stopped behind her. "Yes it is. Denny, Geoff and I spent many childhood hours stalking prey and each other through the gardens with this as our base."

She could feel his warm breath on her neck and his body heat at her back. A large hand settled at her waist and she leaned back with a sigh.

"Poor Denny." Her voice was soft. "I would be devastated if I lost Stephen."

"Not Sheila?" His voice was serious, but there was a hint of humor in its depths.

"Naturally, I would be sorry if something happened to her, but she and I have never been close. As the youngest, she was the spoiled one."

"And you? Were you ever spoiled?"

"No. I was the oldest. I had to be responsible. I suppose Mama spoiled me when I was little, but when Sheila came along it seemed like I was suddenly too old to be spoiled. Although that didn't stop Stephen and I from getting into everything."

"You and Stephen sound like Lisa and Gerald. They would deny it if you mentioned it, but they are very close."

Pamela fell silent. She envied the closeness Lisa and Gerald, and Denny and his sister shared. She and Stephen *had* been close as children, but their lives had taken completely different turns once Stephen went off to school. Always a poor correspondent, Stephen's letters had stopped almost entirely in the last few years.

Being in the company of the Fallmertons and Mellertons demonstrated to her more than anything else how much she missed being part of a family. And she did. Desperately. She wanted someone who would accept her for who she was. If she was never to know her own father, she wanted something to fill that void. And that something was a family of her own.

"Do you think my grandparents know who my real father is?"

The question emerged unbidden. Too late to take it back. Kitt stiffened at her back, the hand resting on her shoulder twitched.

"I would suppose it's possible they do."

It was too late for secrets. He already knew and hadn't turned away from her. Perhaps she could ask for his assistance.

"Do you think they would tell me if I asked?"

He was a long time answering.

"I don't know."

"Mama said he was dead, so I didn't need to know. But...I still want to know."

Kitt turned her to face him, using one long finger to tilt her chin up. Worry lingered in his blue gaze. She dropped her eyes to his cravat. Thinking about families had turned her maudlin. Or, perhaps thinking about Denny's loss reminded her of all she had lost.

Maybe that was the real problem. How did you lose something you never had—even if you didn't know you didn't have it? Her entire life was a lie and she hadn't even known. Trying to please a stepfather who would never have been pleased. If not for Kitt, she might still be at Clark Hall wondering why "Papa" didn't like her.

Did she resemble her real father? Did her presence remind Sheila's father of her mother's transgression? Sheila looked like their mother and Stephen was a taller version of his father, but Pamela resembled no one. Her mother's golden hair on her was mixed with red and no one on either side of the family had green eyes.

She raised her face to his again. "Do you think I should let it go?"

He glanced away for a moment, then back. "Not if you truly want to know." He reached up and smoothed back a tendril of hair at her temple. She was conscious of the strength in the hand at her waist that held her securely without force. "But you might want to ask yourself why you want to know, and what you would do with the information once you had it."

She grimaced. "You're no help. Wouldn't you want to know if you discovered your whole life was based on a lie?"

She did not expect the short bark of derisive laughter that erupted from him. Both arms closed around her and he hugged her close.

He took a deep breath and let it out. "Ah, sweet. If you only knew. Shall we compare our lies?"

"What lies?"

He was quiet for a moment. Considering. "Did Denny tell you where I'd gone?"

"No, but Lady Parkington said she thought you might have gone home."

"Did she tell you why?"

"No."

Kitt's arms dropped and he turned away to stand between two pillars, looking out over a wide sweeping well-manicured lawn. In the distance was a statue she thought must be a fountain because she could see water sparkling in the sun around it. Beyond that was a large hedge which she knew to be a maze.

"I did go back to The Ridge." His voice came back to her over his shoulder. "I don't even know why. There were no answers to be had there, but I needed to go. It's not as if I could have pulled my father from his grave and demanded to know why, but I certainly wish I could."

She moved to his side and slipped her hand into his. His fingers closed over hers and squeezed them briefly. Warmth shot up her arm.

"What would you wish to know from your father?"

He turned then and she saw the bleakness in his eyes. Instinctively, she moved closer in an attempt to provide comfort.

"I'm not sure. I've believed the worst about my mother for so long that learning the truth has undermined my confidence in anything my father ever said." She felt the tension in him as he struggled with his thoughts. "It's humbling to discover your idol has feet of clay—that he was merely human after all." He drew her back into his arms. "It's possible that's why we're both struggling with the past."

With both hands resting on his chest, she could feel the steady rhythm of his heartbeat and the warmth of his skin. His fresh, clean scent enveloped her.

"Perhaps..." He leaned closer and her mouth went dry. "Perhaps we should forget the past and just move on."

Heat washed through her. "But we can't just ignore it!" Her legs were slowly dissolving at the look in his eyes. "Can we?"

His lips touched hers, just a brush. "Yes." He grazed across her cheek. "We can."

His lips settled against hers again. This time the touch was anything but brief. She forgot to breathe. All mental activity ceased and her heart took over, doubling its pounding in her chest. Sensation slithered along her skin, her arms slid up around his neck. He broke the contact, but only long enough for her to remember to take a breath before his head descended again and all thought was lost.

She was warm putty in his arms, her soft curves melting into the unyielding wall of bone and muscle that was Kitt. Resistance would have been useless had she considered it, but his kisses were precious to her and she willingly participated in each and every one. Someday they might be all she had to remember him by.

Her lips parted at his urging, welcoming his tongue into the moist cavern of her mouth. She thought she heard him groan as her tongue met and dueled with his. He tasted faintly of brandy, but dwelling on that fact was beyond the capability of her fog-bound brain.

Without warning, Kitt stiffened and raised his head. She sighed in disappointment as approaching voices intruded on her consciousness. Her cheeks warmed at the realization that they could have been seen.

"You'll be too busy shopping to notice the passage of time," Denny's deep voice said.

"Shopping!" came Lisa's horrified voice, "I'm not shopping for a black wardrobe."

"It needn't be black. You're not in mourning."

"I am if you are."

Pamela and Kitt looked at each other and grinned. Lisa would keep Denny on his toes for the rest of their lives.

"No black!" Denny's voice was adamant. "I don't like you in black. If you insist, buy half-mourning."

"But...but..."

"No black...or we'll wait until I'm out of mourning," he threatened.

The pair rounded the hedge in time for Pamela and Kitt to see Lisa stick out her tongue at Denny. The childish gesture was too much and both erupted in laughter. Lisa turned in surprise.

"There you are!" Lisa exclaimed. "Aunt Claire was wondering where you'd gotten to."

Pamela sobered. "Perhaps I ought to go back, then." She started down the steps, but Lisa stopped her.

"Don't bother. I think she just wondered where you were, but when we realized his lordship was missing, too, well, we just assumed you were together."

Pamela felt her cheeks warm. Denny said nothing, but she knew his eyes missed little.

"I was telling Pamela war stories from our misspent youth," Kitt said to Denny, drawing attention away from her. "Do you remember the time Geoff hid Muriel's favorite doll in the maze?"

The four of them fell into an easy camaraderie and they spent the rest of the afternoon listening to Kitt and Denny reminisce about the adventures they shared with Geoff as boys. Pamela watched with pride as Kitt put aside his own troubles to lift the melancholy hanging over Denny.

As the afternoon waned and the sun sank lower in the sky, Pamela sat in a chair across from Kitt while Lisa and Denny occupied the sofa. Comfortable among friends, Lisa curled her feet up under her and leaned against Denny's shoulder. Pamela wondered if she would ever feel so at ease with Kitt. During a gap in the conversation, Lisa brought up her favorite subject.

"A double wedding would be wonderful. Papa said he would give you away—with your permission, of course."

"Your wedding day ought to be your special day," Pamela demurred.

"But it would be truly special if you shared it with me."

Pamela had no answer to that. Looking to Kitt for help, she found none. The expression in his eyes merely said the decision was hers. Drat!

"I'll think about it," was all she would promise.

Chapter Fourteen

Devon's clear, sunny skies gave way to low hanging clouds and a fine drizzle as they neared London. Lisa rode with Pamela and Lady Parkington for the first leg of the trip. Although reluctant to leave Denny, she was making the best of the situation. That meant planning a wedding including Pamela and Kitt—if not as a second couple, then at least as a bridesmaid and best man.

"I don't know if she will survive the disappointment," Pamela said to Lady Parkington when they were finally alone. "She has her heart set on a double wedding." Staring out the coach window at the passing countryside, Pamela's spirits lowered along with the clouds. "And Kitt is practically encouraging her."

"Then perhaps you need to re-examine the problem."

She turned back to the interior of the coach. "Which one? The betrothal that doesn't exist? My background that is a lie? The Season you and my mother contrived to give me that failed?"

Lady Parkington pursed her lips. Her hazel eyes studied Pamela for long minutes before she spoke again.

"First of all, your Season did not fail." She held up her hand when Pamela would have interrupted. "Oh, I know there were some minor setbacks. But it was not a failure."

Pamela disagreed but kept her thoughts to herself.

"Second, among those that matter, your background is only important to you." She held up her hand and counted on her fingers. "I do not care. Nicky and Charlotte do not care—at least Charlotte doesn't anymore. Those in the *ton* who think they

207

care won't in a year. In fact, they will have forgotten it by then. Kitt doesn't care—at least not anymore." She wagged a finger at Pamela. "You, my dear, are the only who considers it an insurmountable obstacle. And as for the betrothal that doesn't exist—once again, you are the only one who thinks that."

Pamela's mouth dropped open momentarily before she quickly snapped it shut. "I...I'm the only..." Her mind raced with the implications. Had Kitt said something to his godmother? She looked back over the last month. It passed in a blur, but scenes stood out. The most recent of the four of them at Mellerton Chase. Kitt never demurred over a wedding. On occasion he even joined in the "planning".

"Kitt intended the betrothal to be real from the beginning," Lady Parkington explained. "He told me himself, but he didn't think you'd agree to marry him. The Season was a benefit and, before you ask, your mother really did send me funds for it. That was not a fabrication." She smiled and Pamela noted the mischief dancing in her eyes before she continued. "But don't ask whether or not I actually spent them."

Dazed, Pamela had but one question. "Why?"

"Why what?"

"Why go through all this trouble for me? You didn't even know me until I answered your advertisement in *The Times*."

"True, but once I began corresponding with your mother and learned more of your story, I knew I had to help. Then Kitt arrived."

"But why would Kitt suggest a sham betrothal?"

"I don't know. I realize you and Kitt knew each other before meeting in London, but I have not asked. And I suspect whatever history you have was the original reason for the engagement. But whatever the reason was to begin with," she waved a white hand in dismissal, "it has changed."

"Changed? How?"

The coach came to a stop and both ladies peered out the window to discover they had arrived home.

Entering the small house, there was no time for Pamela to ask her question again. Carter and Mrs. Diggs greeted them effusively. Pearl came tearing out of the back parlor, barking furiously, her little paws scrabbling for purchase on the polished wood floor.

Lady Parkington picked her up. While she spoke to the two servants, Pamela turned to direct the two footmen concerning their luggage. In a short time, they were ensconced in the familiar cozy parlor, tea set out on the low table between them. Lady Parkington was scanning a number of missives that had arrived while she was away. Pearl curled contentedly in her mistress's lap. All was blessedly normal again. Or was it?

Pamela wasn't sure. *Kitt intended the betrothal to be real from the beginning.* Did he truly want to marry her? Why? *...whatever history you have was the original reason.* He felt responsible for her, for her current situation. She knew that. But she didn't want to marry someone who felt nothing more than guilt over a situation not of his doing. Kitt might still think her banishment was his fault, but understanding that her entire life as she knew it was false, she now understood he had merely been the impetus for the inevitable. Whatever else might have transpired, she could not have remained at Clark Hall forever. Eventually circumstances would have compelled her to leave. She just could not envision what, or how, it might have happened.

It had taken a desperate situation to rouse her mother into action. For years, she relied on Pamela to keep the household running smoothly. With the housekeeper growing old and failing, without realizing it, her mother fell in with her husband's wishes.

Thinking of her mother, Pamela looked up.

"Is there no letter from Mama?" Her voice cut across the comfortable stillness.

Lady Parkington's eyebrows rose in surprise. "Why, no. Now that you mention it, I haven't heard from Anne in quite a while."

Kitt sat at the desk in his library, a glass of amber liquid at his elbow, sorting through the stack of correspondence which had accumulated in his absence. Sighing in frustration, he broke the seal on yet another missive from his steward at Kitt

Ridge. Spread out before him was correspondence from his solicitor, steward, tradesmen, and even his banker, but nothing from Wyatt.

A fortnight had passed since he and Wyatt eavesdropped on Sheila and Pamela. Two whole weeks for Wyatt to have accomplished his task. So why hadn't he written?

He forced himself to concentrate on the report he held. His steward was extremely competent and Kitt trusted his judgment implicitly, but the man insisted on soliciting Kitt's approval for every little expenditure, and explaining his decisions in great detail. Finishing the steward's account of the damage wrought by a passing storm and expenditures needed for repairs, Kitt reached for a piece of foolscap and a quill.

He was sanding the last reply when Tibbs entered with the day's post. The top letter bore his name and direction in Wyatt's hand. Anticipation hummed through him as he reached for the envelope.

"Cook would like to know if you will be dining at home this evening, my lord."

Intent on opening Wyatt's letter, Kitt didn't answer. Unfolding the single sheet, he scanned the closely written paragraphs. The note was brief but informative and Kitt's heart plummeted at the contents. He looked up and registered Tibbs's presence as the butler repeated his inquiry.

"No, I am dining with the Earl of Fallmerton tonight."

After Tibbs withdrew, Kitt picked up his drink and threw it back in one large swallow. The whiskey burned its way down his throat to his stomach, dislodging his heart from where it landed moments before. Setting the glass down on the polished rosewood surface, the chair creaked as he leaned back, allowed the well-worn leather to surround him and closed his eyes.

When would it end? Once again he was the recipient of information Pamela should have. Information he should not have to pass on. It was not his responsibility, yet he knew he would have to be the one to tell her. Could he soften it some way? Perhaps he ought to marry her first, then tell her.

His lips twisted. No, he couldn't do that. It wouldn't be fair not to be honest with her first, but his protective instincts urged him to shield her from the pain.

Will you marry me? And oh, by the way, I have some good news and some bad news. Which would you like to hear first?

Unable to sit still any longer, he rose from the chair and crossed to the window. Staring out at the nearly deserted street without seeing, his hand absently crushed a handful of burgundy velvet.

You must swear never to tell me you love me unless you truly mean it. Had it only been a little more than a month ago she'd extracted that promise from him? He'd been so sure of himself, then. Of course he'd never say that to her. He'd never said those words to anyone—not even his parents. He didn't believe in love. Or he hadn't until Pamela entered his life.

He wasn't a monk. Growing up with his father and his view of women, he'd been through his share of Cyprians, demireps and the like. His reputation as a rake was well-earned. Even so, once he entered into the betrothal with Pamela, he'd confined his attentions to her alone.

Others had tried to distract him, but Pamela's peace of mind was more important than a casual dalliance. She was already hurt as a result of her family's rejection. He wouldn't add to it. Unfortunately, she knew nothing of his sacrifice. And, knowing the *ton*, she'd probably heard every exploit, every affair, every lark he'd ever participated in.

Worse, though, were those who simply refused to acknowledge the betrothal. Lady Wilmot fell into that category and he was tired of listening to her attempt to shred Pamela's character whenever they met.

The talk in the clubs was just plain cruel. The betting book at White's had begun to sprout wagers until he, Denny and Gerald made it plain they considered them offensive and insulting. Then the wagers miraculously disappeared. Tracing a few of the rumors back to their sources, he was relieved Pamela's grandfather was not at the end of the trail.

It was obvious to him her grandmother was the root of the problem. For some reason the Countess of Marscombe intensely disliked her granddaughter. He didn't want to use the word "hate", but it was the only word that fit. He wished he knew why. Perhaps it was mere embarrassment turned to spite as his godmother suggested. Whatever the obstacle was, it seemed such a waste to dwell on it.

Turning from the window, it occurred to him that Wyatt's news affected another person. Picking up the letter, he refolded it and slipped it into his pocket. Leaving his normally clean desk covered with correspondence and bills was indicative of his distraction as he crossed the carpet toward the door.

"I will be at White's."

His butler merely nodded in acknowledgment and closed the door behind him. Striding down the street, his long legs eating up the distance, he wished he could meet up with Denny to discuss this latest wrinkle, but since that was not possible, the Earl of Fallmerton would have to do.

It was the most daring gown she owned. Emerald green silk clung to her curves, the color intensifying the green flecks in her eyes. The delicate white lace bordering the low décolletage was the only trimming. The gown's utter simplicity was designed to allow the imagination to take over, something she knew Kitt had no trouble doing as he watched her descend the stairs.

Desire flickered in the sapphire depths of his eyes as he raised her hand to his mouth.

"I'm glad we are only dining with the Fallmertons tonight," was his only comment, but his eyes lingered momentarily on her breasts.

Waving away Carter as he approached with her shawl, Kitt said, "It is quite warm out tonight. I doubt you'll need that."

Pamela blushed and turned away as Lady Parkington entered the foyer.

"My, how lovely you look!"

"And you, too," Pamela responded. The deep purple silk complemented the older woman's fair looks and ample figure without making her look like an overdressed partridge.

The ride to Portman Square was short and soon their party was climbing the stairs to the Fallmerton townhouse. A three-storied plain brick-fronted structure, it looked like many others along the square. The lower windows were all illuminated, spilling yellow light out over the front steps.

The majordomo greeted Lady Parkington warmly and then led them into a drawing room tastefully decorated in green and white. There they found Lisa and her mother, but no sign of the earl or Lord Tinsley.

"They are in the billiard room, my lord," Lady Fallmerton told Kitt, "if you wish to join them."

"I think I will, thank you."

Without the men, the women fell to discussing Lisa's wedding.

"The archbishop has agreed to return to conduct the ceremony," Lady Fallmerton informed them.

"Tomorrow I have an appointment to begin the fittings for my dress," Lisa said excitedly. "And you must have a dress, too, if you are to be my bridesmaid."

"But...but I..." Pamela stuttered, unsure of what to say. She grew weary of being the one to draw back each time, feeling guilty for putting a damper on Lisa's enthusiasm. "I thought it was to be family only, with Denny in mourning," she finished lamely.

Lisa refused to listen to any excuses. "But you and Aunt Claire are family. Besides, Lord Kittridge will be there."

Pamela sighed as she looked from one lady to another. Neither Lady Fallmerton nor Lady Parkington said anything. So much for garnering support. Why didn't Lady Fallmerton protest? Was she in agreement because Lady Parkington would be there anyway? Knowing her godmother, Pamela was sure she would refuse to leave her in London. Perhaps Lady Fallmerton considered it convenient she came with Lady Parkington. It saved them the possibility of inviting someone else to fill the role of bridesmaid.

Of course, Lisa didn't need a bridesmaid. But she wanted Pamela and Kitt as part of her wedding and at this point what Lisa wanted, Lisa got. Pamela smiled to herself. If she'd thought of that in conjunction with Sheila, it would not have been complimentary. Lisa, however, was different. Her excitement wasn't selfish. She wanted to share her joy with one and all, and as their only daughter, her parents were willing to indulge her.

She really needed to discuss this with Kitt before the planning went too far and they were irretrievably trapped. She truly liked Lisa. As a younger sister, Lisa was everything Sheila had never been.

The majordomo appeared and announced dinner. Rising, the ladies all followed Lady Fallmerton to the dining room. Lisa walked beside Pamela, chattering about her trousseau. The men came from another direction, arriving at the same time. The earl greeted both Pamela and Lady Parkington, laughing as his sister took him to task for hiding out in the billiard room.

Pamela was surprised to see Lord Parkington with them. So, apparently, was Lady Parkington.

"Where have you been?" Lady Parkington asked him.

"I went to Kingston to check on some items I ordered. I only returned today because I received Aunt Charlotte's invitation."

Although Pamela knew of Lord Parkington's relationship to the Fallmertons, it seemed odd to hear him address the earl and countess as "aunt" and "uncle". She wondered if the earl had spoken to him about leading Gerald astray as Lady Parkington had once stated.

The dining room was a high-ceilinged room decorated in burgundy and cream. Pamela could tell by the size of the room that more than a few leaves had been removed from the table, yet what was left was still at least fifteen feet long. Kitt escorted her to her seat between Lisa and Gerald, admonishing them not to consider her a wall to argue around.

Dinner was simple but delicious. Conversation flowed freely around the table without regard for societal conventions that proscribed such actions as speaking across the table, or around the person directly beside you. Pamela found herself enjoying the banter among the family and Kitt, who was obviously no stranger to dinners with the Fallmerton clan. Lord Fallmerton, she discovered, was not above being teased by his wife, sister, or children, and even she was drawn into a short-lived argument between Lisa and Gerald. She had not enjoyed herself so much in a very long time, she thought as she related a particularly mischievous prank she and Stephen had pulled as children.

"Mama laughed so hard she cried," she recounted, "but Papa sent us both to the nursery, and we were not allowed in the stables for an entire month."

"I would not have been able to stand it," Lisa cried. "A whole month!"

Pamela laughed. "We wouldn't have either, if we'd obeyed, but we didn't. We just didn't get caught."

As dessert was brought in, she savored the congeniality and relaxed atmosphere in the room. When was the last time she enjoyed herself so thoroughly in company? This last month had shown her a side to life she forgot existed. Feeling sorry for herself and bemoaning what might have been, she'd lost sight of herself as a person. She could not change the circumstances of her birth, but she could change her outlook on it.

If Lady Parkington was to be believed—and Pamela did want to believe her—Kitt wanted to marry her. That he didn't believe in love was only a bump in the road, not the death of her dreams. Could she teach him to love her? Was she willing to take the first step and confess her love first?

She'd have to.

Later tonight, she'd ask him to take her for a drive tomorrow. Perhaps she'd even suggest they go to the Manor. They'd have a nice long talk and hopefully all would be well.

The ladies were crossing the large foyer, having left the men to their port, when Lady Parkington turned to her and said, "Come with me. I have something to show you." Then she headed up the staircase while Lady Fallmerton and Lisa continued on to the drawing room.

At the top, Lady Parkington turned right and Pamela followed her down a short hall. At the end, she turned left and emerged into a spacious gallery lined with portraits. A large, brightly lit candelabra sat on a table with three smaller candlesticks beside it. Lady Parkington picked up two candles, lit them both from the candelabra, then handed one to Pamela.

Intrigued, Pamela followed her as she sailed past a number of paintings before stopping before a small head-and-shoulders only portrait of a young woman. A table beneath it held a smaller candelabra and Lady Parkington lit its candles to provide more light. Once she finished, she merely stood there, studying the picture. Pamela looked at the pictures as she strolled in her wake. Reaching Lady Parkington's side, she looked down and her mouth went dry.

It was like looking into a mirror. Curls the color of a fiery sunset tumbled over bare white shoulders while green-flecked brown eyes surveyed the outside world in private amusement. A tip-tilted nose and wide, smiling mouth above a small determined chin completed the picture. Silence reigned in the room. Pamela could hear her heart beating, feel the blood pounding in her temples. The dryness in her mouth made speech nearly impossible, but she forced herself to ask, "Who...who...?"

Lady Parkington seemed to understand her difficulty. "She was my mother."

The room swayed and Pamela forced herself to stand still and wait for it to stop. She rubbed her eyes with her free hand, then peered at the picture again. It had not changed.

"Do you know why I hired you?" Lady Parkington spoke softly into the silence. "I hired you because of your name."

Pamela turned to look down at her, regaining some of her equilibrium in the process.

"Pamela is not a popular name. In fact, besides you, I know of only a few others—all related." She reached out and traced the shape of her mother's nose. "Was it coincidence that I decided to advertise for a companion when I did?" she mused aloud. "And in *The Times*, when I could have consulted an agency and saved myself the bother?" She paused, then continued. "A gypsy I once met would have said it was fate, Gerald will tell you it's because families are families—even when separated. But whatever it was, it brought you to me when you needed someone. For that, I am eternally thankful. And Gerald, who is a firm believer in family tradition, is elated this generation is not the one to break it."

"What tradition is that?"

Lady Parkington smiled, her eyes lighting up with the familiar mischievous sparkle. "The tradition which dictates the oldest girl in each generation is named Pamela."

Pamela's head began to spin. What was Lady Parkington trying to tell her?

A deep voice came out of the shadows. "Don't go filling her head with nonsense."

Pamela jumped and whirled around to find the earl had approached.

"She may as well know. Gerald will tell her anyway."

He chuckled as he stopped beside them. He looked at the picture, then at Pamela. "I didn't remember the resemblance being so uncanny."

"Gerald picked up on it immediately."

"I know. Why do you think I came to Town so early?"

Lady Parkington looked up at her brother. "Ahh. So you weren't surprised to meet her after all?"

He smiled. "No." His gaze moved from Pamela to Lady Parkington and back. "Perhaps, however, it is time to let her in on the secret."

Lady Parkington turned to her. "I think you'd better sit down." She took Pamela's candle and nodded toward a small grouping of chairs nearby.

Pamela did as instructed, folding her hands primly in her lap. The earl took another chair, stretching his long legs out before him, while Lady Parkington lit a number of candles around them.

"Would you prefer me to leave, Nicky?"

"No. You may as well stay—if not for Pamela's sake, then just so you are aware of all of the complications of this affair."

Lady Parkington sat on the bench in the alcove. The candles cast a warm glow about the three of them, and Pamela felt the beginning of a hopeful expectation. Contentment stole over her, barely overlaying the simmering anticipation singing in her blood.

The earl took a deep breath. "Where shall I start?"

Nearly on the edge of her chair, Pamela plunged. "My father," she said quickly before she lost her courage. "Do you know who he was?"

"Was?" The earl was surprised. "Ahh, yes. That's right. You were told he was dead." He glanced at the murky darkness above them for a moment, then steepled his hands beneath his chin. "I suppose that makes us even, because I was told neither Anne nor her child survived childbirth."

Pamela sat frozen in shock as the implication in his words penetrated.

"When you told me your mother said he was dead, I thought it was James or Anthony," Lady Parkington added. "It wasn't until I put the question to Nicky that he confessed."

"Confessed?" The earl's eyebrows rose. "I do not remember *confessing* to anything."

Pamela considered this information. "But it couldn't have been your oldest brother, because Mama told me he was a younger son. But why did she say he was dead?"

"I suspect her parents told her I was reported dead in Northern France. When I turned up badly injured but alive nearly a year later, they never corrected her knowledge. I suppose by then it was best. She would have already been married. You would have been almost six months old. It would have done no one any good. And I was still a younger son."

Lady Parkington picked up the story. "Anthony went to Egypt with Nelson. He died in '98. I considered it might have been him and was quite angry with him for having had an affair with a married woman. I was just as angry with Nicky until he told me the story."

Pamela looked to the earl. Her father! She was having difficulty digesting the information. She'd never thought to learn his identity, let alone be sitting and speaking with him.

"Anne and I were both much too young, but it didn't seem to matter at the time. It wasn't until she told me she was pregnant that the seriousness of our actions hit home. I think we always planned to marry, despite her parents. It just never occurred to us it wouldn't happen."

"What did happen?"

"I'm not sure," he replied sadly. "She insisted on telling her parents the truth alone. I agreed to arrive the next day to speak to her father. That was the last I saw of her. When I arrived the next morning, they were gone and the servants disclaimed all knowledge of where."

Pamela grimaced. Wasn't that what she had done with Kitt? Sent him away, thinking she could handle the situation on her own? Had she and Sheila only inherited their mother's foolish tendencies?

The earl was looking at her with a question in his expression.

"I don't think I know much more. Mama told me she wasn't aware her parents had arranged a match for her. She'd only met Maurice a few times. When she told them about me, they packed her up and took her to Yorkshire, where she was married by special license almost immediately. They gave her no choice. Maurice agreed to pay her father's gambling debts."

"But none of this explains why Marscombe refuses to acknowledge you. I would have thought they would not have invited gossip in this way," Lady Parkington interrupted.

"I have a theory about that."

Both women looked to the earl.

"I think initially it was because they were embarrassed over Anne's compromise. But I think the most recent reason revolves around Marscombe's heir."

Lady Parkington's forehead puckered in thought. "His heir? I don't think I know who that is."

He nodded. "Until recently, it's been kept deliberately vague."

"Why? And how does that affect Pamela?"

"Let me see if I can shed some light. Anne had two brothers—both rakehells of the worst kind. The oldest, John, was killed in a tavern brawl in Oxford when he was twenty or so. He was close in age to Anthony. The youngest, Charles, I think, was killed in a duel. I don't remember exactly when, but I heard about it shortly before Gerald was born."

"I never knew my mother had brothers," Pamela said, "but what does that have to do with me?"

"Because your grandfather's heir is your brother, Stephen."

Chapter Fifteen

"Impossible!" Lady Parkington exclaimed, outraged. "How do they think to get away with that?"

"If not for Pamela, it would be quite simple."

"Explain yourself, Nicholas James," his sister demanded. A narrow-eyed look accompanied the use of his full name.

"I'm trying to, Pamela Claire," he retaliated.

Pamela sucked in a breath, her head swiveling toward Lady Parkington.

"Don't try to distract Pamela with names," she snapped. "I want to know why you think Marscombe will get away with it."

He grinned at her. "Very well. I think it must have been planned around the time Charles died. The last few days, bits and pieces of the last few years have been bothering me, but it wasn't until tonight when Pamela related the story of her and Stephen as children that it all came together.

"Marscombe has badgered Prinny to bestow a title on his son-in-law for years, but Prinny keeps refusing. Many years back, he was granted a knighthood for service to the Crown, but it's not hereditary."

"So, Stephen won't become 'Sir Stephen' on Maurice's death?" Pamela asked.

He shook his head. "No. The title dies with Anne's husband."

Pamela digested this bit of information.

"About five years ago, Marscombe introduced your brother to a number of his cronies. When questioned about Stephen's origins, his explanation was that Charles had been married.

Stephen was born after Charles's death and because your grandparents weren't sure he would survive, they said nothing. His mother supposedly didn't. Marscombe then said Stephen had been raised by his daughter and her husband as their child, only recently being apprised of his true parentage."

Pamela sat back in her chair, eyes wide in amazement. "They thought I would say something that would expose the story for a lie? How do they think I would have known?"

"I can guess," Lady Parkington said. "How old were you when Stephen was born?"

"Nearly three. I have very dim memories of putting my head on Mama's stomach. And of being told I had to wait to play with Stephen until he was bigger."

"Exactly," she said with satisfaction.

"I don't understand. Aren't there records?"

"I suspect they've covered their tracks very well in this," the earl explained. "You were the only flaw in the plan. You can cast doubts concerning Stephen being Charles's son."

"But why would I?"

"You might not have done so deliberately, but it's possible you could have done so without knowing. Your sister is no threat—she was born after Stephen, so couldn't possibly know the circumstances of his birth. But you were older, and there with your mother through her pregnancy. Think of what you just told us."

Pamela rested her head against the back of her chair and closed her eyes. More lies! Would they never end? And now Stephen was being forced into one, too. Or was he? How would she find out what he'd actually been told? Did he truly think himself their deceased uncle's child? Was that why he'd stopped writing?

She opened her eyes to find her companions watching her closely. There was little she could do now, but there was still information she lacked. She would ponder the other questions later, but there were some that could be answered here and now.

"Why has no one commented on our names being the same?"

"I don't know that anyone knows," Lady Parkington answered. "You are the only one who was ever called Pamela. All of the rest of us are known by our second names. Mine, as you know, is Claire. My mother's was Lynette, and my grandmother's was Lenore."

"But why didn't Lisa say something?"

"Because she isn't named Pamela," the earl replied. "When she was born, my oldest brother, James, already had a daughter, Jane. She died when Lisa was four."

"But Gerald knew?" She paused. "Oh, that's right. The family history. Of course he would know."

They lapsed into silence. The candles still burned brightly around them, keeping the murky darkness beyond at bay. Pamela had no sense of the time, and wondered how long they had been talking. Was everyone else wondering where they were, or did they know?

The rustle of Lady Parkington's skirts as she rose to her feet drew Pamela's attention.

"I will join the others and leave you two to talk a bit longer." She bent and kissed Pamela on the cheek. "I'm sorry it has taken so long, but I'm glad you finally know." Then she picked up a candle and sailed away toward the door.

Pamela watched her go. The silence that fell between her and the earl felt awkward. Then he spoke.

"I must apologize for not telling you before, but so much has happened since I first arrived in Town, and time has flown. If not for Charlotte, I might still be waiting for the 'perfect opportunity'."

His admission reminded her that she hadn't understood Lady Fallmerton's sudden defense of her. But...neither had Lisa.

"Does Lisa know?"

He chuckled. "No. She would have said something—not just to you, but to someone else. As it was, Gerald has nearly said something more than once. Although he was not necessarily pleased to discover you were his sister rather than the cousin he assumed."

Lord Tinsley's comment in Vauxhall came back to her. "I remember. He insisted he didn't need an older sister but wouldn't mind a cousin."

He nodded. "He had assumed, like my sister, that one of my brothers was your father."

"I have to admit I have been baffled by everyone these last few weeks. And at Lisa's ball, I didn't understand why I felt like I was being treated like family. I think Lisa thought it odd as well."

"I would have told you immediately, but I owed Charlotte an explanation first. Unfortunately, she was so busy with Lisa's ball I didn't get a chance to tell her until just before we descended for dinner. Gerald had already taxed me with too many questions as soon as I returned from Claire's, so he already knew. I had to make both of them swear not to tell Lisa."

Pamela grinned at that. "She is irrepressible, isn't she?"

As if mentioning her conjured her up, Lisa came into the gallery.

"There you are!" Hurrying over to them, she reached down and gave Pamela a hug. "Mama told me the truth. Ooooh, how wonderful! But—" she turned to her father, "—shouldn't you be ashamed of yourself, Papa?"

The earl rose to his feet. "Have I fallen off my pedestal, Lisa?" The serious tone in his voice was belied by his smile.

Lisa threw herself into her father's arms. "Of course not, Papa. Mama explained that you didn't know. But it was not well done of you to compromise a gently born young lady."

"The folly of youth," he replied. "It is the reason we keep such close account of impressionable young girls."

He looked from Lisa to Pamela, who had also risen to her feet.

"I don't think I was ever an impressionable young girl." She smiled. "Now, Lisa, on the other hand..."

"You are beginning to sound like a big sister now. Maybe I shouldn't have wished for one after all."

Crossing his arms over his broad chest, the earl rocked back on his heels and looked down at his youngest. "And when did you do that?"

"At the last Michaelmas fair. Madame Irina said my wish would come true within the year." She glanced from her father to Pamela. "I suppose we might have found you sooner if I had wished sooner. I've wanted a big sister since Jane died." She looked crestfallen. "I'm sorry. I should have wished for one sooner."

Pamela could contain herself no longer. Bursting into laughter, she hugged Lisa tightly.

"Oh, Lisa, you are such a dear. A bit of a widgeon, but a dear one all the same."

"I will tell Denny you said that!" Lisa threatened as she returned Pamela's hug. "At least now you *have* to be my bridesmaid..."

Pamela grinned. "Very well."

"...unless we have a double wedding. Then Papa will give both of us away."

London's perennial early morning fog still shrouded the city as Kitt arrived at the house on Arden Street the next morning. Inside he found Lady Parkington sitting down to breakfast, but no Pamela.

He took a seat. "Still abed?"

Lady Parkington shook her head. "She said she needed to think, so she took Pearl out a little earlier than usual this morning. I think they normally head for Hyde Park."

"Perhaps I shouldn't bother her then. A lot happened last night."

Carter set a heaping plate before him and a cup of coffee at his elbow. Picking up the cup, he took a sip of the steaming brew then put it down and tucked into his breakfast.

Lady Parkington talked while he ate.

"I was worried she would not take the news well that Nicky was her father." She chuckled. "*I* did not. Explaining how it happened helped, but I wonder what Anne will think when she discovers Nicky still alive. I think Pamela plans to write her today."

Kitt's head snapped up. His whole body went still.

"He didn't tell her?"

"Who?"

"Fallmerton. He didn't tell Pamela what I told him yesterday." He put down his fork and sat back in the chair. "I should have guessed. She didn't look upset when they returned to the drawing room. But it was hard to say anything to dampen Lisa's excitement."

"Tell her what?"

Kitt picked up his cup and took another sip. Why was it so many people learned Pamela's secrets before she did? Fate was being fickle these days.

"Lady Clarkdale died a fortnight ago. I received a letter from my cousin yesterday with the news. Pamela was deliberately not told and no announcement was put in the paper."

"Bastard!"

Kitt stared in shocked surprise at his godmother. "To whom are you referring, madam?"

"Her stepfather, of course. Although I wonder if Marscombe knew while they were at Rawlings's funeral."

"She needs to know." Kitt rose from the table. "I did not want to be the one to tell her. I thought your brother would last night, but apparently he didn't."

"I could tell her."

He was sorely tempted to take her up on the offer, but shook his head instead. "No. I will do it. There is more than just that information. I can also put her mind at ease regarding her sister."

"What about her sister?"

"Sheila and Wyatt were married by special license a week ago. According to his letter, he spoke to Lady Clarkdale before she died and, as he put it, set her heart at rest concerning Pamela."

"That's good, but Lord, that child has been through much in the last four months!"

"I will be back." Then he strode down the hall and out the door.

The fog was lifting as he walked, patches of watery yellow sun beginning to show through the gray. He didn't know how to approach Pamela with his information. How would she react? Twice at Clark Hall, he'd comforted her when she was distressed. The first time, he'd kissed her—and tasted tears. Except for that one time, he'd never known Pamela to cry.

Hyde Park came into view. Stopping just inside the gates, he wondered which way she might have walked. Perhaps he should have brought Gabriel. He could cover more ground on horseback. He looked around him. Maybe the river, he thought, and headed in that direction.

Were there more people here than usual? Or was it because he was looking for someone? It seemed as if all the nannies in the city had decided to walk their charges in the park this very morning. He skirted two women so engaged in their conversation they didn't seem to realize they took up the entire width of the path. Two young boys played with a ball on the grass under the watchful eye of a young man. Another young woman sat on a blanket in the grass with two toddlers and watching another two rolling about together. As he passed another woman with hair nearly the same color as Pamela's, he sighed. Where was she?

He was about to turn back when he rounded a tree and saw her. His feet slowed on the path and his blood turned to ice. She was in the arms of a fashionably dressed young man. Seated on one of the benches on the riverbank with Pearl stretched out contentedly on the grass at their feet. The young man had his arms around her, and Kitt could see his hand stroking up and down her spine. He moved closer, concealed by a nearby tree, and watched.

Suddenly, Pamela turned her face into the young man's neck. Her shoulders rose and dropped as she took a deep breath, then lifted her head to look up at him. He spoke to her and she nodded. When she reached up and brushed a kiss on his cheek, Kitt saw red. Jealousy roared through him with the force of a hurricane, and he moved without stopping to think.

The pair was rising from the bench as he approached. Her companion put his arm around her waist as she leaned her head against his shoulder.

"I suppose Pearl is as good of an excuse as any for clandestine meetings." His voice was sharp.

Pamela whirled to face him, her hands flying up to her face. For a second, her eyes brightened in welcome, but they faded quickly as he bore down on them.

"Kitt! I...I mean, my lord. What a nice surprise."

"Is it?" he ground out. "I suppose I ought to be glad I found out now rather than later. Were you going to end our betrothal sometime soon?"

Hurt registered in her eyes, but it had no effect on the feelings seething just below the surface. Although his brain noted and stored away the image and impression, everything filtered through his fury.

"Well?" Reaching out, he caught her by her upper arm, pulling her away from the young man.

"Here now," the man said, "let her go!"

Kitt paid him no heed as his eyes drilled into hers. Speechless, she merely continued to stare at him out of wide, but dry, eyes. He shook her, snapping her out of her paralysis.

"Well?" he demanded again.

She tried to pull away. "Let me go!"

Her voice must have frightened Pearl, for the small dog began to bark and jump around the three of them.

"Answer me!"

"Here now, that's no way to treat a lady. Unhand her."

"Perhaps, but I don't happen to see a lady," Kitt sneered.

When her companion grabbed Kitt's wrist in an attempt to remove it from Pamela's arm, Kitt turned on him and swung, catching him with a punch to the jaw. Pamela gasped and turned on him. She pushed at his chest and clawed at the hand holding her arm.

"Let me go!" Her voice rose, infused with outrage. "How dare you, you oaf!"

Turning, Kitt ignored the young man and began pulling Pamela toward the path. Pearl followed, barking furiously.

"Let me go. What are you doing?"

"I'm taking you back," he bit out, unable to trust himself further.

Pamela glared at the stranger who held her upper arm in a viselike grip, towing her along like so much baggage. Struggling fitfully against him, she dug her heels into the grass and refused to go further. When he yanked her along, she deliberately allowed her legs to collapse beneath her. His hold loosened as she fell and she jerked her arm free, catching her balance. Turning, she ran back to the bench.

"Are you all right? Did he hurt you?" Her companion rubbed his jaw and looked at her, a speculative gleam in his soft brown eyes.

"I'm fine, Pam. But maybe you'd better ..."

Indignation rose in her breast and she ignored Kitt's return. "I will not! He has no right to bully me any more than you do. I won't be forced to go home until I'm ready."

Her head hurt, but the tears she'd shed earlier were no more. She threw herself back into his arms as Kitt reached them. "Besides, I want you to come with me. I want you to meet..."

He set her away from him, eyeing Kitt warily as he did so.

Pamela spun around and moved in front of him, undaunted by the murderous expression on Kitt's face. Hands on her hips, she advanced toward Kitt. She knew her eyes blazed, knew this was all a big misunderstanding, but she was beyond caring.

"How dare you!" she repeated. "How dare you come charging up and interrupt a private conversation and make unwarranted assumptions without asking questions first? Didn't Frisky teach you better manners than that? Or perhaps you learned how to treat women from your father!"

Kitt's hand shot out to grab her again but she darted out of his reach.

"Don't touch me! Never come near me again!" Her voice shook with anger and frustration.

"Pamela." Kitt's voice was a low growl of warning, but she ignored it.

"Don't talk to me like that. I'm not some green girl you can browbeat into submission." She blinked furiously to keep back the tears. She would not cry again.

He moved closer and she felt a moment of fear before it dissipated. A hand found her shoulder and she glanced back at her companion.

"Calm down, Pam," he said reasonably. "If you'd only introduce us..."

She moved to the side and shook off his hand. Looking from one to the other for a few moments, she tried to think. A reasonable person would do just that. Introduce them. It would clear up the misunderstanding and they could talk it out in a reasonable fashion. But she didn't want to be reasonable right now. Too much had already happened this morning and all she wanted to do was go home and be alone.

Kitt's accusations struck deep and the pain in her heart overtook the pain in her head. It all boiled down to one thing and the realization that Kitt didn't trust her increased her rage. Reasonable was the last thing she wanted to be. She was too bloody furious.

"Introduce yourselves!" she snapped, then turned and stalked away, Pearl on her heels.

She wanted to believe it had started raining. That was the only explanation for her wet cheeks. Unfortunately, looking up at a blue sky and bright sun through watery eyes revealed her self-delusion for what it was.

She was crying.

Wiping her cheeks with the back of her hand, she tried to regain her balance. She rarely cried. Crying solved nothing. And it never made you feel better—only worse. Headache, runny nose, red eyes. Crying *always* made you feel worse than before.

"I trusted him," she told Pearl with a hitch in her voice. "Why couldn't he trust me?"

The dog didn't even have the grace to acknowledge her, much less answer.

She sniffed. "He wouldn't even let me explain. And Stephen! I hope Kitt hit him again!"

She didn't really. She knew she didn't, but it felt good to say it nonetheless.

"Introduce us, Pam," she mocked her brother's words. "Calm down, Pam. I don't know why *I* should be the one to calm down. *I* didn't come barging in on a private conversation not knowing who was who. *I* didn't try to drag me away and leave bruises on my arm. *I* wasn't acting like an ass! So, why should *I* have to be the one to calm down and make introductions?"

She wrapped her arms around herself as a chill seeped into her heart. Stephen's news this morning had been distressing enough without Kitt's overbearing display on top of it all. It was too much, and now she knew what needed to be done.

They reached the house and entered. Carter was nowhere in sight as she removed Pearl's leash and hung it on the peg by the door, then slipped into the small study. Sitting at the desk, she found a piece of vellum, a quill, the ink bottle, and began to write.

The tears on her cheeks dried as she wrote and she was relieved the note wouldn't arrive smeared with tear stains. For long minutes, the only sound in the small room was the scratching of the quill as she composed her missive. When she was done, she put the quill back in the holder, leaned back in the chair, and closed her eyes. The heavy sigh seemed to expel all breath from her body and she wilted into the soft leather.

The day had started out so promising. Up early, she wanted a chance to contemplate all she'd learned the night before. Taking Pearl out earlier than usual suited both of them just fine, and they set off for the park.

The gray, misty skies had not dimmed her mood. She'd never expected the sense of buoyancy she felt at knowing who her father was. The sheer happiness at being accepted. Her grandparents had much to answer for, but she no longer cared.

The park was nearly deserted as she and Pearl wandered the path by the river. In typical Pearl fashion, the little dog barked at anything that moved. It wasn't until she began growling that Pamela realized she wasn't the only person on the path. Coming toward her was a murky shadow she only recognized as a man.

"Pam?" a familiar voice reached her out of the gloom.

"Stephen?" The person stopped before her. "It *is* you! What are you doing here?"

"I've been watching for you," he answered. "Blasted fog! Been trying to catch you for the past few days, but I missed you yesterday and before that I looked for you nearly every day, but never saw you."

"We only returned from Mellerton Chase the day before yesterday."

"That explains it."

She slipped her arm through his and the two continued walking. "What are you doing in London? Where are you staying? How is Mama? I need to write to her. Will you be returning to Yorkshire soon?" The questions seemed to spill out of her.

Stephen's steps slowed at her questions. She could feel his reluctance to answer and wondered at it.

"I'm sorry to be the one to tell you, Pam." His voice made her blood run cold. "Mama..." He took a deep breath. "Mama's dead."

Her heart dropped.

She'd forgotten. In the last few months, the correspondence between London and Clark Hall had insulated her from the reality of her mother's illness. Unable to see her day after day, communicating only by letter—even though she knew they were dictated to her mother's abigail—she'd disregarded the instinctive feeling she had when she left Clark Hall that she would never see her mother again. Instead, she allowed the cheerful tone of the letters to lull her into forgetting her mother was ill at all.

Pamela opened her eyes. The dull ache in her chest reminded her that there was a new void in her life. For less than twenty-four hours, she had been whole, complete, and at peace

231

with herself. Now there was a piece gone forever. The tears welled again.

Sun streamed in through the windows, brightening the small room. But nothing could lighten the heaviness in her heart.

Voices in the foyer roused her from her thoughts.

"Drat!"

She'd lost time woolgathering. She was relieved when she heard footsteps disappear toward the rear of the house. Moving quietly, she approached the door and peered out. Taking the opportunity the empty foyer presented, she fled up the stairs to her room.

Chapter Sixteen

Kitt had never been in love before. It was his only excuse. Unfortunately, the excuse sounded pitiful, even to his ears.

Kitt ran his hand over his face and stared morosely into the leaping flames. The library was dark, suiting his mood. The large clock in the foyer chimed the hour but he was oblivious of the passage of time and paid it no heed.

A decanter of brandy sat on a small table at his elbow, but he refused to try to forget his troubles that way. He needed to think.

He'd acted no better than his father would have, maybe worse. His godmother said his parents fought mostly at home. Not him. He had to choose a public park in which to stage his descent into irrational stupidity.

He flexed his fingers, clenching and unclenching them as he remembered the feel of Pamela's skin beneath them. How could he have manhandled her like that? Despite what Lady Parkington told him, he had never *seen* his father do anything of the sort. In his eyes, his father always lived by his own dictums. If he hadn't known about his parents, his own behavior this morning would have shocked him. Instead, it haunted him.

Pamela had been justifiably furious. If he closed his eyes he could still see her, hands on hips, emerald sparks shooting from her eyes as she advanced toward him.

She was magnificent. Even through his anger, his physical reaction was unchanged, his love and pride steadfast. It wasn't until her companion urged her to calm down and introduce them that he realized what a caper-witted fool he'd been. By then it was too late.

More than her anger, though, he worried he had frightened her. She knew something about his parents, of that he was sure. The comment about how his father treated women had not been chance. She was right about one thing. Frisky would have boxed his ears had she still been alive. And his mother... she would have been deeply ashamed of him.

I'm sorry. It seemed wholly inadequate to express the depth of remorse he felt right now. Even so, the words were all he had.

Unfortunately, the words weren't enough. He needed more to convince Pamela he wasn't like his father in that regard. According to his godmother, his father said those same words again and again, promising to restrain himself each time. In the end the hollow promise cost him not only his wife, but deprived his son of a mother and his wife of her son. No, the words were useless without action.

Pamela loved him. He knew she did. She'd all but confessed it to Sheila—it seemed like an eternity ago. Had his actions this morning changed that? She'd said she trusted him. Trusted him enough to doubt Sheila's lies. But did she trust him enough to believe he'd never harm her?

And...did he trust himself enough to believe it as well?

Pamela kept to her room for the remainder of the day. Trays appeared at mealtimes. On the luncheon tray a note from Lady Parkington informed her Stephen would return the next day. There was no mention of Kitt.

She knew she was being given time to cope with the reality of her mother's death, but she needed the time for so much more. Stephen had explained to her the entire story surrounding his acknowledgment as their grandfather's heir. She was proud of him for understanding the ramifications of the charade, but she felt nothing but pity for her grandparents. Their own actions allowed them to fall prey to Maurice's machinations.

Sleep was elusive and she was bleary-eyed the next morning as she entered the dining room. Lady Parkington was already there.

"Good morning, ma'am." She wasn't yet accustomed to calling her "aunt", but the affection was genuine as she bent to drop a kiss on a scented cheek.

"Good morning, dear. Feeling better?"

Pamela took her seat. Carter poured her a cup of tea and set it before her, asking her if she wanted more than her usual toast and egg this morning.

"That will be fine, thank you." She turned to Lady Parkington. "A little."

"I'm sorry about your mother."

"Thank you. I should have expected it. When I left back in March, I knew she wasn't well, but not being around her day after day, I suppose I forgot."

Carter set a plate before her and she took up her napkin.

"What I truly regret is that she died not knowing about my father."

Lady Parkington nodded. For a few minutes, silence reigned in the room as the two women ate. Then Lady Parkington picked up a piece of folded vellum and set it in front of Pamela.

"I found this in the study last evening. Did you want it sent?"

Pamela looked at the note she'd composed to Kitt yesterday. She had been angry, but she didn't regret its contents. It was better this way.

Lady Parkington watched her, speculation evident in her eyes. Pamela wondered if she was disappointed. Even if she hadn't read the missive; the ring lying on top of it likely alerted her to its contents.

Now that she was no longer angry, desolation settled in her chest. Tears welled again and Pamela could not make her lips move to say the words. She nodded. She thought leaving her home was the hardest thing she'd ever done, but she was wrong.

Walking away from Kitt might very well destroy her. But she knew she had to do it.

"I can't be like his mother." Her voice was a broken whisper. "She didn't know what his father was like before she married him, but I have no excuse. Yesterday..."

"Shouldn't you give him a chance to explain?"

Pamela dabbed at her eyes with her napkin. She would not cry again. She'd shed all her tears yesterday. "What is there to explain?"

"I don't know. Suppose you tell me what happened?"

"You don't know?"

Lady Parkington picked up her delicate gold and white teacup and took a sip. "No."

"He came upon Stephen and me talking in the park and leapt to a wholly unwarranted conclusion. Instead of joining us and asking for an introduction, he thrust himself between us, grabbed me by the arm and tried to drag me away. When Stephen tried to stop him, Kitt hit him."

"I see."

"No you don't." Pamela's voice was bitter. She rubbed the spot on her arm where Kitt had held her. It was still sore and a bruise had formed. "I'm wearing long sleeves today for a reason."

"Hmmm." Lady Parkington took another sip. "Your brother said he'd return today. Will you see him?"

Pamela was startled at the change in subject, but answered readily, "Yes, of course. Although he's not supposed to be my brother. Lord Fallmerton was right."

"Right about what?"

"Stephen explained everything to me yesterday. He said he is Viscount Hendry, but that also means he has to own up to Mama's brother, Charles, being his father."

Lady Parkington frowned. "And he has agreed to this?"

"He has no choice. His father has boxed both him and my grandparents into a corner. Not that my grandfather wasn't willing to agree."

"How?"

Pamela took a sip of her now cool tea, then refreshed it from the pot before her.

"The story about my grandfather's gambling debts was true, but it was worse than that. He mortgaged Castleton and nearly lost it when he couldn't pay the note. Stephen's father bought it."

Lady Parkington reached for a piece of toast. "Marscombe's seat isn't entailed?"

"Not the current one. The original one is a very small holding not far from Bath, Daventry Tower. It's entailed, but Castleton was purchased by my grandfather's grandfather around 1700 and it's not."

Pamela picked up her cup. "Stephen's father planned to leave Castleton to Stephen anyway, but what he really wants is the title. Since he can't have it, he wants Stephen to have it. When our uncle died, Stephen's father was the one who came up with the plan."

She sipped her tea, giving her a moment to order her thoughts.

"I had forgotten that just before he was born, Mama and...his father went on a trip." Taking another sip, she put the cup down and dabbed at her lips with her napkin. "On paper, Stephen was never my brother. He was christened Stephen Maurice Charles Davens, Viscount Hendry."

"It would seem your neighbors in Yorkshire would know better."

"It would, except Stephen wasn't born in Yorkshire. He was born at Daventry Tower and christened at Castleton. The staff at Daventry Tower knew my mother gave birth to him, but no one at Castleton did. And they staged it so no one would."

"How?"

"They arrived at Castleton separately. My grandparents, Stephen, and his nurse arrived first. Then Mama and his father arrived a week later. They put out the story that Mama lost her baby, so no one thought it odd she became attached to Stephen while there and eventually took him with her when they left after his christening. Both of his parents were supposedly dead, my grandparents insisted they were too old to raise a baby and on paper, his own parents were actually his godparents."

"I suppose they were lucky he turned out to be a boy. All that planning would have been for naught had he been a girl."

Carter returned and began clearing dishes. The two women rose and adjourned to the rear parlor.

"How did Stephen find all this out? One would have thought they would have continued the charade with him to ensure he wouldn't say something."

"His father told him. Maurice might not be able to tell the world his son was a viscount, but he wanted Stephen to know."

Lisa dropped by to visit later that morning. Pamela and Stephen were in the parlor and Lady Parkington was out, claiming a prior appointment. She promised to return by luncheon.

"I'm sorry about your mother," Lisa said after being introduced to Stephen.

"How did you know?" Pamela asked.

"Papa told me." Seating herself beside Pamela on the sofa, she studied Stephen for a moment, then asked him, "How is it you're a viscount if you're Pamela's brother?"

Stephen smiled in reply. "Because I'm not."

"Stephen!" Pamela admonished, then turned to Lisa. "Even though he was raised with Sheila and me, we were never told he was actually our cousin rather than our brother. I don't even remember my uncle."

Lisa accepted the explanation and Pamela relaxed. They may as well go on as the script was written. It would do little good to try to refute it now.

"Papa said I should bring you back with me. He said he wanted to talk to you some more."

"Are you planning to stay for luncheon?"

"I hadn't. I thought we'd go home."

"Your aunt promised to return for luncheon, so I should be here. And I've invited Stephen to stay."

Lisa gave her a brilliant smile. "She's your aunt, too."

Pamela sighed. "Yes, I know, but I'm still becoming accustomed to it."

Stephen looked from one to the other. "What's this? Whose aunt?"

"It's no wonder we don't know who we are," Pamela told him. "Neither of us knew our own parents." Stephen's brow furrowed into a puzzled frown. "I found my own father just two nights ago."

"How? I thought he was dead."

"Who told you that?"

"My father, no...I suppose that makes him my uncle and godfather." A sheepish grin lightened his features for a moment. "You know, it's difficult to think of them as anything other than my parents."

Pamela nodded. "I know. Even though he disowned me, I still occasionally think of Sir Maurice as mine." She turned to Lisa. "You are very lucky not to have to wonder who your parents really are."

"But I thought your father was dead." Stephen was clearly having difficulty following the conversation.

"No. As it turns out, he was thought dead. But he returned almost a year later."

"They thought he died at Hondschoote in Northern France, but he survived," Lisa explained.

"So, who is he?"

"My father." Lisa said with a grin. She was clearly enjoying herself.

Astonishment crossed Stephen's features. "The Earl of Fallmerton?"

Pamela nodded. She would have laughed at his confusion, but remembering her conversation with the earl two nights ago reminded her of her grandparents' actions.

"Our grandparents told him Mama and I died." Her voice wobbled but she successfully held back the tears.

"*Both* of you?" Stephen's voice was incredulous. "They told him both of you died? I wonder why?"

Pamela shrugged, but her voice was still sad. "Perhaps they worried about his reaction if he discovered what they'd done."

Lady Parkington arrived home just as Lisa was leaving.

"I would stay, Aunt Claire," she apologized, "but I promised Papa I would return with Pamela and I feel I should go home and explain why I didn't."

"Perhaps we'll drop in for tea. I'll send your mother a note."

During luncheon, a packet arrived addressed to Lady Parkington and Miss Pamela Clarkdale. Lady Parkington didn't seem surprised to see it and handed it over to Pamela to open. The two engraved cards drew chuckles from Lady Parkington.

"I wondered how long it would take."

"Why now?" Pamela asked, examining the two vouchers to Almack's.

Lady Parkington took a sip of her wine. Returning the glass to its place beside her plate, she replied with one word.

"Nicky."

"What?"

"I imagine Gerald was the tale-bearer. He has been chomping at the bit to rub someone's nose in the news ever since he found out."

"But why would it make any difference? I'm still a...a..." she couldn't bring herself to say the word, no matter how often she thought it.

"Because Nicky plans not only to acknowledge you, but to dower you as well. You are about to become very popular, my girl."

Stephen grinned. "It's fortunate you're already betrothed."

"But, but—" Pamela's mind raced. It never occurred to her that finding her father might change her fortunes. She was still a bastard. The circumstances of her birth had not changed.

She pushed the vouchers away, tempted to toss them into the fire and pretend she'd never seen them.

"I don't want them."

Lady Parkington picked them up. "Now, don't be hasty," she cautioned. "One should always be gracious in victory."

"But surely you don't expect us to go?"

"Well, of course we will."

Pamela shook her head. "No. I'm in mourning. I won't betray my mother's memory that way." Just the thought of going to a ball brought a lump to her throat.

"She didn't want that," Stephen said. "I told you yesterday. She didn't want us to stop our lives to mourn her."

"I don't care. I couldn't possibly enjoy myself." Pamela turned to Lady Parkington. "The *ton* will think us rag-mannered if we do not observe some period of mourning."

Lady Parkington studied Pamela for a long moment. "I understand what you're feeling, but your mother wouldn't want you to feel obligated to observe a lengthy period of mourning." She toyed with the stem of her wine glass. "However, you are right on this. Perhaps a week or two of keeping out of society will be enough. We can go to Almack's next Wednesday or the one after."

Pamela shook her head. "A fortnight of mourning isn't enough. When I think of all she sacrificed..."

Stephen reached over and covered her hand with his. "Pam, that's not what she wanted."

The tears that were never far from the surface welled again. "But...but, I can't."

"Yes, you can," he urged. "Think about it and we'll talk about it again in a week or so."

Pamela sighed and dabbed at her eyes with her napkin. "Very well. I'll think about it."

Stephen grinned. "When you go, I'll be there, to ensure the tongues do not wag too much."

"You may escort us," Lady Parkington told him. "Kitt detests Almack's. He will not put in an appearance."

Surprise lit Stephen's face. "But surely if Pamela will be there..."

Pamela felt her aunt's gaze on her.

"Yesterday it might have been possible, but today, I'm afraid not," Lady Parkington said.

The silence stretched so long at the table Pamela finally looked up to find Stephen staring at her, censure in his eyes. He said nothing more as they finished their meal, but she knew he watched her, weighing whether to say something or not. In the end, he opted only for a parting shot as she hugged him good-bye.

"Don't let him go, Pam," he whispered in her ear. "You'll regret it if you do."

Then he collected his hat and cane and was gone.

"Did I miss an announcement?"

Kitt's head snapped up and he nearly spilled his drink as he spun away from his contemplation of the fire. Denny stood framed in the door to the library.

"I told Tibbs he needn't announce me. I don't remember hearing of the demise of the Countess of Jersey. Did something happen while I was away?" Denny moved into the room.

Kitt put down his drink and crossed the carpet to greet his friend.

"Where'd you come from?"

Denny raised a golden eyebrow as the two men greeted each other. "I arrived this afternoon from Mellerton Chase. Needed to see my solicitor about Catherine and Helen. Did I tell you Catherine roused herself enough to give the baby a name? Named her Helen. Thought I'd check in with Lisa and pick up a special license while I was at it."

The two men crossed the carpet to Kitt's desk, Kitt detouring to the sideboard to pour Denny a drink. Settling in chairs, Denny studied Kitt as he drank and Kitt steeled himself not to squirm. The knee breeches were suddenly uncomfortable as they were unusual attire for him.

"Did you attend the funeral?" Denny finally asked.

Kitt finished his drink and put the glass down on his desk. He should find Denny's comments funny, but he was desperate. He was afraid tonight might be his last chance to make things right with Pamela—and he had no idea how to go about it.

"It's not amusing, Den," he said in exasperation. "I've gotten myself into a pickle and tonight might be my last chance at salvaging the situation."

Kitt's uncharacteristic sobriety in the face of a long-standing joke, sobered Denny instantly. Throwing back the rest of his own drink, he put his empty glass down beside Kitt's and gave his closest friend his undivided attention.

"What can I do to help?"

"It's not that simple. In fact, it's rather complicated...and I don't have that much time."

"Very well." Denny accepted the statement. "Let's start with an explanation of why you are headed for Almack's, even though I distinctly remember Lady Jersey telling you that you would only be admitted over her dead body."

"Pamela will be there. And I'm hoping she won't refuse to speak to me in public."

"What's this? Why wouldn't she be speaking to you?"

Briefly Kitt recounted the scene in the park.

"Damn it, Kitt, it's only been a little more than a fortnight since you left the Chase."

"Don't remind me." Kitt rested his head against the back of the chair and closed his eyes. "Unfortunately, it took me less than a week after we returned to make a complete fool of myself."

"So what are you planning?"

"I don't know. I just know I need to talk to Pamela, and I haven't been able to get near her since the day I proved how much of an ass I could be."

Denny rose to his feet. "Then there's no time to lose. Let's go."

"Go where?"

"I have to go change. If she isn't dead, Sally isn't going to let me into Almack's dressed like this. We can discuss strategy on the way."

"You shouldn't be doing this, Den. You're in mourning after all."

"Geoff would understand," Denny said as they stepped out into the night. "Mama and Muriel might not, but you can explain it to them. They've always had a soft spot for you."

"It's a deal."

"Besides, someone has to get you in, and I'll get to see Lisa."

Chapter Seventeen

The country dance ended and Pamela was being escorted off the floor by a young man when she heard Lisa's excited voice.

"When did you arrive, my lord?"

"This afternoon," was the reply, and Pamela glanced up in time to see Denny brush his lips across the back of Lisa's hand as she rose from a curtsy.

Surreptitiously scanning the immediate area, she didn't understand her disappointment at not finding Denny accompanied by his best friend. Hadn't Lady Parkington told her Kitt wouldn't come to Almack's? She glanced away from Lisa's obvious joy, her heart heavy in her chest. She didn't want to see Kitt, did she? In the past week, he had called at the house numerous times, but she refused to see him. He sent flowers, chocolates, and even returned her ring. She knew Stephen had spoken to him, but she wouldn't allow herself to ask what they discussed.

Lady Parkington had become a bystander in the affair. Keeping her own counsel, Pamela assumed she was trying not to take sides. Lisa, a frequent visitor, wondered aloud at Kitt's absence, and Pamela found herself making excuses rather than telling her the truth.

Lisa's wedding plans were shaping up. She and Kitt had been cast as the witnesses. Lisa, she knew, still hoped for a double wedding, but Pamela had insisted Lisa alone should be the center of attention.

Once the news of her parentage and new circumstances leaked out, she discovered a new, friendlier, but patently false side to the *ton*. Tonight was her first outing since her break with Kitt and learning of her mother's death. She was already tired of the blatant patronizing. Greeted at the door by Lady Jersey, then Countess Lieven, she uttered all the correct, polite phrases. Thanking them for something she wasn't sure she wanted was hypocritical, but she did so for her aunt's sake. It was a small thing after all.

Lady Cowper arrived as Pamela helped Lady Parkington settle in a chair and introduced her to a young man, sending them off to dance while she smiled approvingly. One after another, the patronesses brought young men to partner her for each set, until she finally tired of the parade and refused Lady Jersey's choice for the first waltz of the evening. Instead she stood up with Stephen.

"Have you spoken to Lord Kittridge?" Her brother's voice was mildly curious.

"No."

"Why not?"

Because I've refused to see him.

"I just haven't," she replied. Stephen swung her smoothly through a turn. He was a good dancer, but her subconscious compared him with Kitt. Waltzing with Kitt left her breathless and lightheaded, her blood thrumming through her veins. Waltzing with Stephen was like, well, it was like waltzing with her brother.

She consoled herself that she wasn't waltzing with any of the young men she'd been introduced to tonight. Many of them had not deigned to speak to her at any of the other balls she attended, but tonight they all wanted to partner her. If she didn't think it was pathetic, she would have found it amusing. As it was, she compared them all to Kitt—and found them lacking.

Stephen asked no more questions as they finished their dance, but she knew the subject was not closed.

Lisa laughed and Pamela looked back over to where she, Denny and her parents stood in a small circle. Lisa's eyes shone as she looked up at Denny, her adoration obvious. Denny smiled down at her, his expression indulgent. Pamela's heart twisted and a sharp pain caught her unawares. If only Kitt looked at her like that.

He might if you'd see him, a small voice needled her.

"You jest, my lord!" Lisa's loud exclamation in tones of patent disbelief had heads turning in their direction. "Why everyone knows he would never..."

If Pamela hadn't been watching her, she would not have seen Lisa look up and stop speaking in mid-sentence. Eyes wide, Lisa seemed to be searching for words and she turned to look back up at Denny, who only nodded with a broad smile.

It was then that Pamela noticed the room had gone unaccountably quiet. People were turning, obviously trying to see something behind her. Then the whispers started.

"Never thought I'd see the day..."

"Don't believe it..."

"Wonder why now...?"

"Had to happen eventually..."

Awareness crept up the back of her neck. Lady Parkington appeared at her side. "Remember," she said cryptically. "Be gracious in victory." Then she looked up, over Pamela's right shoulder and said, "Good evening, Kitt."

Pamela spun around so fast she would have fallen had Kitt's hands not shot out and steadied her. Her mouth went dry and she stared up at him, unable to force even a mundane greeting between frozen lips.

Gracious in victory.

Victory? What victory? What had she won?

He didn't look any different. He still towered over her, his long, lean frame exuding the raw masculinity and strength that had often provided her with reassurance and comfort. His broad shoulders were still solid beneath the material of his black evening jacket, the hands steadying her still large, but gentle.

Yet there *was* something different, and it had nothing to do with the dark smudges beneath his eyes. It was the expression *in* his eyes that gave her pause. To the casual observer, it wasn't much different, but she wasn't a casual observer. She knew him well enough to know something was wrong. There was a wariness in his eyes she'd never seen before. An uncertainty that told her he wasn't sure of his reception; that he half-expected her to turn her back and walk away.

Gracious in victory.

She glanced around her. All eyes were on them. What did they expect? How much did they know? Enough, she surmised. She wasn't wearing her ring after all.

Then the fog lifted and she understood. Kitt stood before her, in a place he detested, in front of people he had very little respect for, his mantle of self-assurance on the floor at her feet. She had been given the power to ruin him. Just like that, he put his future in her hands.

In the space of those few seconds, her love exploded within her, and her gaze returned to his. For the first time, she realized what she'd been given. Kitt had always accepted her for who she was. When the rest of the *ton* shunned her, Kitt was there for her. When the rumors and gossip were at their worst, Kitt had been there for her. When her confidence faltered, he was the one to bolster it. When her grandmother and Sheila threatened, he held them back. And through it all, he'd wanted to marry her.

She might be slow at times, but she was not stupid. She'd not throw away the one thing in her life that made it worthwhile. The one person in her life who knew all her secrets, but wanted her anyway.

Another glance at the faces around her confirmed her decision. Except for her family, not one of them could be trusted. The men and women circled like vultures, waiting for one or the other to make a move. Then they would move in for the kill. The men to court the newly acknowledged and well-dowered daughter of the Earl of Fallmerton, and the women to console Kitt on his loss. She could not let it happen. Kitt was hers.

She turned and raised her eyes to Kitt's. The uncertainty in his gaze tore at her heart.

Gracious in victory.

Kitt watched the play of feelings and emotions as they drifted across Pamela's face. He expected surprise, but steeled himself to face her anger and disdain. When they didn't appear, hope inched its way in. As she continued to stare up at him, he noted her confusion.

When she glanced away, his heart clenched. Would she walk away from him? What would he do if she did? Helplessness was not something he was accustomed to, but he could not stop her if she turned her back and walked away.

Then she turned back and the confusion had disappeared. He wasn't confident enough of her reaction to believe he saw understanding and trust. The stranglehold on his heart, however, relaxed a tiny bit, his breathing became less difficult and his shoulders dropped a fraction. A small light flared in the wooded depths of her eyes, then she glanced away again.

His cravat was suddenly too tight, the room much too warm. He forced himself to concentrate on keeping his breathing even. Sweat beaded his upper lip. The silence in the room was broken by the orchestra tuning its instruments, preparing to begin the next set.

Pamela returned her gaze to his and smiled. Not just any smile—a brilliant, glorious smile that shone in her eyes. A warm, inviting smile that sent relief cascading through him and increased his heartbeat.

The first notes of a waltz floated across the room as she spoke.

"You're just in time, my lord. I thought I would have to sit out the next set."

He did not hesitate, but offered his arm with a bow. "I would not be so remiss as to leave you without a partner."

The crowd parted as they approached the floor. Kitt paid no heed to the faces he passed; he was concerned only with Pamela walking sedately beside him. Once on the floor, he looked down into adoring—was that truly what he saw?—eyes and could not stop the question on his tongue from emerging.

"Why?"

She dropped her gaze to his neckcloth. The hand in his trembled and she missed a step. He pulled her closer and steadied her against him, savoring the feel of her breasts pressed against his chest and the brush of her emerald green skirts against his legs. His hand tightened on her waist.

"Because..." her voice was soft, breathless.

He waited for her to finish, but she didn't. He wanted to whisk her off the floor, to someplace where they could be private. They needed to talk. He looked up. *Damn!* They were still the focus of too many eyes. Every move, every word, every gesture would be scrutinized, dissected, analyzed and assessed. By tomorrow the *ton* would have decided whether they were still a couple, or merely acquaintances too well-bred to make a scene.

"Pamela, look at me."

She raised her head. The expression was still there, and his heart sped up.

"Because...?" he prompted. He needed to know the rest.

She shook her head. "This is not the place." Her voice was still soft, but she had regained her equilibrium. "I...we...need to talk."

He grinned. "Your wish is my command."

The lamps seemed bright in the confines of the carriage. Pamela alternately considered it good and bad. She wouldn't dwell on how quickly Kitt whisked her off the dance floor and out the door. She was just glad no one stopped them.

Because I love you.

She'd nearly blurted it out in response to his question on the dance floor, but lost her nerve. She did not want to risk so much in front of so many. There were still unresolved issues between them. They could not go forward until the air was clear.

She gripped her reticule in her hand, feeling the contents through the silk. An impulse earlier in the evening led her to drop her ring into the little bag before she left home.

Kitt finished speaking to his coachman and entered the vehicle. It shrank in size, becoming far more intimate than she would have wished. Conversely, she was disappointed when he sat across from her rather than beside her.

His indigo eyes looked black in the yellow glow of the lamps and his unwavering regard made her nervous.

The carriage began to move.

She wet her lips nervously. "Where are we going?"

"Nowhere," he replied. "I told Rupert merely to drive around until I gave him further instructions."

He watched her for a long moment. Was he waiting for her to begin? What should she say?

Kitt leaned forward and captured her hands. They trembled, but she managed to keep her eyes steady.

"I must apologize," he began, "for my unforgivable behavior toward you."

There's no need. The words rose to her lips, but were never set free. It was a lie and she knew it.

"I have already apologized to Stephen."

"He said nothing to me." Probably because he knew she was too angry to listen.

A small smile tilted his lips. "Perhaps he felt it was not his responsibility. He was not the one guilty of trespass."

"You...you were very angry," she said slowly.

"I was jealous," he replied. "I have no excuse except that it was an unfamiliar emotion." He closed his eyes momentarily, and Pamela noted the weariness in his face before he opened them again. "It wasn't until you walked away that I realized how inexcusably stupid I'd behaved."

She had nothing to add to his analysis of his actions. He behaved badly, true. But in her anger and grief, she'd allowed the situation to escalate.

"I'm sorry," he said. "It seems like such an inadequate phrase to excuse the wrong, but it's all I have to give. I don't even know if I can promise it won't happen again."

"It won't." Her voice was firm with conviction.

"How do you know? How can you know?" His voice was hard. His eyes deepened to obsidian and she felt him withdrawing from her. "My father promised my mother time after time he would never hurt her again, yet he did. How can you be so sure I won't turn out just like him?"

She sighed. "Very well. I don't know." She reached up and laid her hand against his cheek. "I don't know that you aren't like your father and maybe I don't know that you won't resort to violence like he did. But you are not your father and now you know the truth about your parents..."

He turned and placed a kiss in the palm of her hand. She trembled. "I'm only a man, Pamela. I can only promise you I won't and swear to you that I would never break my word willingly."

His vulnerability touched a chord deep down and her heart warmed. She trusted him enough not to believe her sister, and she'd never asked him for his side of the story. Shouldn't she be willing to rely on his word now when he'd explained voluntarily?

He expelled a long breath and reclaimed her hand. "I have never hit a woman and I don't intend to begin this late in life. You..." He paused, then looked directly into her eyes, capturing her gaze with his own. "You are the only woman I have ever been jealous of. And the only woman I have ever acted toward in that manner. It was unconscionable and I have yet to forgive myself for the hurt I caused you because I cannot do so unless you can find it in your heart to forgive me first."

She wanted nothing more right then than to throw herself into his arms and hold on to him forever. There had never been a question of not forgiving him. Returning his ring had been her way of letting him go if he wanted to be free, but now he'd come for her and she never planned to let him go again.

He continued to watch her closely in the dim light of the coach. She wondered what he would do if she gave in to the impulse to reach out to him. Perhaps she'd find out—in a moment.

"Of course I forgive you," she said slowly. Her gaze slid to their entwined hands for a moment before rising back to his. "I don't have an adequate explanation for my own behavior that day except I'd just received a shock and wasn't thinking clearly." She smiled ruefully. "I suspect Stephen was the only person thinking clearly that morning."

The expression that entered his eyes could only be described as awe as she spoke.

"Why would you excuse such unpardonable behavior?"

"I can't hold a grudge forever. Besides, you didn't kill anyone and I truly believe you would not deliberately hurt me or anyone else. And..." She licked her lips nervously.

Now was the time. She knew he cared. His actions tonight proved that, but she knew she had to take the first step. Staring up into his eyes, she wanted to watch his reaction to her simple reply.

"Because I love you."

His hands tightened on hers, light flared in his eyes before his lids dropped and shielded them from view. His breathing hitched and he took a deep breath to control it. He groaned.

"Why?" His question asked for more than, "because I do".

Extricating one of her hands from his, she reached up again and laid it against the smooth skin of his jaw.

"Because you came to Almack's to find me."

He turned his face and placed another kiss in her palm. She inhaled sharply as the touch seared its way up her arm. There was no resistance when he reached out and fitted his hands about her waist, whisking her off her seat and onto his lap in the blink of an eye. She rested her head against his shoulder as he held her tight.

"I do not deserve you," he spoke into her hair. "Not now, not ever."

"That's unfortunate," she sighed happily, "because you're stuck with me."

He raised his head. "Do you mean that? Truly?"

In response, she opened her reticule and pulled out the ring.

"When you sent it back, I was still angry. I told my...my aunt I refused to be like your mother. That I couldn't suffer the way she had, but she said there were parts to the story I didn't know."

"Do you want to know?"

She shook her head. "No." She didn't need to know. She knew enough. She picked up Kitt's hand and dropped the ring into it, then held out her own. "There's only one thing I truly want to know."

Kitt stared down at Pamela in amazement. Would he ever be worthy of such trust? There were so many things he wanted to tell her. Things he wanted her to know. But at the moment they all seemed unimportant beside the words he knew she wanted to hear.

"This is hardly the correct position for a proposal," he said in amusement. "But it will have to do." He slid the ring back onto her finger, then raised the hand to his mouth. "Miss Clarkdale, would you do me the honor of becoming my wife?"

Mischief sparked in her eyes. "Why?"

"Because I love you."

She sighed again and smiled brightly. "Yes." Then she leaned her head against his chest and relaxed completely in his arms.

His body burned with a need to possess her, but he held himself in check. There was still much to air out and he knew if he so much as kissed her, no more talking would be accomplished. He should put her back in her own seat, but he could not bring himself to relinquish his hold. Her scent floated around him and he breathed deeply.

His! All his! His heart swelled at the thought.

"Do you want to know when I fell in love with you?"

She looked up and the glow in her eyes nearly made him lose his train of thought. She didn't answer, but there was a question in the forested depths.

"It was when you told your sister you didn't believe I fathered her child."

A blush covered her cheeks. "I suppose Wyatt told you about that."

"No, he didn't. I was there."

"You were...?"

"Wyatt brought me along." He chuckled at the memory of Wyatt telling him about the plan he and Pamela formulated. "He knew I was suspicious of his relationship with you after the dinner party at the Mellertons'. He told me about his understanding with Sheila, then said you wanted him to eavesdrop on a conversation between the two of you and invited me along. He made me promise not to say anything to you about being there until he got Sheila out of Town. The child is his."

Her mouth dropped open and she leaned back to look up at him better. "Wyatt's? But how? Bess told me..." She smacked her palm against her forehead. "I should have known. And he was with Sheila in Vauxhall, too."

"I asked no more questions after his confession. I was too bemused by the fact that you were willing to trust me even though you had no reason to." The carriage swayed as it took a corner. "I did dance with her once, early on in the Season."

"She said you kissed her and..."

"Actually, she was the one who kissed me initially. I just reciprocated. I was trying to discover if she knew me."

"Knew you? How could she?"

"She saw us together in Yorkshire, remember? I wasn't sure if she recognized me or not, but after that kiss she said nothing. That was when I realized she didn't."

Pamela straightened.

"Her father thought I was dallying in the stables with one of the stable hands." She toyed with his cravat, then smoothed her hands down his chest. He braced himself not to react. "He wanted to force me to marry whoever it was." She giggled and the sound bubbled in his chest. "If he only knew."

"What would have forcing you to marry a stable hand accomplish?"

"He thought I would become his housekeeper," she murmured. "Mrs. Creal is getting old, but he wouldn't replace her because I was doing everything. I think he thought he could kill two birds with one stone. He could disown me, but still look benevolent." She raised solemn eyes to his. "You saved me. Even if you didn't know it then. You saved me, just because you weren't one of the stable hands."

He was quiet for a moment, studying her. "So what really happened when you went back inside to speak to your mother?"

"She told me Sheila's father wasn't mine. Even though she was forced into the marriage, she said he promised her that if I was a girl, he would raise me as his own. She was lied to from the very beginning—and I think my grandparents knew all along. Mama believed he only changed his mind after Sheila was born, but after learning about Stephen, I'm convinced he never had any intention of honoring his word."

"What about Stephen?"

Briefly she told him about the change in Stephen's parentage.

"Ah. I wondered how they did it. He introduced himself as your cousin after you left us in the park."

"It seems wrong that they will be able to get away with it, but I suppose my grandfather's title and property would only revert to the Crown otherwise."

"True," he agreed. "And Prinny would just give it to one of his cronies anyway. Fallmerton is right on this one. It's best to say nothing and let things work themselves out."

She leaned her head against his shoulder and shifted in his lap. He suppressed a groan. It was time to take her home. Before he lost control.

"Did you arrive with Denny?"

The question caught him off guard and he had to think for a moment before he answered.

"Yes, but you weren't the only person I had to apologize to tonight. I stopped to speak to Lady Jersey before I came in."

"Is she the reason you dislike Almack's?"

"Partially," he replied. "Sally—Lady Jersey—blacklisted my father."

"Why?"

"She took exception to the way he treated one of his mistresses—a woman with whom she was acquainted. I, of course, didn't believe my father would abuse any woman. It was a side to him I knew nothing of."

"I'm sorry you had to find out."

He shrugged. "I needed to know. Otherwise I would have continued to think of women as faithless and fickle. My godmother is the only woman I ever trusted—until I met you."

"You were right about one, no two, things."

"I was? About what?"

"Almack's was a horrible crush and the refreshments were even worse. Why does the *ton* put up with it?"

"Who knows?"

Lifting his hand, he tilted her face to his and bent his head. The wait was over. He needed to taste her now.

"Perhaps someday, someone will debate the importance of Almack's and wonder at its purpose, but for now, for us, it's not important at all."

Her last words were lost against his lips as he took possession of her mouth.

Epilogue

"I now pronounce that you are man and wife. What God has joined together, let no man put asunder."

Sunshine spilled into the small chapel, brightening the whitewashed walls and adding luster to the flowers adorning the altar. The small group clustered near the front cheered as the groom turned to his new bride and kissed her.

As the couple left the vestry after signing the register, the bridesmaid handed the bride her bouquet and moved to the side of the best man. Hearty congratulations echoed off the stone walls as the group followed the newlyweds from the room.

The best man and bridesmaid remained, forgotten momentarily by the rest of the company.

Pamela leaned back against Kitt and watched Lisa and Denny exit the small chapel surrounded by their families. As Kitt's arms slipped around her waist, she relaxed against him and entwined her hands with his. Glancing down at their interlaced fingers, she admired the way the sun glinted off the diamond-encrusted wedding band she wore.

Two days after the night at Almack's, she and Kitt said their vows in a small ceremony in the Fallmerton's drawing room. Lisa was disappointed at not having a double wedding, but Denny convinced her that this way was best.

Lord Fallmerton had escorted her down the aisle. When he bent to kiss her cheek before handing her over to Kitt, she could not stop the tears. She wished her mother had been with her, but having Stephen present provided some consolation. Her grandparents had retired to Castleton after returning from

Mellerton Chase, and Stephen informed her their paths probably would not cross often.

She and Kitt spent the next two weeks at Covington Manor; far enough away that Lisa could not come to call every day, but close enough for them to remain in contact. Now, with Lisa finally married, she and Kitt would spend the rest of the summer at Kitt Ridge. She looked forward to becoming acquainted with her new home and spending time with her husband.

She turned in Kitt's arms and looped her own about his neck. Raising up on her toes, she drew his head down to hers.

"Do you suppose they've missed us yet?"

"Does it matter?" he asked against her lips.

"No."

He kissed her deeply, their bodies melting against each other. When he raised his head and dropped a kiss on the tip of her nose, she gave him a brilliant smile. He grinned in return.

"Who knew that being robbed and shot would bring me such a priceless gift?"

"My life hasn't been the same since I found you by that stream. Perhaps I ought to thank my stepfather for throwing me out after all."

He chuckled. "I suspect Wyatt has filled him in by now. But if he hasn't, Stephen most assuredly has."

He kissed her again, raising his head only when footsteps sounded in the hall.

"I think we have been missed," he murmured against her lips. "We'll have to finish this tonight."

Pamela blushed as they turned toward the door.

Lady Parkington met them as they emerged into the hall. Glancing from one to the other, she raised her eyebrows but said nothing.

Pamela giggled. "Have you decided whether to advertise for another companion?"

"No," was the reply. "Next year I expect to be too busy with grand-nephews or nieces to need a companion."

Pamela felt the heat in her cheeks as Lady Parkington turned and preceded them to the dining room. Walking beside

Kitt, she knew Lady Parkington was right. The fabrications and falsehoods she and Kitt once lived with were now laid to rest. They could look forward into the future where their own children would never have cause to doubt their parents or their parents' love.

About the Author

Born in an Army Medical Center that no longer exists, Denise has lived her entire life around the military. First an Army brat, then an Army officer, then married to a (now retired) Army officer, she has traveled extensively in the United States and Europe. Living in Europe with a vivid imagination was all it took for her to start writing. Once she started reading her mother's Barbara Cartland romances she was hooked on historical romance, the Regency period in particular.

Writing took a backseat to life while she married and started a family, but she never stopped reading and enjoying romances—especially historicals. She and her aunt used to joke about writing their own someday, but when she died in 2002, Denise realized they'd waited too long, and if she ever wanted to write, now was the time to do something about it. As a form of therapy, she began writing again and when the smoke cleared in 2004, she had written four complete novels.

Juggling church, a full-time job, tennis leagues, and her craft and sewing addictions doesn't leave much time for herself and writing, but being busy is what keeps her going.

To learn more about Denise Patrick, please visit http://denisesden.blogspot.com. She loves receiving emails at denisepatrick@gmail.com.

Look for these titles by
Denise Patrick

Coming Soon:

Gypsy Legacy: The Marquis

hot stuff

Discover Samhain!

GET IT NOW

I9781599987958
FICTION PAT
Patrick, Denise.
The importance of Almack's /

JUL 14 '08

9 781599 987958

PRA-05/308